W9-AUR-053

PAULA DETMER RIGGS

Forgotten Dream

SILHOUETTE·INTIMATE·MOMENTS®

Published by Silhouette Books New York

America's Publisher of Contemporary Romance

SILHOUETTE BOOKS
300 East 42nd St., New York, N.Y. 10017

ISBN: 0-373-07364-X

First Silhouette Books printing December 1990

PAULA DETMER RIGGS

discovers material for her writing in her varied life experiences. During her first five years of marriage to a naval officer, she lived in nineteen different locations on the West Coast, gaining familiarity with places as diverse as San Diego and Seattle. While working at a historical site in San Diego, she wrote, directed and narrated fashion shows, and became fascinated with the early history of California.

She writes romances because "I think we all need an escape from the high-tech pressures that face us every day, and I believe in happy endings. Isn't that why we keep trying, in spite of all the roadblocks and disappointments along the way?"

For Matthew

Prologue

He was drifting, disconnected from everything but the hot throbbing in his head. He heard someone groan. The voice was familiar. His.

He fought to clear his head. Where was he? What happened? Gray wisps of memory floated just beyond his reach, like artillery smoke. Nothing was clear; nothing made sense. The last thing he remembered was a blinding light, then vicious, twisting pain.

When was that? This morning? Yesterday? Why was he here, flat on his back in this cold place?

He tried to sit up, but he couldn't move. Panic pierced the thick fog that held him, and he cried out. He couldn't feel his arms or his legs, only the bayonet jabs stabbing his head.

Through the torment he heard a voice—soft, sweet, like soothing music. Gentle as a spring shower. He had heard . . . once . . . when . . . ?

"Susanna?" His voice was a raspy groan pushing through his parched throat and cracked lips. He swallowed, tried to beg her to come closer, but the words wouldn't come.

Her image floated just beyond his field of vision, her slender arms outstretched, urging him to come back to her. Her smile warmed the cold places inside him. Her laughter filled him with happiness for the first time in his life. Her eyes, softly shimmering with vibrant life, pulled him into their golden depths until his soul touched hers.

For so long he had tried to forget. Years and years. But always she was there, an ache in his gut that never left him, no matter where he was or what he was doing. He was so tired of hurting. If he could just find her...

Opening his eyes a crack, he searched for her. The room was blinding white, so white it hurt his eyes. He tried to turn away from the glare, but it was all around him.

"It's okay, Sergeant Cruz. You're safe now." The voice was calm—a woman's voice. Different from the one he sought. Desperately he tried to focus on the face wavering in front of him, but the image moved in and out.

He narrowed his gaze, wet his cracked lips. "What...where...?" He couldn't seem to make the words come out right. Was this a dream? A nightmare? Why couldn't he move?

"You're in Walter Reed Hospital, Sergeant. You're going into surgery soon. Everything will be fine. Try to relax. The shot I just gave you will kick in soon."

No, he thought, fighting against the numbness that held him prisoner. He had to find her. To tell her...to explain...to beg her to forgive him.

He couldn't let her go. Not again. This time it would kill him. But even as he struggled, a suffocating cloud closed over him, carrying him into blessed oblivion.

"What did he say?" one nurse asked the other as they wheeled the unconscious soldier into the OR.

"Something about a letter. I didn't catch it all."

"Who's Susanna? I thought his wife's name was Trina."

''It was. Not that it matters, though. After the surgeon gets done fishing the bomb fragments from his brain, he'll be lucky if he remembers his own name.''

Three weeks later, when Staff Sergeant Mateo Cruz woke up again, the only thing he remembered was the pain.

Chapter 1

Susanna Spencer was exhausted. She'd been awake and on her feet for almost forty hours, delivering two babies in as many days. This little one was taking his time, she thought with a weary glance toward the first rays of the sun shimmering through the dusty window. The last hour had been the worst—for both her and the weary young woman in the sagging iron bed.

Pressing her gloved hand against the ache in the small of her back, she forced life into her low husky voice. "We're almost there, Robin. Don't give up on me now, honey. Remember what you learned in class. Breathe with the pain."

A low moan answered her as seventeen-year-old Robin Clearwater struggled to bring her first child into the world. Her young husband, Romero, held her hand, his broad copper face stiff with worry. Both were residents of the Santa Ysabel Pueblo in central New Mexico, where Susanna had been the midwife for the past five years. Romero, like his father and grandfather before him, had been born in this bed, in this room.

The crude adobe dwelling had no plumbing, no electricity, no telephone. The only light came from three kerosene lanterns burning on a rickety table by the bed. The only heat came from the wood-burning stove in the corner.

Years of poor nutrition had made Robin's body unsuited for childbearing. Susanna had tried to convince the frail young mother to deliver her baby in the clinic. However, Romero had stubbornly insisted that his son be born on his ancestral land. He and Susanna had exchanged heated words several times about the danger, but she hadn't been able to change his mind.

Although the baby hadn't been due for two more weeks, Susanna had become more and more worried about Robin. Yesterday, even though she had just spent a day and a night delivering another woman's baby miles from the Clearwater ranch, on a hunch she had gone to the primitive little house. She had arrived to find Robin in hard labor, with only Romero to help.

"That's it, Mama," Susanna intoned, trying to keep her voice above a whisper. "Breathe into the pain."

Her dark brown hair, dampened by the sweat dotting her forehead, framed her pale face with waiflike ringlets, making her look nearly as young as the teenage mother-to-be, even though she would be thirty in the spring.

But unlike Robin, her body, though small, had already acquired the sensuous ripeness of motherhood. Her breasts were full and rounded, although her child had long ceased suckling. Her waist, though trim, bore a womanly curve, and her hips carried a generous fullness above the long length of her slender thighs.

"Push, Robin," she ordered, her lilting voice pitched low. "Now. That's it, push harder."

Wiping the sweat from her eyes with the sleeve of her sterile gown, she crouched between Robin's legs, nervously biting her lip. No matter how many babies she brought into the world, she still experienced a moment of panic just before the baby came into her hands.

"Push!"

With one final straining effort from the panting mother-to-be, the tiny infant slid into Susanna's gloved hands. "A boy!" Susanna cried. "And he's perfect!"

Her mouth curved into a tired grin behind the mask covering half of her face. The baby had sturdy shoulders and a little barrel chest, with a full head of silky black hair and a broad face that marked his Native American heritage.

His satiny skin was still wet and warm from the womb, and his tiny hands were clenched into miniature fists, as though he had come prepared to fight. Susanna quickly removed the fluid from his mouth, then gently rubbed his back, watching anxiously for the first breath to fill the round chest.

Her delighted smile disappeared abruptly. Nothing was happening. Adrenaline flooded her veins, but she forced herself to remain clam. She laid him on his back, arching his head backward to open his windpipe. Then, jerking down her mask, she placed her mouth over his and breathed. She removed her mouth, waited, her heart pounding in her throat. Still nothing.

A chill took her, even though the room was warm. She had less than four minutes before the lack of oxygen would damage the child's brain—if he lived at all.

As she bent her head to the baby's mouth again, Susanna heard Robin's frantic voice begging her to save her baby.

She had no time to reassure the frightened young couple. If the baby lived, there would be no need. If he didn't . . .

Working methodically, she breathed life into the still, little body. Over and over the small chest fluttered, then grew deathly still again.

Fighting tears and exhaustion, Susanna refused to believe she had lost him. "Breathe, baby," she pleaded hoarsely, shaking him. "Please breathe. Don't give up on me. Not now."

She started to lower her head again, but just then, as though responding to her desperate cry, the baby jerked. His minuscule lashes fluttered as he opened his mouth and sucked in. His chest expanded, filling with life-giving oxygen. His solemn-featured face wrinkled into an intense baby frown a second before he started to cry.

The blue tint faded from his coppery skin, replaced by a warm pink tinge. He waved his tiny fist in the air, and the pink deepened to an angry red. With each wail, he gained strength, until the room seemed to reverberate with his lusty squalling.

Susanna grinned, even as her soft mouth trembled in relief. "Listen to him bawl," she murmured with a laugh. "Baby has a temper."

Robin's face relaxed into a shaky smile. "Like his papa," she murmured, clinging tightly to her husband's hand.

Romero's face was flushed, but his features were composed. Like most men of the tribe, he was reluctant to show strong emotion in public.

"A son," he said in a low voice. "I have a son."

"Indeed you do," Susanna murmured, stripping off her mask and gloves and throwing them into the plastic bag she had waiting. "And by the look of that square little chin, you're going to have your hands full."

Romero's strong throat worked. "If you hadn't come when you did—" He bit off his words, a grim expression tightening his face. "I was wrong."

"Robin and the baby are fine. That's what counts."

She took a deep breath, fighting the sudden urge to lie down next to Robin and close her eyes. Forcing strength into her tired body, she bathed the baby's face, her fingers stiff from fatigue.

"You did it, Mama," she told Robin as she swaddled the now whimpering infant in a soft, sweet-smelling blanket and tidied his straight silky hair with her fingers. "I'm proud of you."

Robin tried to return the smile, but failed. "Thank you," she whispered, her voice choked with fatigue and emotion. "You brought back our son from the dead."

Romero cleared his throat. "My table will always have a place for you," he told her with formal courtesy in Tewa, the language of his people.

"Just take good care of baby. That's all the thanks I need." She raised the swaddled infant to her shoulder and closed her eyes. Just for a second or two, she promised herself. Not enough time to feel the stirring of love for another woman's child, but long enough to feel his sweet warmth. This was the only payment she needed, the only reward that mattered. A new little life, perfect and special.

The baby's whimpers subsided. He turned his head into her neck and began to suck on one wrinkled fist. She lowered her chin to rest lightly on his dewy crown. The tiny boy hiccuped, then sighed. He tried to snuggle against her. A deep sadness settled in her heart, reminding her of the still, dark emptiness that was always inside her.

"Go to Mama, sweetie," she whispered as she settled the baby into his mother's arms. Robin was so lucky, she thought. Lucky to have a new son. Lucky to have a man who loved her.

As soon as Susanna removed her hands from the baby's back, he opened his eyes and began to wail. Robin looked up helplessly. "What should I do?" she asked in a tremulous voice.

"Rub his back. He just needs to know his mama loves him." Sadness, black and limitless, touched Susanna briefly before she forced it away. This was a time for rejoicing, not bitterness.

Robin began stroking her son's back as the proud father looked on with anxious dark eyes. Gradually the shrill cries subsided into sleepy silence. Robin pressed a gentle kiss against the baby's head, then looked up.

"You should have children, Susanna," she said softly. "You love them so much."

"Maybe someday," she said with false cheer. "Right now I'm too busy taking care of other expectant mamas." She rubbed her hands over her arms, trying to force life into the tired muscles. She couldn't remember when she had eaten last. Or had eight hours of uninterrupted sleep. She fought off a yawn.

"You three need some time together before I finish up. And I need some fresh air to wake me up."

She shrugged into her warm denim jacket and left the small house, closing the door softly behind her. The early-morning air smelled of drenched sagebrush and damp earth.

Huddled against the chill, she walked slowly toward her Jeep. To the east, the sun was an orange circle in the dark dawn sky, sending lonely shadows over the pebbly sand.

Beyond the towering red wall of the mesa, the residents of Santa Ysabel were waking up. The women would be preparing fry bread and bitter coffee for breakfast, and the men would be feeding goats and sheep, or mucking out horse stalls. But out here on the edge of the pueblo, the only sounds were the whistle of the wind through the aspen leaves and the cackling of the chickens in the pen below.

Leaning wearily against the Jeep's dust-coated fender, she let the familiar sounds settle around her. She had healed in this place. Even though she had lived half her life in Albuquerque, she belonged here. The quiet mornings and simple ways of the people were a part of her soul.

Hunching the woolly collar of her jacket closer to her neck, she lifted her face to the wind coming down from the north. Tendrils of warm brown hair escaped the haphazard knot on top of her head and blew across her cheek.

She closed her eyes, savoring the pungent smells she detected in the cool breeze. Sage blossom, burning mesquite from countless fires, dying leaves.

Autumn had come early to New Mexico. Halloween was more than a month away, yet the leaves were already turning. Soon the snow would come, softening the harsh contours of the mesas.

According to long-established custom, winter on the pueblo was a time of reflection, a time for family and friends, a time to renew one's spiritual ties with the mystical forces of the universe that had guided the lives of The People for countless centuries.

She had been thirteen that first winter when her widowed father, an artist of great promise but few sales, had married Hannah Charley, a woman of the tribe with two daughters of her own.

Having grown up in the city, Susanna had been ill-prepared for the slow, often archaic life of an Indian pueblo. At first she had been appalled by the primitive living conditions and near-poverty level of existence.

For centuries the land had remained the same, awakening slowly, in rhythm with nature and its never-changing cycles.

The people were as unchanging as the land. The Spanish conquerors had given the people surnames and horses, and in a few cases a new religion. But most of the beliefs practiced within the boundaries of the reservation had their origins in antiquity. The medicine man was as important as any priest. Women were revered for their ability to bring forth new life and were accorded a special place in pueblo life. Men owned only their clothes and their saddles. Women held claim to everything else. Even the duplex Susanna lived in—and still did—had belonged to her stepmother and another woman who lived in the other half.

Her name was Lily Cruz. She had one son. Mateo.

Susanna had often seen pictures of the handsome young soldier with the laughing eyes and sexy smile, but she had never met him—until that summer when Lily died suddenly and he came home on emergency leave to attend her funeral.

Her stepsisters had talked a lot about the good-looking army corporal that summer. "None of the unmarried girls are allowed to be alone with him," ten-year-old Spring had whispered, her eyes glittering with fascination.

"Mother says he's wild, like a stallion running on the range," Summer had chimed in. "Not even the strongest woman can tame him."

But Susanna had known better. From the moment they'd met, she had been enthralled by Mat. They spent long, secret hours together, walking and talking, or simply holding hands and enjoying the beauty of the land around them.

Tough and taciturn with others, Mat listened to her in a way that made her feel as though she could trust him with her deepest secrets and most fragile hopes.

Shy herself, she had been used to the awkward fumbling of boys, but Mat was a man. He took instead of asked, but he also made her want to purr and smile and sing at the same time.

For three wonderful weeks her world had been defined by Mat and his kisses. Nothing mattered more than the time they spent together. He wanted her, and she wanted him.

When they made love for the first time, her world took on the rainbow hues of perfect happiness. To protect her reputation he had insisted upon keeping their love affair secret. With a thoughtfulness that made her love him even more, he had taken care to ensure she wouldn't get pregnant.

"Neither of us is ready for that, sweet Susie," he'd said before kissing away her fears.

When his leave had been up, he'd promised to write. When he hadn't, she'd made excuses for him. Mat loved her, she'd assured herself over and over. He wouldn't lie to her. Six weeks later Susanna discovered that the precautions had failed. Mat had gotten her pregnant.

Church-mouse poor and only nineteen, she'd been terrified. And yet, she had wanted the baby desperately. Her lively imagination began spinning out a wonderful life for the two of them. Mat would come home, and they would be married. He would take care of her and their child. They would be a family. She believed in Mat. She believed in love.

She had been a fool.

A scavenging crow screeched in the distance. Susanna shuddered and averted her face from the wind that seemed to grow sharper by the minute.

For nearly six weeks she had known this day would arrive. For six weeks she had been fighting the urge to pack her belongings into her Jeep and leave this place she loved.

After ten long years, Mateo Cruz was coming home.

* * *

"...and Aurora Olvera called about her appointment next Friday. She has to go to Gallup that day and needs to reschedule."

Stifling a yawn, Susanna scribbled Aurora's name at the bottom of the long list of calls she needed to return. It was nearly ten. As soon as she had walked through the door of her duplex, she'd called the receptionist at the clinic for her messages.

"Anything else?" she asked the woman on the other end of the line.

She heard the sound of an exaggerated sigh. "Nothing else, except that I'm in love."

So what else is new? she wondered privately. Lupe Becenti was eighteen and cute as a spring lamb. She was also man-crazy.

"I thought you were bored with Ralph Horse Herder." Susanna rested her elbow on the desk and leaned against the receiver, letting her eyes drift closed.

"Forget Ralph. I'm talking about our new Police Chief."

Susanna's eyes opened with a snap, and her head came up so fast her senses whirled. "He's here already?" The question was out before she could stop it.

"Is he ever! I saw him arrive when I was walking to work." This time Lupe's sigh sounded more like a moan. "I read all the stories in the paper, didn't you? About how he almost died when that bomb exploded under his car and all. In Colombia or Bolivia or one of those South American countries where they're having all those drug wars."

"Brazil," Susanna corrected, staring at the words on her pad. They wavered in front of her, and she closed her eyes tightly. "He was on duty at the embassy there."

"Whatever. Anyway, it was so awful, all that blood, and his poor wife being killed 'cause she was driving instead of him."

Susanna opened her eyes and raised her gaze to the ceiling. Her eyes stung. "If that's all the messages—"

"People say he was in the hospital for months and months," Lupe continued as though she hadn't heard. "You can tell, too, 'cause he walks with this sexy limp, and he has scars on his face, not bad ones exactly, only you can't help but notice them. My sister said he was the best-looking boy in her class. All the girls were crazy about him. 'Course, now, he's not what you'd call handsome, but there's something about him, like those guys in the movies who're always taking on the bad guys alone because everyone else is too scared."

Susanna felt herself stiffen. "Take my advice, Lupe. Stay away from Mat Cruz." Her voice came out fast and harsh, but she was too tired to care. "He's not your type."

There was a sudden pause. When Lupe spoke again, her voice was sharp with curiosity. "Hey, this sounds interesting, Ms. Spencer. I didn't know you knew him."

Susanna cursed the rash impulse that had made her want to protect her young friend. "Forget I said anything," she said, suppressing a sigh. "I need a nice long nap."

"Rough night, huh?"

"Two rough nights—and days." She glanced toward the bundle of soiled surgical scrubs she had dropped by the front door. Tomorrow or the next day she had to find time in her crowded schedule for a trip to the Laundromat in Chamisa.

"One more thing, Lupe. Please tell Dr. Greenleaf that Robin Clearwater will bring her baby in tomorrow for a postnatal exam. I've already signed the birth certificate."

Lupe repeated the message in the precise way Susanna had taught her. One of the first things she'd learned when she'd first started delivering babies was meticulous accuracy. A mislaid call from a client could lead to terrible consequences.

"What time will you be in?" Lupe asked when she finished.

Susanna glanced down at her khaki pants. Two days ago they had been crisply ironed, and her blouse had smelled of sunshine from the line. Now they were both wrinkled and limp. She was beginning to feel the same way.

"Late this afternoon, unless I get an emergency call. I'll see you then."

"Right. Oh, and Ms. Spencer?"

Susanna stifled a sigh. "What?" she asked as pleasantly as she could manage.

"When you see Mateo Cruz, you'll understand what I'm talking about."

Susanna mumbled something and hung up. Mateo Cruz was the last person she wanted to see.

Putting aside her pen and pad, she dropped her head and tried to rub the kinks from her neck. Like it or not, however, she had to see him one more time, if only to prove to herself that he no longer had any power over her.

What they'd had was as cold as yesterday's ashes. Nothing he could do or say would bring it to life again.

Another yawn escaped her, and she grimaced. More than anything she craved a bath and a nice long nap. And maybe, if she had the energy to prepare it, a cup of the herbal tea Grandfather Horse Herder had blended for her when she'd had the flu last month. To keep harmony in her body, he'd explained. Lord knows, she could certainly use a lot more of that right now.

"Move, Susanna, or you'll turn to stone right here." Feeling every aching muscle, she pushed herself to her feet and made her way down the hall to her bedroom.

She lived alone. Her nearest neighbors were John and Aurora Olvera, who lived on a large horse ranch three miles north. The Santa Ysabel Medical Clinic and Tribal Headquarters were four miles south. Until last week, Old Man Nez, a distant relative of Lily Cruz, had lived next door.

She was still angry about that. Couldn't they have found their precious new police chief another place to live? she grumbled to herself. Someplace closer to the center of things? Who did he think he was, anyway? Some kind of hometown hero, come back to thrill the locals?

"So he has a chest full of medals. Big deal," she muttered, as she kicked off her shoes and flopped onto her big white bed.

Well, this was her side of the duplex, leased to her because she was Hannah's stepdaughter. Mat had better learn to respect her privacy but quick.

Annoyed that her heart suddenly seemed to beat faster every time she thought of him, she let the serenity settle around her. The house was so quiet she could hear the wind rustling through the bare branches of the aspen trees outside.

She took a deep breath and held it, then slowly released the trapped air. Suddenly feeling tense, she stood and walked to the window. The day was crystal-bright, and the dry brown vista wavered in front of her eyes like a shimmering mirage.

A gust of wind blew against the pane. Even though the bedroom was warm, she shivered. She had been gazing out this same window on a hot July dawn when she'd seen Mat for the first time. He had been standing next to the crumbling wall that marked the boundary of the leasehold, watching the sunrise.

He'd had the look of a man who had just gotten out of bed. His glossy black hair had been tossed into careless disarray, as though by his pillow. His hard-hewn jaw had been covered by a dark stubble. Above the strong bridge of his nose, his brows had been drawn in a thunderous frown, as though he were angry at the awakening day.

He was naked to the waist, and barefoot. His snug jeans rode low on his hips, the top two buttons carelessly left undone.

His chest was wide, his waist lean and hard, his shoulders capped with the thick muscles of an extremely strong man. His skin, the color of hand-rubbed copper, was smooth and glistening in the sunlight.

Susanna must have moved. Or perhaps her thoughts had somehow intruded into his. Before she could duck out of sight, he had turned to impale her with dangerous black eyes that made her pulse flutter like a butterfly caught in a net.

A slow, audacious grin creased the hard planes of his face as, with what seemed to be deliberate slowness, he dropped his gaze to the rounded contours of her small breasts outlined against her thin cotton nightgown.

Something powerful and reckless flashed in his midnight pupils. One lean hip cocked higher, as though beckoning her to him.

She went hot all over. And then a strangely pleasurable feeling began in the pit of her stomach, spreading quickly to fill her with unaccustomed excitement.

Run, she had told herself at that instant, but already it had been too late. She had fallen in love with him.

"I never had a chance," she whispered, disgust turning her hazel eyes to a dull, lifeless gold.

Susanna jerked her gaze away from the barren yard. She seemed a stranger now, that lonely, naive girl standing mesmerized at the window. "Maiden with shining eyes," her stepmother had called her that summer.

When Mat had finished with her, she had no longer been a maiden, and the shine in her eyes had been caused by tears.

Susanna glanced toward the old cedar chest at the foot of her bed. *Don't!* screamed a part of her. *Leave the past alone.*

But that wasn't possible now. Mat Cruz was back in the pueblo, living in the house where he had been born. For better or worse, they would be living only the width of a wall apart.

Sooner or later, he was sure to bring up that summer when they had been lovers. Why not? As far as he was concerned, everything had turned out fine. He'd had his summer fling and walked away without a backward glance.

Muscles aching, she knelt on the cold tile and opened the chest. Her winter sweaters were stored here, along with her mother's wedding veil and an old album of family pictures. Tucked into the pages of the album was a letter.

Her fingers felt clumsy as she opened it. The black ink was tear-splotched and faded, but the words were still there, written in spiked, heavy letters, as though the pen had stabbed at the paper.

Susanna knew them by heart, but she made herself read them again.

Susanna,
I'm not much at writing letters so I'll make this short. You might be pregnant, but the baby isn't mine. I made

damn sure of that. And even if it were, I'm married now. My wife is expecting a baby. Find someone else and marry him. Give your baby a name. Forget about me, just as I plan to forget about you.

It was signed "M.C."

Susanna went cold inside, just as she had done on that long-ago morning. At first she hadn't believed him. It had taken some doing, but she'd tracked down his phone number and called Mat in San Francisco.

A woman had answered. "Trina Cruz," she'd said in a voice filled with pride. Mat hadn't lied. He'd been married. Maybe he'd been married all along.

Susanna heard the brittle crackle of paper and looked down. Her fist was clenched around the letter, her knuckles white, the veins in her slender wrist distended.

Forget? How could she forget the moment when she stopped trusting? When she stopped believing in happy endings and started hurting? How could she forget the child she had lost—the child he had denied?

Oh no, she thought with a deep bitterness. She would never forget.

Relaxing her hand, she carefully smoothed out the crumpled letter, then refolded it. She returned the letter to the album. Then, quickly, before she could change her mind, she lifted the album aside. Nestled in the bottom of the chest, wrapped in tissue paper, was a rag doll, her own handmade version of Raggedy Andy.

Shaggy black yarn framed a round face sporting black button eyes. Tiny gold freckles marched across pink cheeks. The bright red grin was mischievous and just a bit crooked.

Her hands shook as she lifted the doll from the chest and smoothed her palm over the miniature denim overalls. The hair was matted where sticky hands had clutched. The stubby foot was ragged where a small mouth had chewed. A spot of strained plums stained Andy's cheek.

She pressed the soft toy to her lips, inhaling the faint scent of baby powder. "Bobby," she whispered, choking on the pain. "Mama misses you so much, so very much."

A choking sob convulsed her throat, and she bit her lip to keep it from escaping. She wouldn't cry. Not again. Crying only made her weak. And it couldn't bring back her son. Nothing in this world could do that.

Carefully, as though it were made of the most precious materials, she replaced the doll in its cocoon of tissue paper. Then, head bowed, she reaffirmed the vow she had made years ago. She would never forgive Mateo Cruz.

Chapter 2

Mat Cruz braced his strong right hand against the wall and stared through the window at the dusty plaza. Outside, the air was crisp and the wind was brisk. The cottonwoods hugging the banks of Wildcat Creek had already lost their leaves. The gnarled branches seemed weary and vulnerable, like a formation of infantrymen struggling home after a bloody battle.

Like me, he thought, rubbing his aching temple.

"Don't overdo, Sergeant," the doctor had warned when he'd given in to Mat's demand and discharged him three weeks early. "You're still weak."

Weak, hell, Mat thought in savage frustration. He felt as shaky as a raw recruit after his first day on the obstacle course. But that would change, now that he was out of that damn hospital and away from the nervous Nellies who kept nagging at him to take it slow. He'd taken it slow for months, and what good had it done?

He needed to push himself to the limit, find out what he could do and what he couldn't. And then he would work on the things he couldn't do.

Talk about instant humility, he thought with sardonic self-mockery. One night he'd gone to bed thinking he'd had it all wired—a clear shot at the top of the heap, a job he loved, the respect of his men.

Three weeks later he'd opened his eyes in an army hospital, helpless as a newborn, great gaps in his memory, unable even to say his name. His wife was dead, his kids shipped off to San Francisco to stay with his sister-in-law, his career blasted apart by the same shrapnel that had ripped into his left side.

The doctors had all but written him off. He would be lucky if he regained ten percent mobility, they'd told him with brutal man-to-man honesty. But the army took care of its own, they assured him. He would always have a home in one of the VA hospitals.

The hell he would, he'd shouted at them, struggling so hard to move they'd had to sedate him. He'd gotten mad then. Killing mad. The smug bastards with their degrees might have given up, but he hadn't. A man was only defeated it he stopped trying. Mat Cruz could handle anything but defeat.

Jaw tight at the memory of those nightmare months, Mat turned his wrist so that he could see his watch. 1200 hours, he thought, and then frowned. No, it was noon. He was a civilian now. He'd better get used to thinking like one. After all, this was his first day on his new job. Chief of Tribal Police.

He tightened his hand into a fist and studied the place that was to be his home. The tall adobe buildings reminded him of the Presidio in San Francisco, where he'd been stationed when he'd married Trina. Only those buildings had been red brick, and these were mud. Most of the structures were also years older than the nineteenth-century fort, perhaps hundreds of years older. Exactly when they'd been constructed no one knew for sure.

Unlike the bustling hospital that had been his home for the past nine months, no one seemed in a hurry in Santa Ysabel. A knot of local men, some wearing traditional garb and black reservation hats, others in jeans and flannel shirts, stood in front of the Tribal Headquarters, smoking and talking.

A few tourists wearing expressions of curiosity on their Anglo faces wandered here and there, their designer finery and expensive cameras looking distinctly out of place.

Overhead, the sky was the pale blue of early fall, without clouds to soften its monochrome monotony. Against this flat background the sun shone with a chilly brilliance, casting a shadow over the sturdy footbridge where his nine-year-old daughter, Melissa, sat reading a story to her baby brother, Cody.

Three or four picture books lay scattered on the sun-bleached planks like bright patches of life in a dead landscape. Cody, not yet two, bounced up and down on his fat little rump, his attention divided between the book in Missy's lap and two half-grown yellow dogs wrestling in the dust a few feet away.

"I need candles for Cody's birthday cake," Trina had said that last morning. "I'll drive you to work so I can have the car."

The moment she'd turned the key, the bomb had exploded. Because he'd been in the passenger seat, he'd been thrown clear, his left side a bloody, unrecognizable mess. Trina never had a chance. The assassins hired by the drug cartel to thwart the war on drugs in South America had claimed another innocent victim.

No matter how many times or in how many different ways the shrinks told him it wasn't his fault, he would always feel responsible.

When the war on drugs turned hot, he had asked for assignment to the American Embassy in Brazil, where the international task force was headquartered. They had needed an experienced noncom, a man used to working as a military policeman, to head up an elite twenty-man security detail.

He'd been the perfect man for the job. Hell, he'd even called in a few favors to get the billet. He had wanted to be where the action was. And why not?

Mat Cruz had been a man with a goal. Six stripes by the time he was forty. Master Sergeant, the best of the non-coms. A soldier's soldier, respected by privates and generals alike.

He clenched his left hand. A hot splinter of pain shot through his wrist, followed by an icy numbness in his long blunt fingers. When he had finally emerged from the drug-induced fog they'd kept him in for weeks, to discover his left side completely paralyzed, they'd told him he was lucky, that he still had the use of his right hand. The bastards hadn't even considered the fact that he might just be left-handed. The only thing his right hand could do as well as his left was caress a woman's body.

At the moment, however, a woman could be a walking centerfold and he wouldn't be interested. Not that he didn't miss sex. He did. But he'd been without it a long time, so long he no longer counted the months. He had stopped sleeping with Trina after she'd told him about her affair with his CO, the one designed to cadge him a plum job in the Pentagon. When he'd refused to accept the new assignment, she'd been coldly furious. One by one, sparing him none of the details, she had recounted the other affairs she'd had over the years.

That night he'd left the house in a rage, determined to find a woman who would welcome him home with an eager smile and a loving hug instead of bitter complaints and accusations. To his chagrin, he'd discovered he wasn't a man who could cheat on his wife, even though she'd been unfaithful. Instead, he'd gotten blind drunk every night for a week. After that, he no longer cared what she did, as long as she was discreet.

Sensation returned to his fingers, sharp stinging needles running up his wrist. It sometimes went on for hours like that. It had been a long road back, nine endless months of grueling hard work learning to walk and talk and live again.

No matter what else he did now, no matter how many hours of therapy he put in, his once-powerful body would no longer be perfect. Partially disabled, the army doctors had termed it when they'd retired him on a disability pen-

sion. A damn cripple, was what they meant. At age thirty-
six, after eighteen years in army khaki, he'd been out of a
job, scrapped like an obsolete weapon.

It hurt like hell.

"Feel at home yet?"

Mat half turned toward the deep voice. John Olvera,
Chairman of the Santa Ysabel Tribal Council, stood in the
doorway. "Not yet," Mat said with a twisted grin. "But I'm
working on it."

Olvera dropped his dusty Stetson onto the desk and joined
Mat at the window. The Tribal Chief was a rancher by
choice, a diplomat by education. He was past forty, and
looked it, but the lines in his face and the experience in his
eyes gave him a quiet strength that Mat respected. He'd seen
the same look on countless combat veterans, the ones who'd
fought the hardest and talked the least.

"If you need more time to settle in, take it," Olvera said.
"We've done without a Chief of Police for a few hundred
years. We can survive without one for a few more days."

Mat managed a smile. His face was still stiff from the re-
pairs made by the plastic surgeon. The doctors had done the
best they could. At least his face no longer looked like
hamburger, but he had a feeling it would be a long time before he was comfortable with the stranger in the mirror.

"Thanks, but it's time I got off my duff and made myself useful again."

"It's your call. The Council intends to help all we can."

"You've done plenty already," Mat told the man who was
technically his boss. "Getting the house in shape and the
office ready, putting the Bronco at my disposal. Hell, John,
I'm used to army snafus and red tape. This is 4.0 treat-
ment."

He glanced at the newly constructed cell in the corner of
the office. Considered a sovereign nation by the United
States government, Santa Ysabel had the right to make its
own laws and enforce them, so long as they didn't conflict
with federal statutes.

Olvera ran his finger along a strip of peeling beige paint
on the wall. "Sorry we didn't get the office painted. I ran

out of money." A rare smile softened the stern lines of his face. "That happens a lot around here."

Tribal Headquarters was almost sixty years old. The thick adobe walls had been patched and repatched. Metal tubing snaked up one wall and across the ceiling to the overhead light fixture that had been installed less than ten years ago.

A month ago this space had been a storeroom. It still smelled musty.

Mat lifted his shoulders in a shrug. "Painted walls are the last thing on the list. First we need to hire two deputies, and then we need to get them trained and out on regular patrols. Driving here this morning, I nearly got clipped by some cowboy in a rusted-out Chevy. Must have been going eighty at least. Thank God no one got in his way."

John grimaced. "Tell me about it. With the clinic open to outsiders and the pottery studio selling to tourists on a regular basis now, we've created a nightmare. A day doesn't go by without a complaint, tourists looking in the window, kids tramping over the graves in the burying ground. Even my wife is mad as a little hornet because someone broke into the studio a few nights ago and wiped out the petty cash drawer."

Mat inhaled slowly. It had been a long time since he'd felt like a cop. "Tell her I'll be by today or tomorrow to take her statement."

John laughed. "She'll like that. But be prepared. She'll take you on a grand tour. That studio is her pride and joy."

Mat nodded politely. "Should I know her?" Already this morning he'd run into two people who had clearly remembered him very well. To him, however, they had been total strangers. He still wasn't sure they had believed him when he'd explained about the amnesia.

John shook his head. "She grew up in Texas. I met her when she came to the pueblo as part of a team of archaeologists from SMU. She was their pottery expert."

"How long you been married?"

There was a slight hesitation before the other man answered. "Almost a year this time. We were divorced for five years before I talked her into taking me back. It was a hell of struggle, though. The woman is stubborn."

Mat had the feeling there was more to it than that, but something in John's tone warned him not to push it. Instead, he crossed his arms and leaned his good shoulder against the sagging window frame.

"I looked over the applications for deputy you left on my desk. Three or four look promising."

John raised a black eyebrow. "Which ones?"

Mat hesitated. His short-term memory was still good, but he sometimes stumbled over unfamiliar names. Slowly, he listed the applicants he had decided to interview.

"Sounds good," Olvera said when Mat finished. "What can you tell me about them?"

Mat listened intently as John gave him a concise rundown on the backgrounds of the applicants. As he listened, he also studied the other man.

John Olvera was someone else he didn't remember, though he should have. Santa Ysabel was a big place in square miles, but very small in population—just over two thousand. Over the years most of the families had become intertwined, so that nearly everyone was related one way or another. John belonged to the Fire Clan on his mother's side, as did Mat. According to pueblo beliefs, they were cousins.

Two months ago Mat had just finished another frustrating therapy session and had been lying sweat-drenched and shaking on his bed in the ward when John had walked in, a job offer in his briefcase.

"The pueblo needs a police force," the man with the intelligent eyes and blunt manner had told him straight out. "Two deputies and a chief. That's you, if you want the job. Interested?"

Hell, yes, he'd been interested. Santa Ysabel needed him, even if the army didn't. He'd been given a new start, and he intended to make it work. It had to. He didn't have a second option.

"Any one of them will work damn hard for you," John said when he finished describing the candidates.

"You have any favorites?" Mat's voice was carefully devoid of expression. In the army, the man at the top generally wanted a favor for a favor. Mat had hated it, but he'd learned to live with it.

John looked at him sharply. "If you mean, is there anyone in particular I want you to hire, no." His eyes narrowed at the sun-weathered corners. "This is your department. You run it. You have a problem. You handle it."

Mat felt some of the knots in his belly loosen. "Fair enough." He glanced toward the stack of applications on the desk. It felt good to have decisions to make again.

"Those your kids on the bridge?"

Olvera's question sent a rush of chagrin flooding through him. He'd forgotten all about Missy and Cody. Damn, he thought, calling himself a few choice names, he was off to a great start.

"Yeah, they're mine, though right now I'm not so sure they're crazy about that idea. Missy looks at me like I'm some kind of sideshow freak, and Cody doesn't even remember me."

"Give it time."

Mat glanced toward the bridge. Cody had climbed into his sister's lap, his thumb now firmly poked into his mouth. His son had changed from a baby to a toddler while he'd been at Walter Reed. Those months were gone, lost to him forever. He forced back a sigh. Regret was a useless emotion. It solved nothing and made a man hurt inside.

"Soon as I get settled, I need to enroll Missy in school here. She's having nightmares again, and she's way too quiet. Having kids around her again might help her adjust."

"Hell of a thing, losing her mother that way."

Mat acknowledged the unspoken sympathy with a stiff nod. He hated to think about things that were out of his control. He'd done enough of that when he'd been flat on his back with nothing to look at but the ceiling for hours at a time.

Facing himself, accepting the guilt for the misery his ambition had caused Trina and his kids, had hurt more than the most excruciating physical pain.

He'd made mistakes—lots of them. He'd been selfish and arrogant, taking what he'd wanted from life without a thought to the consequences. But that was in the past. He couldn't change the things he'd done. He could only change the man.

"How about you?" he asked Olvera. "You have kids?"

A look of deep sorrow passed over Olvera's lean face. "We had a daughter. She died at birth. That's one of the reasons we have a midwife here now, and a clinic with a full-time doctor." His expression turned grim, as though he were remembering something painful. Whatever he was thinking, though, he kept to himself.

Mat understood. A man kept his worst pain private where it couldn't be used by his enemies to make him vulnerable.

A door slammed down the hall, the sharp crack boring into Mat's head. His left hand went to his hip, but the .38 Special that had been such a part of him was still locked in his suitcase. He wasn't yet on duty.

Just as well, he thought, opening his hand. The fingers still stung.

John glanced at his watch. "I'm late," he muttered. "Guy from Albuquerque wants to buy one of my mares. He's probably already at the ranch." He pulled a key ring from his pocket and removed two keys.

"Here's the key to the office and the one to your duplex. Yours is the one on the right, same place you lived in before. Soon as I knew you were coming for sure, I had it fixed up for you."

He held out the keys. Mat started to extend his left hand before he remembered and quickly switched hands. If John noticed his awkwardness, he didn't let it show.

"Susanna Spencer lives next door. If you need anything, I'm sure you can borrow it from her. She's been back for five years now."

"Who?" Mat pocketed the keys.

"Susanna Spencer. Robert Spencer's daughter? He married Hannah Charley when Susanna was a teenager. She lived here until she was eighteen, nineteen, something like that, before she went off to nursing school in Albuquerque."

Mat rubbed his forehead. He searched his mind, but the name meant nothing. "Tell you the truth, John, I don't even remember the house, let alone who lived next door." He hesitated, fighting the feeling of savage rage that came over him whenever he had to face one more thing he couldn't do. Or remember. "The first twenty-six years of my life are gone. Lost. The doctors think I'll probably never remember."

"Come to think of it, you were probably gone by the time she came here to live, anyway." He grinned suddenly, taking years from his face. "You'll like her. She reminds me of a little dynamo, always going someplace in a hurry, usually with a smile on her face. Anyway, she's the midwife I was talking about."

"I didn't realize there were still such things as midwives these days."

"There aren't many around. I found that out when I went to hire one. That's why I was so damn glad to find Susanna. She's not Indian, but she knows the customs and the language, so I broke tribal policy and hired her. It was probably the best chance I've ever taken. The infant mortality rate is way down and still falling, thanks to her." A grin broke over his weathered face. "Watch out, though. When she's riled, she's a real pistol. Doesn't take any guff from anyone, not even me."

Mat felt a shiver rip through him, though he wasn't sure why.

"Thanks for the warning, and for . . . everything. A few months ago—" He broke off, suddenly embarrassed by the rush of gratitude he felt for the Tribal Chairman.

Their eyes met, Mat's bleak, John's dark with understanding. "A few months ago I found us one hell of a police chief," John said in a low, strong voice, extending his right hand. After a split second's hesitation, Mat did the same.

John strode to the desk and grabbed his hat. "*Adios,* Chief. Call me if you need anything." He left, the sound of his boot heels gradually fading into the heavy silence of the old building.

Mat pushed both hands into the pockets of his new jeans and shifted his gaze to the bridge. Cody was crying. Again.

At least his son was too young to remember the violence, he consoled himself. But Missy wasn't as lucky. Before anyone had thought to shield her, she had seen pictures of her father's torn face and bloody body on TV and heard the commentator describe her mother's death.

Once she had giggled at the silliest things; now she scarcely laughed at all. Her big brown eyes, once alive with joy, were filled with the kind of sadness most adults never had to face.

I'm sorry, baby, Mat told her silently, regret biting deep. If I could have died to save Mama, I would have. The bastards just didn't give me the choice.

A feeling of helplessness twisted in Mat's gut. He had served two tours in Vietnam without thinking much about dying. He could whip a platoon of hardened veterans into shape without raising a sweat. But being both mother and father to his kids terrified him.

He swore a vicious oath that would have impressed even the crudest gunnery sergeant. It didn't help.

The coffee tasted like battery acid and smelled worse. Mat slugged down the last inch in the cup and waited for the caffeine to kick in.

It was late afternoon, and he and the children had just moved into the small two-bedroom apartment that was to be their home. The kids were in the other room, sorting through the things they'd brought with them from California, their voices shrill and grating on his ragged nerves.

Their first day on the pueblo had turned out to be a disaster. Cody had thrown up all over himself at lunch, Missy had pulled a fit when she'd discovered she was to share a bedroom with her brother, and Mat had gotten lost on the bone-jarring drive out to the house where he'd spent the first seventeen years of his life.

By the time he'd reread Olvera's directions and figured out where he'd taken a wrong turn, he would have killed for a cigarette, a quart of rye and eight hours of solitude without any more problems and frustrations.

He put the cup on the small table next to the cheap couch and rested his head on the lumpy cushion. Eyes slitted, he studied the living room, trying to find something, anything, to jog the memory tapes that had somehow gotten erased by the surgeon's scalpel.

Built low to the ground, with thick walls and small windows to blunt the glaring rays of the summer sun, the house was dimly lit and smelled of old timber and wood smoke. The floor tiles in the living room were pitted with age, and the ceiling showed signs of a leak. A large fireplace took up one wall, its blackened stones suggesting heavy use.

The place reminded him of army housing. Ugly as sin, but built to withstand a direct attack—like one Mateo Cruz, ex-army NCO.

Shifting his gaze to the vista beyond the window, he studied the empty land, praying for some spark, some stirring of remembrance in his mind. But nothing seemed familiar—not the squat red mesa, nor the barren, windswept land surrounding it.

He had studied the unemotional facts in his service jacket until they had been etched into his mind. He knew he had been born in this house, in the very room where he had stowed his few personal possessions. He knew that he had gone to school in Chamisa, joined the service when he graduated, finished first in his class on the army's toughest obstacle course during boot camp. He knew his mother's name, but not his father's, and that he was illegitimate, a half-breed, caught between two worlds. He knew when he had been married, Trina's maiden name, the date his daughter had been born—six months after her parents had wed.

But the details, the feelings, the living, breathing memories of those things, were gone. He knew his mother's name, but not her face or her voice. He knew his ancestry, but not the boy who had grown up Indian. He knew why he had married Trina, but had no memory of ever loving her.

It was driving him crazy.

"Welcome home, Cruz," he muttered, closing his eyes. In a minute he would drag his tired body into the bedroom and unpack. The house was clean. He would give it that. And someone had stocked the cupboards and refrigerator with staples. Now, if he only knew how to cook, they would be in great shape.

At least his sister-in-law had potty-trained Cody while the kids had lived with her. That was one less thing he had to learn how to do.

Suddenly a scream cut through the silence. "Stop it, Cody," Missy shouted from the bedroom. "That's my stuff."

"No, no. Mine." Cody's outrage matched his sister's—in volume, anyway.

What now? Mat thought, closing his eyes. He'd always thought he was as good a father as the next man. Now he was beginning to discover just how ignorant he was when it came to the day to day hassles of raising two independent, strong-willed kids. In that, at least, Trina had been exemplary.

"Let go, or I'll tell."

"No, mine."

Mat sighed. Another battle to mediate. He ran the palm of his hand down his face. It'll be better tomorrow, he told himself, sitting up.

"Daddy!"

The sharp sound of breaking glass accompanied Missy's anguished cry.

"Look what you did!" she shouted. "You broke my perfume."

Cody began to scream.

As he shot to his feet, Mat's heart kicked into a gallop. Raw fear shuddered through him for a split second before the icy calm that had saved his life under fire more than once took over. Whatever it was, he would handle it.

When he reached the bedroom, the cloying scent of strong perfume nearly made him gag. "What the hell?"

Cody sat on the floor, surrounded by bits of frosted glass, his chubby foot clutched in his hand. As soon as he saw his father, his screams grew louder.

"Ow-ee," Cody wailed, letting go of his foot and holding up both hands.

Mat scooped Cody into his arms, patting his back awkwardly. "It's okay, scout. Daddy's got you." He glanced around the sparsely furnished room, then sat down on one of the beds.

Cody cried louder, peeking at his father through long wet lashes. Quickly, Mat examined the damage. The cut was small. A Band-Aid and antiseptic should take care of it.

Some of the fear eased from him. He hugged Cody tighter. "It's just a scratch. Don't even need the medics for this one."

It was then that he noticed Missy. She stood a few feet away, her face whiter than the walls. Her eyes were huge pools of terror.

"Cody hurt," the little boy said, twisting like a pretzel until he could see his foot.

Mat dropped a reassuring kiss on Cody's silky black head. "Yes, I know. Daddy will wash it off and put some ointment on it in just a little bit. First I need to talk to your sister."

He redirected his attention to his daughter. "Your brother's still a baby," he told her with the awkward gentleness of a man who was more at home barking out orders to men almost as tough as he was. "He didn't mean to drop your perfume bottle."

Missy stared at the drop of bright red blood on the tile, both hands pressed over her ears. "It's not my fault, it's not my fault," she said over and over.

"Missy, I didn't say it was. I heard you tell him to put it down."

"I tried to take it away from him, Daddy," she cried, her shrill little voice quivering. "I told him it was mine." Her fawn brown eyes filled with tears. "Aunt Patty gave it to me so...so I could...remember...Mommy." The tears turned to sobs.

Mat swore silently. He could back down the meanest drunk with just a look, but one crying little girl made him go weak inside.

"Sweetheart, calm down. Don't cry, okay?" He hesitated, then reached out his hand, and she came to him, folding into the circle of his arm like a terrified kitten seeking shelter.

"It's okay, baby," he said into her tangled curls. "We'll get through this, you'll see. You and me and Cody, we'll be a family again."

He felt Missy shake her head against his shoulder. "We can't be a family without M-Mommy."

Mat dropped his forehead to Missy's little girl shoulder, then raised it quickly before she could feel the weight. As gently as he could manage, he lifted her small chin until she was looking at him again. "Yes, we can, baby," he said quietly but firmly. "If we help each other, take care of each other—"

"Aunt Patty said you can't even take care of yourself," Missy blurted out in a rush, as though she'd been holding the words in too long. "I heard her tell Uncle Mark that you shouldn't even be out of the hospital yet. She said me 'n' Cody would just make it harder on you to...to adjust."

Fury twisted in him like a barbed hook. Trina's sister had been barely civil to him the few times she'd brought the children to see him in the hospital. It hadn't taken much to figure out that she held him responsible for Trina's death.

"Aunt Patty is wrong," he said, his voice barely in control. "I need you and Cody to help me remember how to be a daddy again." His hand trembled as he wiped the tears from her cheeks.

"Okay now?" he asked.

Missy sucked her lower lip between her teeth and nodded. She didn't look okay, but at least she'd stopped crying.

Mat tightened his left arm around Cody's chunky body, then stood up. "There's a first-aid kit in the duffel bag in my room," he told Missy in a calm voice. "Get it for me, will you please?"

Without another word she walked across the hall to the other bedroom.

Mat carried Cody into the kitchen and sat him on the counter, his feet in the sink. He washed the blood from the fat little heel, then lifted Cody's foot to the light streaming through the window over the chipped bowl.

The cut continued to ooze slowly as he wiped the sticky blood away with his fingers. Cody cried out, and tried to pull away. "Hurt Cody," he said with wide-eyed indignation.

"Sorry, scout," Mat muttered. "The sliver is still in there."

"Daddy?" Missy stood at his elbow, her mouth trembling, the first-aid kit clutched tightly in her hands.

"Thanks," he said, taking the small metal box from her. Missy's gaze jerked from his face to the blood on his hand. Her face paled even more.

"Missy?" Mat asked urgently. "What's wrong?"

"I feel sick," she choked. Before he could say another word, she spun away from him and ran from the room. A second later he heard the bathroom door slam shut.

What next? Mat thought, rubbing his stiff jaw.

Next you bandage up your son, he thought grimly. Then you try to find a way to make things right for your daughter without screwing up any worse than you already have.

He found a clean towel in the second drawer he tried, then set about removing the splinter of glass. But it was embedded too deeply to remove without tweezers. Which he didn't have. And even if he did, his left hand couldn't begin to manage the precise movement needed. His right had the strength, but not the dexterity.

He would have to take Cody to the clinic near the center of the plaza.

"Saddle up, soldier," he said as he lifted the boy into the crook of his left arm. "We're going to take a trip back into town."

Cody brightened. "I' cream?" he asked eagerly.

Mat laughed. "I guess I can stand another trip to the Prickly Pear Café if you can," he said, carrying the boy into the living room. Missy would have to go with them. He couldn't leave her alone.

He started toward the hall. A flash of red caught his eye, and he walked to the window, staring thoughtfully at the Jeep parked in the ramshackle carport. His memory stirred. Hadn't Olvera said something about the woman next door going to nursing school?

What was her name? Susanna something?

"What the hell, it's worth a try." He ruffled his son's hair. "Right?" Without waiting for an answer, he shouted to Missy that he was going next door for a minute, then headed out the front door, Cody still in his arms.

A sharp gust of wind hit him head-on. The air had turned from crisp to cold. When he reached his neighbor's front door, he turned his back to the wind, trying to protect the boy from the chill.

He knocked on the bright pink panel, then waited. Another gust of wind, more biting than the first, blew his hair over his forehead and kicked bits of gravel over his boots. Cody ducked his head into the curve of his father's neck.

Mat knocked again, harder. His hand went numb. He bit off an obscene curse. "C'mon," he muttered. "I know you're there."

Just as he raised his fist to beat on the door one more time, it opened. The woman who stood there was tiny, barely tall enough to reach his shoulder. She had obviously been sleeping. Her cheeks were flushed, her mouth soft, her exotic gold eyes half-open and blinking drowsily, reminding him of a small barn owl. A large white T-shirt reached to midthigh, covering her body like a soft drape, delineating every generous curve.

Mat sucked in. Something moved in his head like a shadow passing over a darker background. He frowned. Had he known this woman? he wondered.

"Susanna?" he asked politely.

The moment he spoke the sleepy-owl look fled from her eyes. Her soft mouth compressed, her chin came up, her face hardened.

"Hello, Mat," she said, her voice cold and unfriendly. "Welcome home."

Chapter 3

The rest of the cold words Susanna had rehearsed stuck in her throat. Mat had a child in his arms, a solemn, black-haired little boy peeking at her through lashes as dense and blunt as his father's. His small cheek was pressed to Mat's leaner one. His square chin had the same stubborn line, his miniature black brows bore an identical slant. But unlike the man's world-weary black eyes, the boy's were an innocent brown. Like Bobby's.

She forgot to breathe. A longing to hold his sturdy, healthy little body against hers grew inside her until she had to press her hands to her stomach to keep from reaching for him.

"Hi," the toddler said shyly, his mouth opening in a toothy grin. "Cody wants i' cream."

He was dressed in blue corduroy rompers with extra padding on the knees and a blue-and-white striped T-shirt. The one little brown foot she could see was bare, the chubby little toes curling in.

Making herself smile brightly, she reached out to tweak those tiny toes. But even as she smiled at Mat's son, she was coldly furious at the man himself.

How dare he bring his son to see her like this when he had denied the child the two of them had created? she seethed silently.

Then she remembered. Mateo Cruz would dare anything. Integrity was only a word to him. Rules meant nothing. He thought only of what *he* wanted, what *he* needed, what *he* could take.

"Hello, Cody," she murmured to the little boy, ignoring the man who held him. "I'm afraid I don't have any ice cream. Would a lollipop do?"

The little boy shook his head. "I' cream," he said in a stubborn voice.

Mat drew a slow breath, seeking to ease the tension that had gripped him the moment his new neighbor had looked up at him, her eyes only half-open, her mouth full and soft from sleep. He felt as though he'd taken a nine-millimeter slug in the gut, but for the life of him he didn't know why. Maybe because, for the first time in months, his body had quickened at the sight of a pretty woman.

"This is a hell of a way to say hello, I know," he said as politely as he could manage, "but I need your help."

Her eyes narrowed, and he found he liked the way they confronted him through the thick gold-tipped lashes. He appreciated directness in a woman.

"Cody stepped on a piece of glass. It's still in his foot. I can't get it out." He lifted Cody's leg so that she could see.

Susanna inspected the small wound with critical, experienced eyes. The cut seemed superficial; it had already begun to clot. No sutures would be necessary, just a Band-Aid and a generous measure of TLC.

Relief traveled through her. Ten minutes and the child would be walking on that foot again. A tiny smile grew in her mind. Running is more like it, she thought, holding his sturdy little foot in her palm.

"Ow-ee," Cody said, wrinkling his brow as though trying to decide what he was supposed to do next.

"Yes, darling, I see," she said softly, all too conscious of the man watching her so intently.

"Where do you want him?"

Reminding herself that Mat had never held her son in his arms, never kissed him or hugged him or contributed a penny to his support, she stepped back and opened the door wide. "Take him into the kitchen. The light's best in there."

Mat stepped over the threshold, then waited while she closed the door against the afternoon chill. The wind caught her before the door was fully closed, plastering her shirt against her like a body stocking. Shivering, she shoved the door the final inch until the latch clicked.

He'd been right, he thought with an unexpected rush of masculine interest. She was small, but her body was surprisingly ripe, the kind that raised a man's blood pressure to dangerous levels.

"Maybe you should change into something . . . warmer," he suggested, his frank gaze shifting to her breasts for a heartbeat before returning, unrepentant, to her face.

He let his gaze rest on her mouth long enough to imagine what it would feel like against his, but not so long that it appeared obvious.

Blood surged to her cheeks. How dare he look at her that way? she raged, somehow keeping her temper in check because of the child between them. Did he think he could waltz back into her life and pretend nothing had happened? Was that how he saw her—a convenient lay right next door? Sweet, stupid Susanna, an easy target?

Not this time, she vowed silently. This time she knew better than to mistake sexual need for love. The next time she took a man to her bed, she would know that he loved her for herself and not what she could give him.

"I'll get my medical bag." Leaving him standing there staring after her, she retreated to her bedroom and closed the door.

She rummaged through the drawers of her bureau for clean clothes, then stripped off her shirt. Cool air from the open window hit her naked body, and her nipples hardened, as though possessive hands had brushed over them. Deep inside her body a whisper-soft tension spread to the most intimate part of her.

Dropping the shirt in a heap at her bare feet, she quickly pulled on a bra and panties, her most disreputable pair of jeans, an old sloppy sweatshirt. She didn't bother with shoes. Nor did she comb the sleep tangles from the unruly brown hair waving past her shoulders.

Why should she care if Mat Cruz found her desirable or not? She shouldn't, she answered firmly, punctuating the thought with a determined nod of her head. He wasn't worthy of another thought, another ounce of energy. If it hadn't been for the little boy, she would have slammed the door in his face.

Her voluminous medical bag, stocked with emergency supplies, sat in its usual spot by the door. She reached for it, then paused to take a few bracing breaths.

Involuntarily, her gaze went to the pristine white wall opposite. The master bedroom in the other apartment was separated from hers by ten inches of adobe. In the quiet of a summer night with the windows open he would be only a whisper away.

"So I'll sleep with the windows closed," she told herself with a grimace.

Squaring her shoulders, she opened the door and left the safety of her white bedroom. It was a short distance—a few steps down the hall, to the living room and then into the kitchen.

As soon as she entered, Mat looked up. The man must have terrific peripheral vision, she thought sourly, glancing down at her bare feet. As far as she knew, she hadn't made a sound.

He stood by the sink, holding his son with one strong forearm under the boy's chubby bottom. His shoulders were still massive, wider than most, and slanted toward his strong corded neck in heavily muscled lines that suggested sinewy strength. Beneath the crisp cotton of his pale blue shirt, his torso was hard sinew and lean muscle tapering slightly to the low-riding line of his belt. If his massive injuries had restricted him in any way, it didn't show.

Turning away, she switched on the overhead light, then placed her bag on the kitchen table and snapped it open.

Busying herself laying out her supplies, she studied him without seeming to.

His face had a hawklike leanness and a stillness that suggested enormous restraint. His jaw was hard, inclined to be square, and his mouth, too ruthless to be sensual, marked him as a man used to being in command.

Those things were the same, but there were differences, too.

Deep lines now bracketed lips that looked stiff, as though he had forgotten how to smile. On the left side of his face, faint white scars angled away from the corner of his eye to disappear into the glossy thickness of hair now threaded with a generous measure of silver. Another thatch of scars scored his rigid jaw, reminding her of a wind-scoured granite cliff.

He still stood tall, nearly six feet, but he clearly favored his left side. His feet, shod in boots that looked new, were planted wide; his lean hips still angled in that same raw male aggressiveness she'd seen before, but the cocksure arrogance that had once been such a part of him was missing. Had Mat learned humility? she wondered, and then dismissed the thought out of hand. Nothing could humble this man.

"This where you want him?" he asked in the faintly accented voice she remembered.

"That's fine. Put his foot in the sink."

"Can I help?" Mat asked, his deep voice sounding incongruous in the room that had heard only female voices since she had moved in.

"I'll manage," she said in the curt professional tone she'd developed as a student nurse to ward off unwelcome advances from overly aggressive male patients.

Surprise flickered in eyes that still reminded her of sun-warmed ebony, but instead of the devilish laughter she remembered, she saw shadows there, the kind that came from hours of haunting agony.

Something twisted inside Susanna, but she refused to give the emotion a name. If it had no name, it didn't exist.

"Here you go, scout," he told his son, hefting him onto the edge of the white porcelain sink. "Sit still for a minute, okay?" He dropped a quick kiss on his son's head, then stood back to give her room.

Susanna, in the act of turning around, didn't see him move until it was too late. She slammed into him, the breath escaping her lungs with a soft gasp. Hands full, she was thrown off balance. His reflexes were quicker than hers. One arm looped around her waist, holding her steady until she found secure footing. She had an impression of musky warmth and coiled strength before she pushed away.

"You okay?" he asked, his hand still outstretched to catch her if she fell.

"No problem," she managed to get out. For all the changes she had noted, there was one she hadn't explored, but the momentary pressure of his body against her told her that, in one very elemental way, Mat had not changed at all. He was still powerfully male.

Susanna cleared a sudden flurry of nervousness from her throat. "So, Cody," she said as she washed her hands and dried them on a clean towel. "Let's see if we can get rid of that nasty old piece of glass, okay?"

The little boy bobbed his head. "'Kay," he said, popping his thumb contentedly into his mouth. He seemed fascinated by the whimsical clay rabbit with floppy ears that sat on the counter.

"This is Skippy," she said, rubbing the bunny's ear. "He's a tickle bunny."

Cody removed his thumb long enough to ask quite seriously, "What's that?"

"Here, I'll show you." She picked up the small figure and poked it gently into his stomach, tickling him until he curled his tiny body over her hand. He giggled helplessly, his sturdy legs kicking in excitement, the cut in his heel temporarily forgotten.

Mat felt an odd sensation in his gut, a kind of softening that took him by surprise. They looked so right together, the shy little boy and the spirited woman with sunshine in her smile. She was good, a natural with kids. Cody was obviously smitten.

His left leg, the one that had been in a cast for months, began to stiffen up on him, and he shifted position, waiting for the painful knot to ease.

"Get out of my light." Her voice was cold.

Mat obeyed, then caught himself. He was the one who usually gave the orders. He wasn't used to taking them, especially not from a pint-size pixie who couldn't weigh more than a hundred pounds. I'll give you that one, lady, he told her silently. Just don't push it.

Aloud, he said in what he thought was a friendly tone, "He's shy with strangers."

Susanna spared Mat a cool look. "He doesn't look shy to me." She glanced pointedly at Cody, who was busy playing with a drip from the faucet, his head pillowed trustingly against her breast.

"Hey, scout," Mat said in a plaintive voice. "You just made your old man look like a jerk in front of this lady, you know that? You and me, we're supposed to be pals."

Susanna refused to smile. When he'd been in a playful mood, Mat had been irresistible. In fact, that was one of the things she'd loved most about him—his ability to make her laugh. Thank God she was no longer susceptible, she told herself firmly.

She put the miniature bunny into Cody's hands, then skillfully, talking nonsense to distract the squirming toddler, set to work.

Mat stood behind her, careful to stay out of her light. As he watched her work, he noticed how small and capable her hands were. They would be strong, he thought, and gentle against a man's face.

Like a hawk swooping toward prey, his imagination carried him into the bedroom. Into bed. With this woman next to him, her hands exploring his body. Caressing. Stroking.

His belly rippled involuntarily, then hardened. Below his belt, his body reacted. God help him, it had been a long time since a woman had touched him intimately. He hadn't realized until now just how much he'd missed that.

In the hospital he had been surrounded by women—nurses, therapists, even a fair number of doctors. If he had wanted sex, it had been available.

He simply hadn't been interested. But he was now.

He shifted his weight, trying to ignore the sudden stirring in his loins. The woman had a serenity about her, an air of ladylike dignity, that fascinated him.

In the sunlight her hair seemed to change color with each slight movement of her bent head. Sometimes it was a deep rich brown with a hint of red, suggesting a hidden temper. Sometimes it was threaded with gold, like a priceless tapestry he'd seen once in a museum in London, and so soft looking it begged to be stroked.

Beneath her tumbled bangs, her face had a classical fragility of line and a daintiness of structure that made a man want to slay dragons and fight duels in order to win one of her smiles.

Her eyebrows were the richest shade of brown he'd ever seen, her lashes equally dark and lush, casting little shadows on her cheeks.

And then there was her mouth. Full, naturally red, with soft corners and a surprisingly sensuous curve to the bottom lip. He'd never seen a mouth more suited for kissing.

Mat reached for a cigarette in his breast pocket, then remembered that he had quit in the hospital. Damn, he needed a smoke.

"There. All done." Susanna kissed the plump little foot in her hand, then smoothed her finger over the Band-Aid she'd just applied.

"Aw done," Cody echoed, a smug look of satisfaction crossing his face.

Susanna hesitated, then lifted him into her arms. His short little arms twined trustingly around her neck. "Cody aw done," he said again, snuggling against her, his breath warming her neck. One hand still clutched the tickle bunny.

"You were such a brave boy," she murmured into his ear. "I'm so proud of you." She began to rub his solid little back.

"My son likes you," Mat said quietly, leaning back and resting his elbows on the counter.

"He's a darling. How... how old is he?"

"Almost two. His birthday's in January, the same as my daughter, Melissa. She'll be ten."

January, Susanna thought numbly. Bobby had been born in March. Mat hadn't lied in the letter. Another woman *had* been carrying his child when he'd made love to her that first time.

Abruptly she turned her back on him and walked to the table, Cody still cradled in her arms. With one hand she rummaged in her bag and came up with a red lollipop.

"This is for being such a good boy," she told the wide-eyed toddler with a grin.

"Lolly," he said joyfully. Somehow he managed to get the cellophane off and the lollipop into his mouth before Susanna could settle herself in a chair.

Leaning back, she shifted him in her lap so that he was cradled in the curve of her arm. I'll only hold him until he finishes the candy, she told herself firmly, resting her cheek on his head. Just a few more minutes, until he feels safe again.

Mat hesitated, then pulled out the chair opposite and sat down. As he stretched out his legs, Susanna noticed that the left one didn't quite straighten all the way. It was thinner, too. Not much, but enough to be noticeable, especially when he was wearing tight jeans.

Her gaze jerked back to his face. The deepened lines around his mouth and the hard look of frustration in his eyes told her that he had guessed her thoughts.

"I had some trouble a few months back," he said with a definite edge to his voice.

"I know," she said, a chill creeping across her face. "I read about the bombing in the newspaper. I'm... I'm very sorry about your wife."

"So am I," he said in a weary voice. "I keep slowing things down in my mind, trying to change the way things happened. But no matter how I replay it, I can't put myself in her place." His hand slowly formed a fist. His jaw, flushed with dusky color, was equally tight. Something told her that he hadn't spoken of these things to anyone before.

A part of her wanted to believe he deserved the pain he was feeling. Another part wanted to hold him in her arms and comfort him.

She inhaled sharply. Had she lost all sense? she thought disgustedly. Hadn't she learned anything in ten years?

Yes, she had learned to protect herself from men like this who preyed on a woman's natural instinct to feel compassion for the suffering of others.

The sympathy that had started to bud inside her withered and died.

"At least you're still alive," she said more harshly than she'd intended.

"Yeah, that's what I told myself about a thousand times in the beginning," he said sardonically. "It finally got through my thick head to be grateful."

Cody mumbled something she didn't catch. She looked down to find his little face lifted toward hers inquisitively. His cheek was red where it had rested against her sweatshirt, and he looked rumpled and sleepy.

"All done?" she asked. He nodded, and she pulled the soggy sucker stick from his mouth. She kissed his sunburned nose, then pressed his head to her breast.

Mat leaned forward to touch the little boy's shoulder. "Cody, say thank you to Ms...." He gave Susanna an apologetic look. "Sorry, I forgot your last name."

Forgot?

Susanna nearly choked. This was too much. Mat knew her as intimately as he must have known Cody's mother. He had been her first lover, her only lover. She had loved him, trusted him, believed in him. He had given her a son as darling and sweet as this one. How dare he treat her as though she were a stranger?

Susanna met his questioning gaze with ice. "I know I've changed, but not all that much," she said, turning down the chill in her voice another few degrees. "Surely your memory isn't that bad?"

Something savage and hard ripped across his face. "As a matter of fact, it is," he said with steel in his voice. "I can't remember anything that happened to me before Melissa was born."

Susanna gaped at him, her breath ruffling Cody's hair.

"Are...are you saying you're suffering from partial amnesia?"

"That's what they tell me." One side of his mouth moved upward, giving his scarred face a saturnine hardness. "Fancy term for a damn nuisance."

A nuisance, she repeated in stunned silence, her pulse drumming in her head. He didn't remember. He truly didn't remember making love to her—while she remembered everything. The nights under the stars when he groaned out her name on a wave of hot throbbing release, the stolen hours in his arms spent dreaming of the life they would share, the desperate aching sadness when he kissed her goodbye with such fierce longing. "Think about me," he had said before he'd climbed onto the bus in Gallup.

And she had. His rare slow smile, his devilish eyes, his sexy laugh, had been with her every day, every hour, every moment. She'd seen him in the face of his son. She had loved him in her dreams, even as she told herself she hated him. While she had been praying to forget, his memories of her had been wiped away in one blinding second.

"Maybe your memory will come back," she said, letting her gaze slide from his face.

"Maybe it will," he agreed.

But did she want it to? Did she really want him to remember the foolish, adoring girl who'd all but begged him to marry her?

No, she thought. This way she was safe. This way *she* had the advantage.

"Maybe you could help me fill in the blanks," he asked when she looked at him again. "When did we meet?"

She knew that her cheeks were burning and that her mouth was tight with the need to choose her words carefully, but she forced herself to speak in a matter-of-fact tone. "When you came home for your mother's funeral. You had a special leave."

Mat nodded. She would have been a kid ten years ago. Fifteen, sixteen, something like that. No doubt she'd had every buck on the pueblo chasing after her. Hell, she probably still had her pick of men.

"Were we friends?" he asked, his voice dipping into the seductive huskiness she had once loved.

Pain tore through her, almost as fresh as it had been ten years ago. It isn't fair, she wanted to shout. She wanted to tell him the truth, to rail at him, to recite his own words back to him, the cold cutting words that had shattered her dreams.

But she didn't dare. It was better to keep the past buried.

"No, we weren't friends," she told him, her tone putting a period to her words.

And we're not going to be, Mat finished for her. The message was as clear as if she'd shouted it in his face. What the hell had he done to make this woman dislike him? He quickly thought back over the time he'd been with her.

Sure, he'd given her a few admiring glances. So what? Most women who were as good-looking as this one were used to masculine admiration.

He inventoried his vocabulary. Surprisingly enough, he'd kept things clean, and he'd been polite. He'd even let her boss him around. So why the cold shoulder?

"Is there something I should know?" he asked, in the deadly still tone the men in his command had come to fear. "Something that's got you putting up a No Trespassing sign before you even know me?"

Susanna didn't know how she'd lost the upper hand. She only knew that she had. She gritted her teeth and angled her chin.

"I like my privacy," she said stiffly. "Most people do around here."

He digested that, his features edged with a dangerous hardness. And then he grinned. The hardness changed instantly to an even more dangerous charm that made her catch her breath. At the small sound, his grin widened.

"I'd better get my tired little soldier home," he said, his gaze dipping lower. "Looks like he's worn out."

Susanna realized that Cody had indeed fallen asleep, his small face pillowed on her breast. Awkwardly, trying not to wake him, Susanna lifted the little boy away from her.

There was a damp circle on her breast where his mouth had rested. She pretended not to notice. So did Mat. But she knew that he had.

As he took his son into his arms, Mat was tempted to brush against her soft breasts. Nine out of ten guys wouldn't think twice, but that wasn't his style. At least, it wasn't now. He didn't know what he'd been like before he married and settled down.

"Thanks for the help, Susanna." He stopped, then grinned. "I still don't know your last name."

Her silence ended in a terse "Spencer."

Mat filed that away, along with the picture of her small chin rubbing the back of Cody's head and the image of her suntanned thighs peeking out from under the T-shirt she'd worn earlier.

He extended his hand. "I'm glad we met. Again."

She hesitated, then accepted his touch. His hand was so much larger and callused to a hard smoothness on the edges. "I owe you one," he said quietly, his fingers exerting a warm pressure.

"Forget it," she said, tugging her hand free. She didn't like the way her skin burned where he had touched her, or the familiar tightening in her stomach as her hand slid into his.

Casually, as if it were the most natural thing in the world, he reached over and fingered a strand of her hair where it curled against her neck. His knuckles brushed her skin, and she stiffened. Beneath the sweatshirt her heart pounded so hard she was sure he could see each thundering beat. Her face felt frozen. It took all the control she could muster to keep from jerking away from him.

"Goodbye, Mr. Cruz," she said coolly.

Mat fingered the soft strand of hair. "Like Thai silk," he said, as though talking to himself. "Beautiful." As casually as he'd taken it, he dropped the long strand.

"Goodbye, Ms. Spencer. You may not know it yet, but we *are* going to be friends."

Without another word, he turned and walked out of her kitchen.

Susanna stared at the shadows stretching across the ceiling. It was late. She should be asleep, but bits and pieces of her conversation with Mat swirled like a maelstrom in her mind.

No doubt he was sleeping soundly on the other side of the wall, the things they'd said to each other already forgotten. And why not?

He didn't remember the feel of her hand on his body the way she remembered his. He couldn't hear the low moans of passion that she had whispered into his shoulder the way she still heard his fierce groans.

She stirred restlessly, trying to find a comfortable spot. Her mouth was dry, and her body felt oddly heavy. Even her breasts felt unnaturally full, and the nipples hurt every time she moved.

Sighing in exasperation, she kicked at the covers that were suddenly too constricting. Sensations she had forgotten ran up her spine, spreading heat and longing into every inch of her. She had known only one man's body. Mat's.

Timid at first, she had soon grown eager to explore every corded muscle. Her mouth had tasted his mouth, his flat nipples, his salty skin. Her hand had burrowed through the soft hair below his navel, exciting tiny ripples of reaction under her fingertips. His skin had been smooth and hot, as though his blood ran faster than hers. And his chest had been wide and solid as granite, but wonderfully comfortable as a pillow for her head after they'd made love.

Arching her back, she stretched her legs toward the foot of the bed, trying to drive the tension from her muscles and the ache from her bones.

Her skin felt tight, and her lips tingled. She turned onto her stomach and rubbed against the mattress, trying to ease the strangely pleasurable tightness between her thighs. But it only grew worse, provoking powerful stirrings inside her.

She had felt this way before, right after Mat had returned to San Francisco. Then she had welcomed the intimate trembling tormenting her. Each time her breasts had ached in this special way, she'd remembered his mouth closing around the throbbing tips. Each time the familiar yearning had settled between her legs, she'd remembered his potent body thrusting into hers as though staking his claim.

Her soft mouth compressed, she pushed herself upright and stared through the window at the thin sliver of moon rising over the mesa.

A lovers' moon.

No! she told herself in desperation. Think of something else. Anything.

Frantically she searched her mind.

Tomorrow. Think about the things you have to do tomorrow.

Tomasa Delgado was due for her monthly checkup at nine. Then Dr. Greenleaf had a hysterectomy to perform at ten, and she was scheduled to assist.

Susanna sighed. She still had to get out to the Clearwater spread to check on Robin again. Sometime in the afternoon would be best. If it was a nice day, she would pack a lunch and eat on the way. Out by the ruins maybe, or in the Canyon of the Chosen.

She would take a blanket, get some sun, maybe hike into the shadowy canyon spot known as the Meeting Place of the Gods.

The first time she'd gone there, Mat had been with her. She could still see him, his worn boots planted firmly on the uneven boulders, his bare chest as unyielding as the copper brown wall of rock behind them.

He'd worn threadbare jeans and boots that had been in the back of his bedroom closet for years. One square hand had rested on the red shirt he'd rolled into a makeshift belt and tied around his lean waist. His hat, an old one with a braided leather band, had shaded his eyes.

Susanna tried to blink away the vision. Tried and failed.

This time she knew very well the signals that her body was sending. From the moment she'd emerged from the haze of sleep and seen him standing on her doorstep, she had been aware of him, not as a man she had tried to forget, but simply as a man, a rugged, hard-edged man with eyes that didn't smile and a look of loneliness about him. She had seen that look before.

On the day of his mother's funeral.

Groaning, she turned her head on the pillow and closed her eyes, determined to blank out the painful memories. No, she thought suddenly. It was better to remember. The pain would act as a barrier to the attraction that still lay heavy inside her.

Susanna shifted restlessly, sinking slowly into the past.

It had been late afternoon, but the sun was still warm. Shadows filled the sacred place, making her move closer to Mat's strong body.

"You ever been here before?" he asked almost absently, breaking off a piece of sage to sniff its pungent scent.

"No," she said in a hushed voice. "Have you?"

"Lots of times." His jaw clenched, then relaxed. "First time I came I was a year old, the time when a father takes his son to the medicine man to ask for a special blessing. For the fierceness of an eagle or the bravery of a mountain cat or the strength of a grizzly, mostly, though I've heard about men who ask for the sharp eye of a hawk or the wisdom of an owl."

Susanna sat on a smooth rock still warm from the sun and studied him from beneath the rolled brim of her floppy hat. Lily Cruz had never mentioned Mat's father.

"What did your father ask for?" she asked, trying to imagine an older version of Mat.

This time his jaw remained tight. "He wasn't there. My mother brought me. The elders refused to allow her to speak." His mouth twisted. "They told her the gods would be angry to hear from a woman without honor."

Susanna cast her mind over the various customs Hannah had described for her. She had no memory of this one, but she knew the ceremonial rituals were often kept secret from outsiders, especially those that were held most sacred.

"Where . . . where was your father?"

He shrugged. "I don't know," he said, his voice taking on a chill. "My mother never talked about him except to say that he was a white boy she met while she was attending the Indian boarding school near Gallup. A *rich* white boy whose parents wouldn't let him marry a dirty heathen."

A soft gasp escaped Susanna's lips. "Don't talk like that. I like the beliefs of your people, especially their feeling for nature and its . . . its loveliness. Sometimes I wish I'd been born Indian."

Mat tugged his hat from his head and rested it on one crooked knee. Sunlight caught in his short-cropped hair, giving him a dark halo.

The farther they'd gotten into the canyon, the more he'd seemed to change. It was as though he were becoming a different man in a different time, shedding step by step the patina of civilization until he seemed as primitive and as potentially volatile as the dormant volcanoes to the west.

"When my mother was your age she was one of the prettiest girls in Santa Ysabel, but none of the young men would offer for her because she had given birth to a white man's child."

His brows met together over his blade straight nose. She saw the flash of pain in his eyes, and the rigid control around his mouth.

"She told me once that my father loved her. That he would have married her if it hadn't been for his father's money. She never stopped loving him, for all the good it did her. For all the good love does anyone." He made it sound like a curse, bringing a soft protest from Susanna that he ignored.

Susanna didn't consider the prudence of her actions. She only knew that Mat was alone and desperately unhappy.

Rising from her place on the rock, she went to him and wrapped her arms around him, resting her cheek against his thundering heart.

After a startled instant, his powerful arms closed around her small body so tightly she couldn't move. He smelled wonderfully male, and his skin was hot, like the sun-washed rocks surrounding her.

A deep satisfaction spread through her. This very strong, very dangerous man needed her. She'd read somewhere that the greatest gift a man can give a woman is to need her, and now she understood what the author had meant.

Suddenly the torturing pressure on her arms relaxed. The agony bled from his eyes. His mouth lost its hard tortured edge as it brushed hers.

Instantly, small shivers shot through her.

He stared at her, an arrested expression on his face. "Don't tell me that's the first time you've ever been kissed by a man?" He sounded shocked and just a bit nonplussed.

Still shaking, she could only nod.

"Did you let me kiss you because you feel sorry for me?" he asked with silky softness.

Susanna saw pride flare in his eyes, along with a bleak look she couldn't identify. "No," she whispered. "I wanted you to kiss me. I've wanted that since I saw you that first morning."

"Why?" He sounded as though he didn't quite believe her.

She shook her head. "I just know I want it inside. My father told me to always do what feels right, deep down."

His mouth jerked in a small movement that might have grown into a smile if his face hadn't been so tense. "Does this feel right?"

This time his mouth moved lazily over hers, exciting a rush of sensation flooding through her—like the heady feeling she always got when she stood at the edge of a steep cliff and looked down.

"Yes," she whispered when the brief kiss ended. "It feels right, like . . . like I've been waiting all my life for you."

His touch was gentle, even deferential. His hands moved down her arms to capture her hands. He lifted them to his shoulders, then angled his head and kissed her again.

This time the sensations coursing through her were laced with a heady exhilaration, unlike anything she'd ever felt before. Is this what it's like when a woman wants a man? she thought, her eyes springing open in wonder. The sensation localized, centering in a place deep inside.

"I want to make love to you," he said without pretense. "Here. Now."

Yes, she thought, oh yes. "Why?" she asked, suddenly afraid.

His hands circled her waist, pulling her against him. "Feel that? That's why." He began rubbing against her, his pelvis moving in a tantalizing circle. She knew the rudiments of male physiology, but she'd never before felt the power of a man's sexual arousal.

"You make a man crazy, Susanna. Your body is so ripe I'd kill to know what it feels like to be inside you. But your eyes keep asking me questions I can't answer." He groaned, his jaw clenching. "I've never met a woman like you before."

Heady feelings of instinctual feminine power shot through her. He wanted her. Shy, awkward Susanna Spencer. Mat thought she was special.

She swallowed the fear rising to her throat. "Make love to me, Mat," she whispered. "Please."

Instantly, as though waiting for a signal, Mat released her. A dark flush colored his high cheekbones, and his eyes glittered in a way she'd never seen.

"I'm not like my father, Sweet Sue," he said. "I won't make promises I can't keep. And I won't make you pregnant."

Susanna realized she was crying. Impatiently she dashed away the tears, her heart pounding, her mouth trembling. He had done both, and she had paid the price.

Close by the house, a coyote howled suddenly, sending a shiver down her spine. An answering cry came, not as close. And then another.

The pack was hunting, prowling for prey, the more vulnerable the better.

Some of The People believed it was bad luck to hear a coyote howl on the night a child was born. In the old times, if such a catastrophe occurred during a birthing, the father would send for the medicine man, who would do a sing to ward off the evil spirits.

Bobby had been born in Albuquerque, in the hospital where she'd been taking her training. She had been alone. If a coyote had howled that night, she hadn't heard it. But she *had* called Mat's name, over and over, until she'd had no more voice.

In the distance the marauding pack began yipping shrilly. They'd made a kill.

Susanna felt a sudden chill. Body clenched, she slid lower into the white nest of covers and huddled there, alone in the middle of the bed that had never seemed so large before.

Remember the day you lost your son, Susanna. Remember the days and nights you cried. Remember the empty feeling that's always with you. Remember that you no longer love Mat Cruz.

Susanna turned over and pressed her hot face into the pillow. It didn't help.

Chapter 4

Susanna turned off the ignition and breathed a sigh of relief. The black Bronco with the Santa Ysabel Tribe emblem on its side was gone.

Mat wasn't home. For two days she'd avoided him. For two days she'd tried not to think about him. For two days she'd tried not to worry about the little boy with the sweet smile and mischievous eyes. She hadn't succeeded.

Dropping her keys into the oversize bag that served as a briefcase as well as a purse, she opened the door of the Jeep and stepped out into the brisk afternoon wind.

Something pink flashed past the corner of her eye, and she let out a startled gasp. A child, a small brown-haired little girl looking dejected and forlorn, sat cross-legged under the aspen next to the carport. She was dressed in a hot pink Snoopy sweatshirt that was several sizes too big and purple jeans.

So that was Mat's daughter, she thought. The child another woman had been carrying while he had been making love to her.

Sad brown eyes watched her warily as she approached, her sneakers crunching the leaves covering the hard dirt.

"Hi, my name is Susanna," she said with a friendly smile. "You must be Melissa."

"Missy," the girl corrected gravely. Intelligent brown eyes studied Susanna with open curiosity. "Daddy says I have to call you Ms. Spencer."

Susanna was careful to keep her anger at Mat from showing on her face. "But then I would have to call you Ms. Cruz, and that gets very complicated, doesn't it?"

The little girl giggled. "I guess so." Her stiff shoulders relaxed, and her mouth lost its melancholy droop.

"What're you reading?"

The child glanced down at the well-used book in her lap. "*Huckleberry Finn*. It's my favorite."

"Mine, too." Susanna grinned. "Looks like you've read it a few times." Her own copy was almost as tattered.

Missy frowned. "Most of my books 'n' things are still in some big warehouse where we used to live in Brazil. This is Daddy's, but he said I could have it until all our stuff comes on the boat. Some people gave it to him in the hospital when he was learning to read."

Susanna stared at the child. "Learning to read?" she asked, certain that she had misunderstood. Mat had been one of the brightest people she'd ever known.

Missy stood up and carefully brushed the leaves from her jeans. She was thin, all arms and legs. "Daddy was in a…a coma for three weeks. They wouldn't let me 'n' Cody see him or talk to him 'cause he was so sick. When he woke up, he couldn't talk or read or…or anything. Aunt Patty said the nurses had to feed him and give him a bath and help him go to the bathroom." She clutched the book tightly. "I asked him if he felt funny going back to school again, 'n' he said it was a humbling experience, whatever that means."

Susanna forced a smile. "I imagine it means he didn't like it much."

In her imagination she saw Mat as he must have been then, lying as still as death, his strong body mangled almost beyond repair, his mind groping to relearn things most people took for granted.

It must have been a living hell for such a restless, virile man, trapped by the damage in his brain to lie immobile for hours on end, wondering if that was how he would spend the rest of his days.

Before she'd left nursing to become a midwife, she had treated patients like him in the trauma ward. Every day she had shared their despair and their pain. Every night she'd gone home and cried.

"Did I say something wrong?"

Susanna looked up to find Missy staring at her uncertainly. How long had she stood frozen, thinking of this girl's father? she wondered. A minute? Two? More?

She swallowed. "No, of course not. I . . . hadn't realized that your dad had been so badly injured, that's all."

Missy's frown smoothed away. "He doesn't talk about it much. But sometimes, at night, he can't sleep very well."

Susanna refused to let herself care. She knew herself all too well. Once she opened the door a crack, the compassion she invariably felt for those who had suffered would come flooding out. She couldn't afford to feel sympathy for Mat Cruz. She couldn't afford to feel *anything* for him.

Just being near him had sparked feelings in her body that threatened the cold anger she'd used as a knife to cut away the love she'd had for him. But now that she knew she was still far too vulnerable to him, she would make sure she stayed as far away from him as possible.

"Hey, I have a book you might like," she said, changing the subject.

The child brightened instantly. "Great. I'm tired of reading Daddy's books," she said with a lilt in her thin voice. "What's it called?"

Susanna shifted her heavy bag to the other shoulder. "*Island of the Blue Dolphins*. Have you read it?"

"No. Is it about dolphins?"

Susanna nodded. "And a little girl a lot like you." She held out her hand. "C'mon. I'll show you."

She was touched at the eager way Mat's daughter slipped a small hand into hers. Her thoughts flew backward to the black days after she'd lost her own mother. For months she'd been lost—a shy little shadow haunting the shabby old house that suddenly seemed too empty and too quiet.

At the door, she hesitated, struck by a sudden thought. "Where's your brother?"

Missy scowled. "Grandmother Ettaway is giving him a bath. He dumped a whole bag of flour all over himself. Daddy's really going to be mad when he sees the mess in the kitchen."

Susanna opened the door. "Grandmother Ettaway? Is she your baby-sitter?" She gestured for Missy to enter ahead of her.

"Sort of, I guess. Daddy says her grandchildren moved away, and she needs a couple of kids like us to take care of so she won't be lonely." Missy couldn't quite stifle a sigh. "Mostly I like her, but sometimes her tongue gets all twisted and the words come out funny."

Susanna knew what Missy was trying to say. The old woman had grown up speaking her own language, learning English only when her children had insisted.

"I couldn't understand her, either, when I first came here," she told Missy sympathetically. "But it wasn't long before I picked up enough of the language to get by." Now she was fluent enough to understand all but the most obscure words.

Susanna dropped her bag onto the floor and closed the door. Grandmother Ettaway had been the first woman to welcome her to the pueblo when she'd returned. Because the motherly old woman had lost her youngest daughter in childbirth, she'd convinced many of the younger women to break tribal custom and allow Susanna, a stranger not of the blood, to attend their deliveries. After the first few times, the resistance had melted away. Now virtually all the mothers-to-be consulted her.

Susanna was very fond of the old woman. But Grandmother had to be in her late seventies. Surely Mat didn't expect her to keep up with an active toddler.

A frown tugged at her eyebrows. She told herself not to interfere, but she couldn't help worrying. Children were so terribly vulnerable.

"Do you live here by yourself?" Missy asked, avid interest sparkling in eyes shaped like Mat's but holding nothing of her father's glittering hardness.

"Yes, all alone." She dropped her arm gently over Missy's thin shoulders. Together they walked down the hall and into the spare bedroom she'd converted into an office. She kept duplicate records in the battered old filing cabinet in the corner, along with every textbook on midwifery and obstetrics she'd been able to find.

Missy stopped short, her features taking on an enchanting expression of pure delight. "Gosh, you must have more books than the library," she exclaimed in an awestruck tone.

Susanna laughed. "It sure feels that way when I have to dust them, that's for sure."

As though seeing the room through Missy's eyes, she ran her gaze over the bookshelves that covered three walls floor-to-ceiling. They'd been custom-built for her by the husband of one of her first patients.

"I wish I had these many books," Missy said in a wispy voice. "'Cept Cody would probably ruin 'em. He's always messin' with my stuff, even when Daddy yells at him not to."

Susanna came to stand next to her. "Sounds like it's hard being the big sister."

Missy shrugged. "It's okay, I guess. 'Cept he snores."

Susanna nodded sympathetically. "How about your friends? Do they have little brothers that bug them, too?"

"I don't have any friends here." A sad little note crept into her voice, and her shoulders slumped again.

Susanna's heart went out to her. Moving closer, she gave the child a gentle hug. "You'll have friends here, soon, kiddo."

Missy didn't respond. Susanna knew exactly how strange Santa Ysabel could be for someone who had never lived within its vast boundaries. But there wasn't anything she could do to take away the strangeness. She couldn't afford to become involved.

She dropped her arm and assumed an air of concentration. "Let's see, where is that book?" she muttered, trailing her hand over the rows of books.

Sun streamed through the west window and puddled on the huge, recycled school teacher's desk in the middle of the room. The air smelled musty, like the library stacks at UNM.

"Aha, here it is!" she exclaimed. She tugged the small volume free, then ran a caressing hand over the worn cover. A soft reminiscent smile lit her face. "I can't tell you how many times I've read this. I know it by heart, and I still love it."

Missy breathed a soft sigh of anticipation. "I'll take very good care of it," she said in an eager voice. "I promise."

Susanna hesitated, then strode to the desk and took a pen from the drawer. Turning to the front page, she wrote a neat inscription: "For my friend Missy. Happy reading."

To her surprise, tears welled in her eyes. For this lonely little girl whose best friends were books. For her adorable, motherless brother. For...

No, she thought. Not for Mat. Never for Mat.

She spun around and held out the beloved book. "This is for your collection."

Missy's mouth dropped open. "You mean it? For keeps?" She tucked the worn copy of *Huckleberry Finn* under her arm before taking the book from Susanna's hand.

Susanna nodded. "I told you, I know it by heart. Besides, if I want to read it again, I'll just borrow it from you."

Missy started to grin, then seemed to think better of it. "Susanna?"

"What, honey?"

"Can I come visit sometimes? When you're not busy, I mean? Daddy said not to make a pest of myself, but..."

Susanna saw the hopeful look in Missy's eyes and went soft inside. What could it hurt, really? It might be nice to have company now and then. "Sure, you can visit. Anytime at all."

"Maybe I can bring Cody some—"

The sound of hard knuckles on harder wood, demanding and insistent, reverberated through the quiet. Susanna realized she was grateful for the interruption.

"Someone sounds pretty darn impatient," she muttered, then grinned. "Sometimes babies come early. Might be an anxious father-to-be who doesn't have a phone."

She left the room, followed by Missy, who looked intrigued. "Are you a doctor, like the one Mommy went to when Cody was born?"

"No, I'm a midwife. Sort of like a doctor, but not really, because I mostly help mommies have their babies at home."

Still smiling at Missy, she swung open the door.

Mat stood two feet away, half turned away from the door, the uncompromising angles of his profile distinctly outlined against the sky. He wore a new brown Stetson, pulled low against the sun. Aviator sunglasses with gold rims hid his eyes.

He was dressed in khaki, and for an instant past and present merged before she realized it was a different kind of uniform, with the tribal insignia emblazoned on a patch below his shoulder. A large black, businesslike revolver snapped into a worn leather holster rode low on his left hip.

At the click of the latch he turned. One lean hand swept off the Stetson, while the other smoothed his thick unruly hair into rough order. His jaw was shadowed, giving him the rumpled look of a man who'd put in a long day at hard labor.

"Hello, Ms. Spencer," he said. "We meet again." One eyebrow slanted mockingly, as though saluting the sudden frown on her face.

Susanna recognized the low throb of masculine interest in his greeting and stiffened inside. She didn't want to respond when this man spoke to her. She didn't want to notice the tautness around his mouth or the lines of strain in his face.

"So we do," she replied coolly. What she really wanted to do was slam the door in his face, literally and figuratively until he got the message. *Do Not Disturb. Ever.* But, with her conversation with Missy fresh in her mind, she had to be careful to display no overt hostility. She could care less about Mat Cruz, but she would rather suffer his presence than hurt Missy.

He hesitated, as though he intended to say more, then shifted his gaze a fraction to the child at her elbow. "Missy, Grandmother Ettaway was worried about you. She didn't know where you were, so she called me at the office. Next time you go visiting, tell her where you're going."

"Yes, Daddy," she said meekly, hanging her head.

Susanna wanted to belt him. Couldn't he see how lonely Missy was? she thought indignantly. Couldn't he see the sad little droop to her mouth? Or the hurt in her face when he barked at her like that?

She gathered herself up to her full height, which unfortunately brought her mouth on a line with his strong throat. She had to arch her neck in order to look him squarely in the eye.

"It's my fault," she told him quickly. "We got talking. You know how it is." For Missy's sake, she fashioned a winning smile.

His face didn't change, but Susanna felt a prickle of uneasiness move down her spine. Something dangerous and dark was bottled up behind his rough-hewn features.

"Missy knows the rules." He raised one eyebrow and looked at his daughter. "Don't you?"

She bit her lip and nodded. "I'm sorry, Daddy," she said in a low voice.

His mouth relaxed into a brief smile. "Don't do it again, okay?"

"I won't."

"Go apologize to Grandmother."

Susanna ached for the little girl, who seemed so miserable all of a sudden. Slipping behind Mat and his daughter, she gave Missy a hug.

"Come back soon," she said with her best chin-up smile. "Any time you want to borrow a book or just . . . talk."

Some of the hurt left Missy's face. "Bye, Susanna."

"Melissa!" Mat rebuked her sternly. "What did I tell you? It's Ms. Spencer."

"It's okay, Mat," Susanna interjected quickly with a smile for the upset little girl. "I told her she could call me Susanna."

The corner of Mat's mouth moved, not much, but enough to tell her that she had intruded on dangerous territory. "I know what's best for my daughter, Susanna. Try to remember that, and we'll all get along fine."

Missy burst into tears. Before Susanna could comfort her, she was running toward her own front door.

As soon as Missy was safely out of hearing, Susanna rounded on the man standing so silently next to her. "Did you have to order her around like a damn drill sergeant?" she demanded, hands on hips. "She's just a little girl, not some...some recruit."

"Better she gets her feelings hurt some than die out there on the mesa because she doesn't listen to orders," he said, the steel in his voice sharpened to a razor edge.

Susanna's gaze followed the jerk of his head. Just last year a tourist from Vermont had ignored the council directive against camping within pueblo boundaries and gone wandering among the rugged foothills to the north. He'd fallen, broken his leg, and died. Alone.

She repressed a shudder. "You're right," she admitted grudgingly. "But you could have been more understanding. She's still...adjusting. She needs love, not harsh words."

"What the hell is that supposed to mean?" he asked in a deceptively soft voice. "I love her. She knows that."

"Oh yeah? Well, you sure could have fooled me."

For an instant his face went white before dusky color flooded his cheeks. "What are you, the resident expert on child psychology?"

"It doesn't take an expert to see how unhappy she is. She's been through a hard time, losing her mother, nearly...nearly losing her father. Tell her you love her more often. Show a little patience and understanding."

"Patience and understanding," he repeated meditatively, his voice silky. "Like you've shown me, right?"

His words were slipped under her guard with the deftness of a sniper hitting a target in the dead of night in a high wind. It took her a second to realize she'd been bloodied.

"Goodbye, Cruz." She stepped backward, but before she could slam the door, he flattened his palm against it.

Susanna leaned against the door and shoved, one hundred and ten pounds of determination against nearly two hundred pounds of muscle and grit.

"Take your hand off my door," she said through tight lips.

Deliberately ignoring her chilly order, Mat dropped his head and stared at his dusty boots. These days, he was never sure he was making sense when he spoke, especially when he was tired. Or like now, when he'd been taken by surprise.

Surprise? He'd damn near been bowled over by this pint-size tigress. Hell of a thing, hearing this woman with a stranger's face defending his daughter against him.

Thankful that his dark glasses hid the frustration seething in his eyes, he raised his head and took a deep breath. He was bone-tired, discouraged and hungry as a grizzly after a winter sleep. All he wanted was a bath hot enough to steam out the knots in his muscles and a few hours of peace.

"Look," he began slowly, watching an angry flush creep into the faint hollows below her cheekbones. "It's not that I don't appreciate your interest in Missy. Believe me, I do. It's just that I've had a ballbuster of a day and—" He broke off.

"Sorry about that," he muttered, slapping his hat against his thigh. "Bad habit. I'm working on it."

Suddenly he grinned, a devilish, intensely sexy grin that nearly rocked her back on her heels. She stiffened her spine.

"I was a nurse for two years before I became a midwife," she said tartly. "I'm not bothered by vulgar language."

"But you *are* bothered by me." He moved closer, sliding his shoulder along the door's hard panel until his wide chest was only inches from her breasts. He smelled of leather and sweat and dry New Mexico dust.

Her heart began to beat too quickly. "I hardly know you. Why should I be bothered by you?"

He shrugged, a controlled movement of muscles and tendons that hinted at the power hidden under the plain uniform. "You tell me."

"I just did."

Mat found that he was watching her mouth rather than listening to her words. Her lips looked enticingly soft, even when they were stretched into an angry scowl. He had half a mind to kiss that furious little mouth into a sweet sigh of pleasure.

The thought gave way to an instant reaction in his groin, faint at first, then more insistent. Whipped as he was, he was still susceptible to one Susanna Spencer. Physically, at least. Emotionally, he was walled off from everyone but his kids. And that was the way he wanted it.

He dropped his hand and shoved it into his back pocket. "Let's stop the sniping, shall we? I don't need to have a brick fall on me to figure out we have some history between us. Right?"

Susanna stood mute, refusing to reply. Her hand curled around the knob until the knuckles stretched the skin to the point of pain. Hidden behind her flannel shirt, her stomach was doing flip-flops.

She didn't want him to know the truth, not ever. She didn't want him to remember her lying naked and eager under him. She didn't want him to remember how she'd moaned helplessly when he made love to her. It would give him power over her, and that would be unthinkable.

"Right," Mat continued, answering his own question. "Since you're obviously not interested in filling in the blanks for me, I'll have to do it myself."

Panic gripped her like a strangling hand before she forced it down. There's no way, she reassured herself grimly. No one knew. Not her people or his. They'd met secretly, mostly at twilight, when she'd been accustomed to taking long walks after dinner. No one had seen them alone together. Mat had wanted it that way. He'd *insisted*.

A small smile of irony escaped her rigid control. Caught in his own trap, she thought with bitter pleasure. "Don't waste your time. There are no blanks to fill in."

Slowly, making every move count, he reached up to remove his dark glasses, then pinned her with a look that had invariably sent the recipient diving for cover. "Then why do your feathers ruffle like an angry little owl's every time we're together?"

Susanna knew she had only seconds before the shaking in her knees became too noticeable to ignore. Not that she was afraid, far from it. She was furious—with herself, for letting him push her into a corner like this.

She braced her feet and took a tighter grip on the doorknob. "This half of the house is mine. Tribal Law says a person's house is sacred territory, not to be entered except by invitation. In case you haven't noticed, I haven't issued one."

He reached out to straighten the open collar of her shirt. As he slowly withdrew his hand, his knuckles brushed the thin skin between her throat and her breasts, instantly releasing a heat that quickly spread to her face.

"I'm the police, remember?" he said in a voice as rough as a winter thistle against the skin. "How're you going to enforce that law if I refuse to cooperate?"

Susanna didn't hesitate. "With a 16-gauge shotgun." Fiery eyes the color of expensive whiskey challenged him to push it.

Mat fought down a grin. Damned if she'd didn't have the guts of a horse thief, this one.

"Okay, you win," he said, the steel in his voice now tempered with quiet patience. "This time."

He was a practical man, without false modesty. Years as a noncommissioned officer had taught him how to control men as well as lead them. There wasn't a man in ten who would even think of challenging him the way Susanna Spencer had done more than once. But one skirmish didn't make a battle.

He threw her a lazy salute, grinned and walked away. Susanna didn't even have the satisfaction of slamming the door in his face.

"Daddy, Daddy."

Mat jerked awake, his heart slamming in his chest. The sheets were wound around his body like a shroud. The bedroom was as dark as a tomb.

It took him a few seconds to realize that the night-light he'd left burning in the children's bedroom had gone out.

The shrill cry came again, sounding like a sob. Mat struggled to escape the constricting covers, then snatched up his discarded jeans and hitched them over his legs, buttoning them as he left the room.

The tile was cold on his bare feet. In his haste, he banged into the doorjamb, bruising his shoulder. He bit off a curse, trying to rub away the pain.

The hall was a lighter shade of black, illuminated by the faint glow of a thin crescent moon shining through the bathroom window.

"Daddy, where are you? Daddy." It was Missy. "Daddy, it's *dark*." The last was a wail of pure terror.

He moved faster than he'd thought he could, reaching her side before the keening sound of her voice died away.

"I'm here, baby," he said, angling his hip onto the bed and pulling her into his arms. "It's okay, Missy. Daddy's here." He leaned toward the bedside lamp and switched it on. The glare stung his eyes.

Missy relaxed slightly, but her pupils were still dilated, and her mouth trembled uncontrollably.

In the other twin bed, Cody frowned and muttered something indistinct; then, eyes still closed, he turned away from the light.

Missy pressed her small body against Mat's bare chest, sobbing. Tears wet his shoulder, and her elbow dug into his ribs. Small, surprisingly strong fingers clutched his arm with a desperation born of a terror only she could see.

"Shh, baby, shh. Daddy won't let anything happen to you." He rubbed her back, trying to reassure her. Her spine was bony, her small body as fragile as a leaf in the wind.

Her sobs lessened, then stopped. She clung to him, her legs drawn tight against his side. Wisps of brown hair framed her hot face. She shivered.

For the first time he noticed the chill in the air. He kissed her forehead, then pulled the blanket over her legs. She'd insisted on wearing a frilly little girl nightie that was much too light for the cold desert nights. He'd been too preoccupied to argue.

"Better now?" he asked in a low voice.

She nodded, her tousled hair brushing his chin. "I woke up and it was so d-dark. I couldn't breathe," she cried, her voice shaking. Mat smiled slightly. He knew all about suffocating black nights. He'd had his share, especially in the bad months before the doctors were able to tell him that he would walk again.

He tightened his arms, trying to let his little girl know he understood. "Tomorrow I'll go into Chamisa and buy another night-light, sort of a backup."

"Aunt Patty said I should try to be brave and sleep without a light." Her small fingers dug into his arms, and her thin body shook.

"Damn Aunt Patty," he said in a rough tone before he remembered he had vowed to clean up his language around his children.

Mat ignored the band of pain beginning to pull tight around his head. "It's okay to be scared, baby," he told Missy in a low voice thick with the frustration he couldn't quite hide.

"You're not."

He reached for the right words, but they weren't there. They never were when strong feeling gripped him. Emotions were powerful things, the doctors had told him. Necessary, even desired. He would only get himself in trouble if he tried to ignore them.

He had understood that. Rage had impelled him to brave a sniper's bullet in order to save a shavetail lieutenant who'd gotten himself in a hell of a mess outside a VC stronghold in Quang Tin Province.

Terror of being a cripple the rest of his life had gotten him through the gut-busting torture of rehab. Icy control had kept him from falling apart when they'd told him his wife had paid the price for his selfish ambition.

Except that control wasn't an emotion. Or so the damn shrink had told him over and over.

"I'm scared of the dark sometimes, just like you are," he said slowly. "And I'm scared people will feel sorry for me because my face isn't very pretty anymore. Most of all I'm scared I won't be a good daddy to you and Cody."

"Really, Daddy? You really get scared sometimes?"

"Yes, I really do. But you know what helps?"

She shook her head. "What?"

"I think about all the good things in my life. Like you and Cody and my new job and the feeling I have when I walk outside and the sun is shining and the sky is blue. I think about all the people, our people, who have lived in this special place, and I'm glad I have a home."

"I don't like this place, Daddy. Everything's brown and ugly. And everyone looks at me funny."

"Be patient, baby," he said, forcing a reassuring smile he didn't feel. "Things will work out fine, you'll see."

"Why couldn't we stay with Aunt Patty?"

"You know why, Missy. Daddy has a job here."

Missy huddled against him, looking small and miserable. She sniffled. Mat looked around for a tissue, then remembered the box was in the bathroom. He used the edge of the sheet to wipe away the tears. She trembled against him.

"I'm sorry, Daddy. I didn't mean to make you mad this afternoon."

Mat felt something rip inside. Susanna Spencer's accusing voice came back to him, harsh and pain-filled. Paradoxically, this time he remembered every word.

"I'm not mad, Missy." He swallowed. "Sometimes I get tired, and sometimes I forget things I should know. I didn't mean to take out my troubles on you."

Mat closed his eyes, listening to the child's quiet breathing. The first time he'd held her in his arms he'd been terrified he was squeezing her too hard. When she'd opened her eyes and looked up at him, he'd felt a dozen feet tall and so proud he thought he would burst. Nothing had ever meant more to him than his new baby daughter. Not even his stripes. Somewhere along the way he had forgotten that.

Regret burned in his stomach. He had forgotten too many things he needed to remember.

"Missy, it's all right with me if you want to call Susanna by her first name."

Her face lit up. "Really, Daddy?"

"Really."

"She's nice. I like her a lot."

Mat realized that he did, too. He wasn't exactly sure why. Maybe because she fought so hard to defend his daughter. Whatever the reason, however, he figured he wasn't all that high on her list of people she liked. But maybe he could change that. For Missy's sake.

He dropped a kiss onto Missy's head. "Think you can get back to sleep now?"

Missy nodded.

"Can your beat-up old dad have a kiss?" he asked, surprised at how husky his voice sounded. In the days before the bombing he had taken kisses from his children as his due. Now he no longer took anything for granted.

Missy raised her chin and kissed his cheek, then, to his surprise, pressed her face to his neck and threw her arms around his chest.

His eyes stung. *Tell her you love her more often.*

He took a deep breath. "I love you, baby," he managed to choke out.

"I love you, too, Daddy," she whispered in a muffled voice. Only he knew how precious those words were to him.

He tucked her in, promising to leave the light burning, then returned to his room. After shucking off his jeans, he climbed into the lumpy bed and turned onto his side, trying to relax.

The silence pushed in around him, constricting, heavy. From the other room came the sound of the children's breathing. Tension traveled down his spine and settled in his legs. He felt every lump and sag in the old mattress. Nothing felt right, not even his skin.

He thought about the room next door, the twin to this one. No doubt Susanna had been asleep for hours, her body as relaxed as his was tense.

His body stirred. From the first moment he'd seen her, he'd been aware of an intense sensuality hidden beneath her cool facade, like a hot ember waiting to be fanned into life.

Knowing he shouldn't, he let himself imagine what it would be like to make love to Susanna. He would take a very long time, using his mouth and his hands to sensitize every inch of her sleek body. He would kiss her breasts and her belly. He would stroke the inside of her thighs slowly and thoroughly, letting his fingers trail higher and higher with each stroke until she was ready for him.

Anger pushed through him, making his muscles tight. What the hell was he doing, tormenting himself over a woman who barely gave him the time of day?

With a groan he turned onto his belly and buried his face in the pillow, trying to escape the need torturing his body and shattering his hard-won peace of mind. But he kept seeing the smile leave her eyes when she spoke to him.

He was a man who liked things clean and simple. No surprises, no hidden agendas. Subtlety escaped him. Evasion made him nervous. When he liked a woman, he made that fact perfectly clear. When he wanted her, he made that clear, too.

But there was something about Susanna that didn't quite feel right. It was as though something was driving her, something that had put her back up against him. But what?

Tomorrow, first thing, he intended to do some scouting around, talk to some people who knew him when, ask a few discreet questions.

The next time she took him on with her chin raised and her eyes smoldering with dislike, he would be ready.

Chapter 5

Mat unlocked the door that now bore his name painted in black on the window. The air inside was hot and smelled musty. Dust motes zigzagged through the afternoon light. His boot heels made a hollow sound on the bare wood floor.

Leaving the door open, he tossed his hat onto the corner of his desk, angled his hip onto the edge and ran both palms down his cheeks. He and his deputies had just put in two intense hours of target practice out on the mesa. His skin still stung from the raw wind slicing down from the north.

He flexed his injured hand. The exercises prescribed by his therapist were helping. He still couldn't shave with a blade, but he could draw his gun now without dropping it.

It had felt damn good, firing his weapon again. The cold weight of hard blue steel against his palm and the acrid smell of the exploding powder brought back a lot of good memories.

Mat stretched the tired muscles of his shoulders, then sat down and propped his feet on the desk. The old swivel chair screeched, bringing a wry grin to his face. Everything in the office had been recycled or patched. Even him.

He let his shoulders slump. His side felt leaden, numb. His leg ached with the steady dull pain that sometimes lessened, but never really went away.

All in all, though, things were going pretty well. In the three weeks since he'd hired his two deputies, Sonny Spruce and Mary Two Skies, he'd spent most of his time training them in the basics of police work, military-style. So far they'd worked out fine.

Burly and tough, Sonny had been employed in Gallup as a security guard, coming home weekends to his wife and four sons. Mat could still see the joy in the young man's face when he'd gotten the job. His words of thanks had been formal and polite, in the way of The People, but outside, where he'd thought Mat couldn't see him, the kid had thrown his hat up in the air and whooped like a warrior on the warpath.

The other deputy, Two Skies, was another story. Lured back to the pueblo by the new life John Olvera and his allies on the Council had breathed into the community, she had an edge on her that Mat didn't like.

But the woman could handle a rifle better than anyone he'd ever seen. She also had a steady look in her eye that suggested the kind of calm temperament a cop needed, especially when faced with a belligerent drunk or an irate wife looking for her straying husband. Santa Ysabel had its share of both.

Mat moved restlessly in the hard chair. His hand was beginning to throb. Jerking open the desk drawer, he took out the bottle of aspirin he kept there and shook out three tablets. He tossed them down without water, grimacing at the bitter taste, then recapped the bottle and returned it to the drawer.

Down the hall, a phone shrilled. Two rings, three, then silence. He glanced at his watch. He had a couple of hours before he had to stop by the pueblo school to pick up Missy. Most of the children walked home, some going miles, but she was city born and bred. He worried about her when she was away from him, probably more than he should.

Poor baby, he thought, resting his head against the wall behind his chair. She still missed her mother. He had a feeling that was why she spent so much time with Susanna Spencer.

"She's nice, Daddy," Missy hold told him when he'd asked her about her new friend. "She knows all about makeup and clothes, and even knows my favorite songs. She makes great cookies, too."

Mat opened his eyes and stared at the ceiling. In the polite roundabout way of his people, he must have asked a dozen people about her. Just as John had mentioned, everyone seemed to like her a lot. He had heard story after story of her dedication to her patients and her valiant efforts to improve the chances of survival for their babies. In the way of his people, some had nicknamed her Woman Who Saves Babies. Others knew her as Woman With Sunshine in her Eyes. The more he found out about her, the more he respected her.

But no one knew any more about her history than Olvera had told him that first day. Not even Grandmother Ettaway, who knew everything that happened within the boundaries of the pueblo almost as soon as it happened, had told him anything that could explain her antipathy toward him.

Mat dropped his feet to the floor and sat up. Forget it, Cruz. You have a job you like more every day, two great kids, a fresh start. The last thing you need is trouble with a woman who can't be bothered to give you the time of day.

The sound of boots tramping down the hall outside caught his ear. A second later John Olvera appeared in the doorway. "How's it goin'?" he asked, crossing to the desk and pulling up the extra chair.

Mat waited until Olvera sat. "Can't complain. How about you?"

John shrugged. "Sometimes I wonder why I asked for this job," he said, his voice laced with dry humor. "If it's not the Bureau of Indian Affairs on my back, it's the Council. One thing about our people, they like to talk things half to death before making a decision."

John yawned, then slumped back in his chair. "Speaking of talking, I stopped by to ask you to come to the Council meeting next Wednesday night. I like your idea of a Tribal Court that combines the old ways of tribal justice with military court-martial procedures. I think it might just work. But I'd like you to explain it to the Council and answer their questions."

"I'll do my best."

John nodded. "That's all any of us can do." He leaned forward, prepared to stand, then frowned. "Oh, before I forget, I ran into your neighbor on the way here. She has a problem you should know about."

Tension sliced down Mat's spine and settled in his belly. "What kind of a problem?"

"Someone broke into her Jeep and took her medical supplies."

Mat spat out an obscenity. "When?"

"Yesterday afternoon."

"Where?"

"Out by Red Horse Rock, near the Delgado place."

Mat nodded slowly, his emotions pulled in tight, the way he kept them when his temper threatened to explode. For three weeks he had worked day and night to prove that he could still cut it as a cop. All it took was one suggestion of weakness, one whispered comment that someone as respected as Susanna Spencer questioned his ability, and he would be in trouble. No one trusted a cop who wasn't tough enough to handle his job.

"You just see her?" he asked, glancing toward the window.

"Twenty minutes ago." John gave him a measuring look. "In case you're interested, she said she was on her way to the clinic."

"I'm interested." He grabbed his hat and headed for the door. "Lock up when you leave," he tossed over his shoulder. "This might take a while."

John's laugh followed him into the hall. "Good luck," he called after him. "I have a feeling you're going to need it."

* * *

Susanna leaned heavily against the desk in the clinic's reception area, staring at the indecipherable words scribbled on the message pad. She had two women ready to deliver. The message could concern one of them.

"Sorry, Susanna," the harried receptionist whispered, darting a quick look over her shoulder. "I took a coffee break, and Dr. Greenleaf covered the phones for me. You know how awful his writing is when he's in a hurry."

Susanna shot Lupe an exasperated glance. She was exhausted, her nerves worn to a frazzle during an especially difficult early-morning delivery, but she had a full calendar of afternoon appointments and a house call to make before she could call it a day.

She rotated her head, trying to ease the painful tightness between her shoulder blades. "Is the doctor in his office now?"

Lupe nodded. "I just put through a long-distance call."

"Okay, when he hangs up, let me know. I'll be in the lounge."

"Yes, ma'am." Lupe started to add something more, but the phone rang, and she broke off to answer it.

Just as well, Susanna thought, as she walked slowly down the hall to the first door to the left. The last thing she needed was a recitation of Mat Cruz's impressive masculine charms.

The staff lounge was tiny, hardly larger than a good-size closet. It contained a lumpy cot, an even lumpier sofa and a huge coffee maker that was never turned off.

Eyes drooping with fatigue, she drew a full cup and took several sips, waiting for the hot brew to cool before drinking deeply.

Voices came from the children's ward at the end of the hall. Someone giggled; another voice joined in. Her stomach clenched. One of those sweet little voices had reminded her of Cody Cruz. In spite of the exhaustion pushing at her, she smiled at the memory of his silky head resting on her breast.

She'd seen him three times since then—twice with his sister, playing in the yard, and once with his father. In spite of her good intentions to stay well away from the father, she was becoming more and more entranced with the children.

Susanna sighed and tried not to think about the fine line she was walking. It didn't take much insight to figure out that Missy was looking for someone to replace the mother she had lost. With every ounce of maternal instinct she possessed, Susanna longed to be that someone. But she didn't dare become too involved with the lonely little girl.

Missy wasn't her child, and she never would be. Nor was Cody. That place was reserved for Bobby. She could never love another child as she had loved him.

Too groggy to risk sitting, she wandered over to the window at the far end of the empty waiting room. Setting her cup on the wide sill, she stared at the afternoon gloom. There was a storm building near the Canyon of the Chosen. Angry thunderheads stretched like an impervious black wall up to the heavens, blocking out the sun. Long jagged shards of lightning slashed at the land, power in the raw.

She ground her teeth. The house call on today's list was in that area. "Naturally," she muttered, crossing her arms over her chest. Twice in the last three weeks she'd gotten mired in the mud after a sudden squall took her unawares. She'd been too preoccupied with thoughts of Mat to notice the clouds piling up overhead.

Nothing had gone right since Mat Cruz moved in next door. A week ago she'd run out of firewood because she'd forgotten to order a cord when she'd run low, then spent a miserable night shivering under a pile of blankets, trying not to think of the man sleeping only a few feet away.

"Sleep," she muttered. "I just need some sleep."

"Me, I need answers."

Adrenaline shot through Susanna like an explosion, overriding the exhaustion. Before she could stop herself, she spun around to face the man she'd been trying so hard to drive from her thoughts.

He stood less than two feet away, booted feet spread, thighs hard with tension, hands loosely clenched at his sides—like a gunfighter watching for the flicker of fear in his opponent's eyes.

He knows, she thought with wild dread, her hand going to her throat. Somehow he's found out. About their love-making. About Bobby. About everything. Her stomach clenched, and her breathing grew shaky. Her heart thundered in her ears like the wildly fluttering wings of a trapped dove.

But who could have told him? She had told everyone that Bobby's father was a fellow student at the university, a Navajo. Not even her family knew about Mat.

"Don't you know better than to sneak up on someone like that?" she challenged, her racing heart giving her words a breathless quality.

Watching her through narrowed lids, he removed his hat and smoothed his hair with strong impatient fingers. He hesitated, looked around quickly like a man used to taking charge, then tossed his hat on the bunk.

"Game's over, Susanna." His mouth slanted into a hard smile that took none of the rawness from his scarred jaw.

She drew her brows together. "What game?" she asked, searching those lightning-kissed black eyes for a hint of emotion, some betraying sign to tell her what he was thinking. But his feelings were buried deep.

He ignored her question. "John tells me you have a theft to report."

She nearly collapsed with relief. *He didn't know.* Pressing her hands together to stop their trembling, she made her voice calm. "Yes. I gave him the details."

His eyes narrowed, not much, but enough to shiver the fine hairs on the back of her neck. "Wrong person. I'm the law here. Or my deputies."

"John is head of the Council," she hedged, sending a sidelong look toward the door, gauging the distance. "I knew he would handle it."

"Are you saying I wouldn't?"

She resisted the urge to swallow. "No, I'm saying I preferred to discuss it with John."

"That's bull—"

"It's not!" she cried in exasperation, her nerves beginning to unravel. "I saw John, I mentioned it, that's all there was to it."

He digested that with a stoic calm she knew was deceptive. Instinct told her that he would be a formidable opponent at chess—or poker. He would play silently, steadily, showing nothing, taking his losses without excuse, until, ultimately, he would risk everything on one final pot. And he would win.

"You got some reason for thinking I can't handle my job?"

"No, of course not."

"Then this is personal."

Her pulse rate accelerated. Her mouth went dry. "How...how could it be personal?"

His eyes took on a cold glitter. "Since I can't remember, I don't have any way of answering that." He moved closer until only inches separated them. She noticed that one side of his mouth didn't move as easily as the other, especially when he smiled without humor, the way he was doing now.

"I saw you watching me." This time the look in his dark eyes was all too recognizable. In fact, that same look, potent and demanding, still haunted her dreams.

Susanna felt disoriented at the sudden change of subject. "What?"

Mat watched her thick curly lashes flutter against her creamy skin. For one crazy moment he wanted to pull her down on the cot, making his frustrated imagining real. But Susanna was a woman who deserved gentle handling, for all her inner steel. Not because she was weak, but because she was strong. Force her, and she would fight to the death. Woo her, and she would surrender. For the right man.

"When I was playing with Cody the night before last, you were at the window, watching. I felt your eyes on me."

In spite of the chilly weather, he'd been wearing shorts and a skintight khaki T-shirt with his name stenciled across his broad back. Every time he'd lifted the laughing little boy over his head, his biceps had bulged with an oiled power that sent small tugs of awareness darting through her tense muscles. When he'd leaned down to return the little boy to safe footing, his shorts had pulled taut over his hard masculine buttocks. He might as well have been naked.

She made her voice strong. "I was watching Cody, not you. To see if he was limping."

He saw her mouth tremble at the corners and knew she was lying. He liked the idea that she was fighting the same battle he was. "Won't wash, Susanna. The cut's been healed for over two weeks."

Susanna shot another glance toward the door. "I don't have time to argue with you now. I have a patient waiting."

"Let her wait," Mat muttered as he pulled her into his arms. Her body jerked, and her hands sought to push him away.

"I want you, Susanna. I've wanted you from the moment you opened the door in that damn skimpy shirt and blinked up at me like a sleepy little owl. And you want me. I see it in your eyes whenever you look at me."

"No." Her voice was too husky to be called a whisper.

"Yes. I may have been out of circulation for a while, but I know when a woman wants to make love, and you, my sweet Susanna, want that very much."

Before she could tell him that he was wrong, his mouth found hers. She sought to struggle again, but a part of her wanted to give in, to yield to the wild sweet force buffeting her.

His kiss was just as she remembered, intoxicating, overpowering, taking and giving with an arrogant demand that couldn't be denied.

Through the material of his shirt, she felt his heart pounding. Her own thundered in a strident cacophony in her ears. His breathing, so deadly quiet a moment before, rasped between them, warming the skin of her face.

Susanna fought the lethargy turning her muscles to warm velvet. In her mind she saw herself pushing him away. In her mind she saw herself walking away without a backward look. Still, she couldn't seem to move.

Feelings built inside her, overriding her resolve. Another kiss, a touch, a demand, and she would be lost. He would ask, and she would give.

From someplace distant she heard a child's cry. Faint at first, it grew until it seemed to pound through her head. It came from the nursery at the end of the hall.

"No," she cried, struggling wildly to push herself out of his arms. She wouldn't let this man into her life again. Not ever again.

"What the hell—" His words came out in a gasp. Somehow she found the strength to escape his hold. In a panic she whirled, aiming for the door.

He caught her before she got away. His hand closed over her wrist, and he jerked her around to face him. A savage look of frustration slashed like a whiplash across his dark features.

"Is it all men you hate, or just me?"

Susanna went cold inside. "I don't hate you." A betraying pulse throbbed in the tender place under her ear. Slowly he raised his fingers to feel the frantic pounding. She jerked away, but his body blocked her passage.

"Susanna, there's something you should know," he told her with a mocking half smile. "I was an army cop for half my life. I've met more than my share of liars, and you, my sweet Ms. Spencer, are a damn poor one."

Her control finally snapped. Maybe it was the truth of his words that made her reckless. Or, more likely, exhaustion.

"You want the blanks filled in," she said in a cold clear voice. "I'll fill them in for you. I lied to you, Mat. We were friends ten years ago, or so I thought."

Mat stared at her, his brows a dangerous black line. "Go on."

"I was only nineteen, an easy mark. It took you exactly three days to seduce me. When I found out I was pregnant, I wrote to you."

His body jerked, as though he had taken a bullet in the gut. "No!" he cried in a violent explosion of sound.

"I was so happy," she went on, as though he hadn't spoken. "I knew you'd be happy, too. After all, you had told me you wanted to marry me after I got out of school."

She lifted her face and looked deeply into his eyes. She wanted to see his face when she forced him to confront the man he'd been, the man he had so conveniently forgotten.

"You were very prompt with your answer. It was short and sweet. The baby wasn't yours, you said. Besides, even if it was, it didn't matter. You were already married, and your wife was pregnant. You were very helpful, however. You advised me to find another man to give my child a name."

Mat inhaled sharply, the air hitting his lungs like artillery fire. She was lying. She had to be lying. A man who would do what she claimed deserved to die a slow and painful death.

Fury knotted his fists at his sides. "I don't believe you."

He watched her face go white. Her small face looked utterly defenseless all of a sudden, and her eyes seemed rimmed with a terrible sadness. "I had your child."

A sharp twisting pain ran up his spine. Oh my God, he thought. She's telling the truth.

He had to clear his voice twice before he could speak. "Tell me about the baby."

Her mouth trembled, but she made herself say the words. "He was adorable, so bright-eyed and alert, with the longest eyelashes I've ever seen on a baby. I named him Robert for my father. Bobby. He…he was a good baby. Sweet. He used to suck on his toes and talk nonsense to himself in the morning before I went in to change him." Her throat stung, but she made herself continue.

"Not that he was an angel. He . . . he had a temper, too. I remember one time when he was learning to crawl. He'd get going so fast he'd get his arms and legs tangled up and fall flat on his little nose. He'd be furious with himself, but he wouldn't give up." Her hands began to shake, and she pressed her trembling fingers to her belly.

He took a step forward, then stopped, his hands clenching at his side as though to keep him from reaching for her.

"What...what happened to him?"

Susanna managed a slow trembling breath. The tears she'd suppressed for so long escaped her control and began streaming down her cheeks. "He...he died when he was nine months and two days old."

"Susanna," he began, then stopped to clear the sudden huskiness from his throat. "I don't know what to say."

He lifted a hand toward her, then let it drop. He was suffering, but she couldn't afford to care. He deserved this pain, she insisted to herself. He deserved to pay for what he had done, just as she was paying.

"Don't give it another thought," she said with a bitter smile. "Ten years ago you told me to forget you, and that's exactly what I intend to do."

Slowly, feeling each beat of her heart pulsing furiously through her rigid body, she turned and walked out of the room.

Chapter 6

Aurora Olvera, Susanna's two o'clock appointment, was waiting in her office when she arrived.

"Sorry I'm late," Susanna said with a too-bright smile as she closed the door behind her. "My father called and left a message with Brad who, of course, scribbled two lines of unintelligible gibberish. I had to wait until the darling doctor got off the phone to have him translate."

"Sounds like John. When he's in a hurry, his handwriting looks exactly like hieroglyphics." Aurora was tiny and vivacious, with laughing gray eyes and a mischievous smile.

Six years ago, during a visit to her mother-in-law in Santa Ysabel, she had gone into labor and had lost the child she had been carrying because there had been no medical facilities on the pueblo. Her marriage to John Olvera had broken up after that.

Susanna didn't know all the details, but she did know that he had been in South America at the time instead of with Aurora, as he had promised, and that Aurora had held him partly to blame for the baby's death.

The women of the tribe loved to talk about the campaign John had waged to change the things about himself that had driven Aurora away. The younger women thought it was wonderfully romantic the way he had lured Aurora back to the pueblo to begin the Artists' Cooperative, then convinced her to marry him again.

Susanna had met Aurora during that time and had liked her immediately. The two had become good friends and, sometimes, confidantes. Susanna had never known Aurora to break a confidence.

Keeping her expression carefully controlled, Susanna slipped into the immaculate white coat hanging on the back of the door, then dropped into the padded chair behind her desk.

In the ladies' room, where she had gone to compose herself, she had told herself over and over that she had done the right thing.

Now that Mat knew why she didn't want anything to do with him, he would leave her alone. There were plenty of available women on the pueblo. It wouldn't take him long to find one willing to satisfy his needs.

Reaching for Aurora's file on the low cabinet behind her, she said over her shoulder, "You look particularly perky this afternoon. I like your hair longer. Reminds me of Katharine Hepburn in the forties."

Aurora fluffed the thick curly page boy that gleamed with coppery fire. Since she and John had remarried, her face had taken on a glow of happiness that Susanna envied.

"John and I made a deal," Aurora said with a grin. "He's promised to take at least one afternoon a week off, and I promised to let my hair grow."

"Is that why I saw you two riding out by the ruins last Sunday afternoon?"

Aurora colored. "We had a picnic, in the place where we made love for the first time."

For an instant Susanna remembered a man as tough as rawhide kissing her, holding her, every powerful muscle in his body taut with restraint. Something softened inside her until she remembered that she and Mat hadn't made love. They'd simply had sex.

Dismissing him from her mind the way she'd disciplined herself to do years ago, she picked up the thick file in front of her and quickly skimmed her notes.

Aurora settled back in her chair and crossed her legs. "So, how's it going with you two?"

Susanna's hand jerked, spilling papers onto the desk. She lowered the file to the desk and awkwardly gathered the papers into a ragged pile. "You two who?" she asked warily.

Aurora looked confused. "You and Brad Greenleaf, who else?"

Relief made a fast trip through Susanna's tense body. Now she was getting paranoid, for Pete's sake. "We see each other now and then. For dinner or a movie. He's a nice man. I like him."

"But no fireworks, huh?"

Susanna shook her head. "Not really, no."

"Well, there's always our new police chief. I'll bet he could generate plenty of heat."

Susanna's fingers pressed so hard on the manila folder that it creased between them. Did every woman in the pueblo want to talk about Mat Cruz? First Lupe, then the women in her prenatal class, and now Aurora.

"For some women, I suppose," she muttered, replacing the papers in the folder.

"John likes Mat a lot. He said that there are some men born with a warrior's spirit, men who never compromise, who never surrender no matter how much punishment they take."

Susanna took a deep breath, then picked up her pen. "So—how're you feeling?"

Aurora's smooth brow creased in a puzzled frown. "Why do I think you don't want to talk about Mat Cruz?"

"I'd rather talk about you, that's all," Susanna managed smoothly.

Aurora gave her a penetrating look. "In other words, mind your own business, Aurora."

Susanna heard a faint note of hurt in her friend's voice and dropped her pen. "I'm sorry, Aurora. I didn't mean to sound snippy." She slumped back in her chair and rubbed her burning eyes.

"Don't ask me to explain it, but whenever the moon is full, I can always count on at least one middle-of-the-night delivery. This week I've had two. I think I'm terminally tired."

The other woman regarded her in silence for a long moment, her eyebrows pulled together in a thoughtful look. "I had that same condition once, right after John came back into my life. I couldn't seem to get enough sleep. Then, when I did sleep, I kept dreaming about *him*."

Susanna gave a humorless laugh. "Tell me about it." She sighed again. Weariness was making her ears ring and her vision blur. "Life is so blasted complicated sometimes. Just when you think everything is going along just fine, something...happens."

"Meaning Mat Cruz?" Aurora questioned softly.

Susanna sighed. "Yes, meaning Mat Cruz. I...met him once, when he came home for his mother's funeral." That much, at least, she could admit. Sooner or later, when the women got together to discuss the return of the prodigal son, she would be asked the usual questions. Did she remember him? Didn't she think it was a shame about his face? Did she have a crush on him like all the other young maidens?

Aurora nodded. "I wondered. I mean, since your families lived in the same place. You must have been young then."

So young and so foolish. Susanna sighed. "Nineteen. I thought he was the most gorgeous man I'd ever seen." Her laugh was bitter. "But you don't want to know all that. It'll only depress you."

"Sounds like you're the one who's depressed." Aurora hesitated, then added softly, "I've never seen you look so upset. If it would help to talk, I'm willing to listen. God knows, you've listened to me go on for hours about trying to have another baby."

Susanna was tempted. The incident in the lounge had shown her just how volatile her emotions could be around

Mat Cruz. She had lost control and that made her intensely vulnerable, something that couldn't happen again.

Telling Aurora might vent the explosive power still waiting to take her unawares. Just saying the words might act as a safety valve of sorts, maybe even a catharsis.

Tell her, a small voice urged. She'll understand.

Susanna took a deep breath. "We were lovers. We were careful, but . . . I got pregnant anyway."

Aurora gasped softly, her face losing its radiant glow. "My God. You and Mat . . . a baby?"

"No one knows that I once had a child except my family, and I never told them the father's name." She picked up the pen she'd just discarded and began stabbing the blotter with the point. In a wooden voice she told Aurora what had happened ten years ago, ending with a description of the scene in the lounge.

The color drained from Aurora's face. Her eyes widened in horror, and she swallowed hard. "He really doesn't remember?"

"No. If you'd seen his face . . ." She sighed. "If I didn't know better, I'd think he really cared. But then, he's always been a great actor."

"Dear God, what a mess!" Aurora commiserated. "No wonder you didn't welcome him home with open arms."

The two women looked at each other in silence, each thinking about the revelations Susanna had just made.

Susanna was surprised to discover how much better she felt after unburdening herself to her friend. Aurora was one of the strongest women she knew, and one of the most compassionate.

"What happened to the baby?"

Susanna stared at the slashes she'd made in the blotter. It was as though she'd made those same jagged rips in her heart.

"I loved Bobby so much, Aurora. I tried so hard to make a home for him. I worked a double shift. I even took in ironing at night, but what with day care and all the things a baby has to have, I couldn't seem to make enough money to stay ahead of the bills. And then I got sick. Pneumonia. I thought it was a bad cold, that I would be fine. One morning my landlady found me unconscious." She bit her lip, breathing in strength to continue. "While I was in the hospital, they put Bobby in a foster home. They...they said I wasn't capable of taking care of him."

"Oh no, Susanna. They didn't take him away from you?"

"No, but there was a hearing. My baby-sitter and my neighbors and even Bobby's pediatrician testified that he was healthy and happy. My landlady told them what a good housekeeper I was, and that Bobby was always laughing and clean when she saw him."

She managed a small smile. "After I recovered, things were better for a while. But then, gradually, I fell behind on my rent. My landlady was sympathetic, but she couldn't carry me forever. Finally, after four months, she sent me an eviction notice. I looked and looked, but I couldn't find a cheaper place that would take a child."

"What about your family?"

"At the time my father was supporting a family of four on the little money he could make selling his paintings at art fairs in Gallup and Albuquerque. He offered to take us in, but you've seen my place. Can you imagine six of us in there?"

Aurora shook her head. "No, I can't. Your place is scarcely big enough for two."

"When things got desperate, I swallowed my pride and applied for state aid. The welfare people said I had to quit my jobs to qualify. But I made more money working than they could give me, so I was caught in a Catch-22."

"What did you do?" Aurora asked quietly.

Susanna took a deep breath. "When Bobby was nine months old, I gave him up for adoption."

"Oh, Sue," Aurora whispered, her eyes filling with tears. "I'm so sorry."

Susanna had trouble speaking. "So am I. I'll be sorry all of my life, but I couldn't stand to see Bobby deprived any longer. I thought about the children I saw in the welfare office, with their shabby clothes and lifeless little faces. They were all so...pale, like wispy little ghosts." She fought off a sob. "I couldn't make him live that way, Aurora. I just...couldn't. Not my precious baby."

It had taken weeks, months, before she stopped searching for Bobby's sturdy little body in a crowd. Even now, the sight of a dark-haired baby boy in his mother's arms tied her in knots for days afterward.

"I tell myself he's happy now. I *know* he's happy. The agency assured me that the couple who...who adopted him were wonderful people."

Aurora wiped the tears from her cheeks with her fingers. Silently Susanna plucked a tissue from the box in the drawer and handed it over.

"Thanks." Aurora blotted her eyes. "What did Mat say when you told him about the adoption?"

Guilt shivered through Susanna. "I didn't tell him. I lied and told him Bobby was dead."

"Why?" Aurora asked in a puzzled tone.

"I can barely stand to think about those terrible times. I don't want him asking me questions, saying things that would hurt. I don't even want to...to remember."

She stirred restlessly in the chair, trying to ease the tightness in her muscles. "I hadn't even intended to tell him about the baby, but it just...came out. Maybe I wanted to hurt him. I don't know. I've thought about it often enough—the words I'd say and how I'd say them." Her mouth twisted, and her voice hardened. "I'm only human, Aurora. I told myself that hating him would only hurt me, but sometimes—" She broke off with a shrug.

"Sometimes you need the hate as a crutch to help you stand the pain," Aurora finished for her in a soft voice filled with understanding.

"Yes, that's it, exactly." She stood up and walked to the window. The day had grown even darker. Like her mood. Slowly she turned, resting her spine against the cold pane.

"Have you ever felt so guilty you wanted to hide in a dark room and scream?" she asked in a dead voice. "Have you ever felt such shame you wanted to shrivel up and die?"

Aurora shook her head. "No, thank God."

"I have. When that social worker looked me in the eye and told me my son would grow up poor and illegitimate because I had too much pride to do the 'right thing' for him."

Aurora gasped. "What a dreadful thing to say!" she cried softly. "And so unfair."

"But true," Susanna said in a sad tone. She felt her face crumple, but she forced down the tears. Crying wouldn't bring Bobby back, or make the truth any less scalding.

"I know I had no choice, Aurora. I know I did the best I could, but sometimes—" her voice wobbled "—sometimes I wonder what might have happened if I'd held on just a little longer. Maybe I could have found a cheaper place or a better job or...or written to Mat again." She bit her lip until the pain grew too sharp to bear. "Maybe that awful woman was right, Aurora. Maybe I had too much pride."

"Sue, don't *do* this to yourself," Aurora exclaimed earnestly. "It won't help. I know. I second-guessed myself for years after Dawn died. If I just hadn't come to the pueblo that weekend, I thought. Or if I had brought my mother with me to drive me to the hospital when labor started." She sighed. "I nearly made myself sick, but nothing changed. Finally, with John's help, I made peace with it."

Susanna glanced down at her scuffed running shoes. Appropriate, she thought. Running was exactly what she wanted to do at the moment.

"There's something else..." Her voice faded away.

"What?"

"Did John tell you that Mat has two children?" she asked, returning to her chair.

"Yes, he told me."

"The little boy is so much like Bobby I can hardly stand to be around him. And yet I can't seem to make myself stay away. When...whenever I'm home during the day I slip next door and play with him. It's...it's almost like having Bobby in my life again."

"Is there any chance at all for you and Mat?" Aurora's voice was quiet.

"Chance at what? An affair?" She skimmed her palm over the arm of her chair. "That's what Mat wants, Aurora. He told me so. And if I know him—and I *do*—that's all he wants."

Aurora gnawed on the corner of her lip. "I understand what you're saying, but I'm wondering . . ." She fell silent.

"Wondering what?" Susanna prompted.

"Well, I felt the same way about John once. He even admitted he hadn't loved me when we were married the first time, but he changed, Sue. He fought for me. He made me believe in him again. Now . . . now I've never felt more loved. Or been happier."

Susanna remembered the expression on Mat's face when she'd told him. She'd seen guilt there, and remorse. And for an instant, before belief had settled like lifeless stones in the black depths of his eyes, fury. What she hadn't seen was love.

"Mat isn't going to fight for me," she said flatly, ignoring the bleak, cold feeling settling in the pit of her stomach.

Her fingers trembled slightly as she opened the folder. "Let's talk about something more pleasant, like a baby for the Olveras. You're here to find out if your . . . picnic was successful."

Aurora drew a nervous breath. "If it wasn't," Aurora said lightly, falling in with Susanna's determined mood shift, "there's always the hayloft."

Susanna smiled. "No hayloft for you, Mrs. Olvera," she said, her voice wobbling. "By my calculations, *and* the results of the tests, you're already eight weeks pregnant."

Aurora stared at her, both hands pressed against her cheeks. "I . . . Oh, Sue. I was afraid to hope." She began to cry, laughing even as the tears splashed onto her cheeks. "John will be so happy."

Susanna nodded, too choked up to speak. She was so happy for her friends. And so terribly sad for herself.

Thunder cracked overhead, reverberating over the empty mesa like a sharp cry of pain. Head lowered against the driving wind, Mat ran along the edge of a dry wash gouged like an open wound into the hard earth.

He moved with a ragged stride, each step clawing at the scar tissue of his legs until he felt as though his skin were ripped open and bleeding. Each rasping breath he took scorched his lungs. Sweat beaded his forehead, and his sweatshirt was plastered to his skin by the wind.

Ahead was the Canyon of the Chosen, its red limestone walls rising like a ghostly city against the stormy dark sky. Behind him trailed a tortuous line of miles covered stride by stride, more miles than he'd thought he could run again.

Exhaustion gripped every part of his body, but his mind refused to shut down. With every punishing yard he traveled came an echo of Susanna's voice. *I had your child.*

A son who would have been Missy's age now—if he'd lived.

A knifelike pain shot through his side, driving the breath from his burning lungs and bending him double. Hand pressed to his side, he half ran, half stumbled, to the shelter of a jagged outcropping of rock at the mouth of the canyon.

Struggling for air, he slumped against the wind-scored boulder, head hanging, eyes closed, waiting for the cramp to release him.

How long had he run? An hour? Two? More? He no longer had a sense of time.

He was alone in this place, with only the ghosts of his ancestors to witness his agony. The burning pain eased enough to allow him to rest against the cold hard boulder that kept him from sagging to the ground.

Slitting his eyes against the driving wind, he surveyed the stark vista surrounding him. Nothing looked familiar, and yet he knew this place. In legend, if not in fact.

The supernatural beings who caused the wind to blow and the rain to fall resided here, along with the spirits of the Chosen Ones. The great leader, Cadiz, was rumored to have been buried in the same spot where he'd once planned his victorious battle against the white invaders.

Mat licked his parched lips and tried to swallow past the choking dryness in his throat. Somehow he knew he had always wanted to be a warrior, too. To be as brave and as honorable as Cadiz.

The army had pinned row after row of medals on his chest. His superiors had promoted him for his skill at leading men and praised him for his courage under fire. A hero, they'd called him. A coward was more like it, and a lousy excuse for a man.

God help him, he didn't want to be the man Susanna had described, the man she so clearly despised. Deep in the dark place in his soul, however, he knew he could have been. Maybe he still was, even though he told himself he'd changed.

Lightning split the sky overhead, followed almost immediately by the sharp crack of thunder. The air smelled of sulfur and rain. Mat's chest heaved, but he couldn't seem to draw in enough air.

He'd done his damnedest to find an excuse, some justification, for his actions. For the past week, alone at night, his children asleep across the hall, he had struggled to remember the lost years, desperate to prove her wrong about him. But the effort only brought on one of his savage headaches.

The baby wasn't yours, you said.

Bitter self-hatred shivered through him, cutting into his gut like the killing thrust of a bayonet. It hurt like hell to know he'd lost a son. It hurt even worse to think he'd denied that son.

Raising his left hand, he stared at the spiderweb of scars. He'd been dead inside when he'd come back to the pueblo. And then he'd met Susanna.

She'd made him feel like a man again. When she smiled, he felt warm inside for the first time in nine cold and lonely months. When she spoke, he had to fight the urge to catch the words with his mouth. When she had pressed a kiss to Cody's dark head, his own body had surged into life. The more she pushed him away, the more he had wanted to get to know the woman behind the reserve.

The hell of it was, he already knew her. At least, he knew the innocent young girl she'd been ten years ago—if only he could remember.

She sure as hell knew him, however.

She also hadn't forgiven him. He had a gut-deep feeling she never would. Why should she?

Mat pressed the heels of his hands to his eyes, trying to blot out the look of unbearable grief on her face when she'd told him.

How had she stood it?

He dropped his hands and raised his stinging gaze to the black thunderheads. Had she been at the hospital when she'd lost the baby? Or home alone, desperately calling for help? For him?

He had known pain, the physical kind that tore at a man until there was nothing left but blinding agony. He had known terror that he would spend the rest of his life a quadriplegic. He had known the sorrow of losing the mother of his children. He had survived those things because he'd had no choice.

But he wasn't sure he could have survived the loss of his child.

His chest heaved. Remorse twisted in his belly like a barbed hook. He'd made a mistake—a bad one. And then tried to shirk his responsibility, like the selfish bastard he'd been then. Susanna had paid the price for his selfishness.

He muttered a curse into the wind. Rain began pelting him with cold stinging drops. He cursed again and pushed himself away from the wall. Taking a shuddering breath, he started jogging toward the home he shared with Susanna, pain searing through his thighs with each excruciating step.

When he'd left the hospital, he'd thought the worst was behind him. But he'd been wrong.

Every day he had to face her. Every day he had to find a way to live with the grief he'd caused her. Every day he would wonder what would have happened between them if he had been a better man.

Mat lifted his face to the driving rain, his vision blurred by the stinging drops that tasted salty, like tears. He had endured months of physical pain that tore at him in blinding agony without crying.

He wasn't crying now. Mat Cruz never cried.

Or did he?

Chapter 7

Mat stood in the middle of the kiva, garbed only in a soft deerskin loincloth. The men seated on the benches lining the perimeter of the large subterranean room watched him with expressionless eyes. John Olvera sat directly in front of him, along with most of the Council members. As a distant cousin and the man Mat respected most in Santa Ysabel, John was there as a representative of the Fire Clan. The others were witnesses chosen by the medicine man, Grandfather Horse Herder, to guard the secrecy of the ancient ritual.

No one spoke. No one made any sign of recognition. Only if he disgraced himself in their eyes would they speak. And then their words would be carefully chosen to heap shame on him.

An inky sky studded with cold stars was clearly outlined in the large square entrance in the roof. Light from the fire crackling in the pit to his right illuminated the large sand painting at his feet.

Mat stood stiffly, glancing now and then at the crude ladder that was the only exit from the sacred place. Was he making a mistake, standing vulnerable and nearly naked in front of the very men whose respect he craved?

Years of living in the white man's world, following his rules and seeking his approval, had taken him far from the simple beliefs of his people. Could he put aside the doubts that flowed in his veins along with his mixed blood and open his heart to the ministrations of a pagan shaman?

He kept himself very still, counting the heavy beats of his heart, each slow beat reminding him of the shame that was always inside him. He prayed that Susanna might someday forgive him. He had no confidence that he would ever be able to forgive himself, even with the help of the Healing Way. Without it, he had no hope at all.

Grandfather drizzled the last of the red sand onto the sacred figure portrayed in the dirt. The kachina was large, with the face of an eagle and talons for hands. He was garbed in turquoise robes and held a coiled whip in his beak. His very name made Mat shudder. Giver of Terrible Pain and Forgiveness.

The painting finished, the medicine man began to chant, his reedy voice suddenly taking on a deeper tone as the ancient words rolled from his barrel chest.

Mat bowed his head in humility and supplication as he had been told to do, trying his best to follow the convoluted song, but the words were unfamiliar, buried along with the memories of his childhood in the black void.

The plea was a simple one. That the man prostrate before Warrior Father be allowed to atone for the dishonor he had brought on himself and his clan. That he be freed from the bonds of his shame so that he might walk in the path of honor again. That he be restored to harmony in his spirit.

Suddenly a man clothed only in a turquoise breechcloth slid down the ladder into the kiva so quickly he seemed a blur.

A mask with the same fearsome features of the kachina hid his face. His body was painted in black, but his hands were coated in yellow. A braided rawhide whip trailed from one large fist.

At a word from the medicine man, Mat dropped to his knees and then to his belly, spreading his arms as the arms of the figure in the dirt were spread.

He closed his eyes and made himself relax. "Whatever you do, don't stiffen," John had warned him. "Otherwise, the lash will cut deeper, and you might cry out."

To cry out was to give in to the shame sickness, and the Healing would be a failure.

Grandfather knelt beside him, chanting steadily. With the tip of an eagle feather and paint made from clay and pollen, he drew three lines across Mat's shoulder blades. The old man's voice droned monotonously, adding to the dread building in Mat.

Get on with it, he wanted to shout, but haste was the white man's way. The Guiding Spirits were deliberate and slow, each word, each action, each movement, precise and meaningful. Nothing could be hurried. Nothing could be omitted. Even the ancient ceremonial vessel sat in the same spot near the figure's outstretched hand where it had been placed throughout the centuries.

In the way of The People, he tried to free his mind of impatience, filling it instead with the shimmering image of Susanna's face. Her smile. Her golden eyes.

The first lash came without warning, snaking across his shoulder like the hot slice of a razor-sharp blade. To purge his body of dishonor.

He bit through his lower lip, somehow keeping his agony inside. Sweat broke out on his brow, and his fingers dug into the dirt, seeking handholds to keep him anchored. His every instinct urged him to run, to escape, but the memory of Susanna's pale sad face kept him motionless. He deserved this humiliation, this pain, and more, for what he had done to her and to his son.

This time he heard the hiss of the rawhide as it cut the air. To purify his mind.

His flesh split in a red line, and he nearly strangled on the sickness springing to his throat. One more, he told himself as he clung to the image of Susanna's golden eyes. Slowly he opened his eyes, half believing that she would be there.

Dimly, as through a haze, he was aware of the fire, the jangle of small bells tied to the ankle of the kachina, the stinging wetness of the sweat dripping into his eyes. He heard the rasping of his labored breathing, smelled the musky scent of the dirt beneath his cheek, felt the fear choke his throat.

The last blow came quickly and, surprisingly, without pain. To cleanse his soul.

His body sagged in relief.

He had done it. He hadn't disgraced himself.

Cool water from the fragile bowl bathed his shoulders, dripping into the dirt. Grandfather scooped up handfuls of the red clay and patted them onto his torn skin, making a soothing balm. With each healing touch Grandfather intoned softly,

"In honor may I walk,
In honor may I walk,
In courage it is finished.
In courage may I be healed."

Chapter 8

Susanna threw down the tire iron and tossed the last lug nut next to the others in a little pile in the dirt next to her flat tire.

"What a way to end my day off," she muttered, staring glumly at the skirt of her best dress. Her sheer nylons, snagged on a mesquite branch as she was getting the jack from the rear of the Jeep, were already ruined. The filmy silk dress didn't stand a chance.

She inhaled slowly, summoning the strength to complete the task. In the distance a bird called to its mate, a mournful two-note song that wasn't answered. The evening breeze ruffled her hair and chilled the skin above the dress's plain round collar. Shivering, she pulled the lapels of her thin jacket closer to her neck.

"You can do this," she said, trying to buoy her spirits. "Piece of cake."

She moved to the rear bumper, where she had already attached the jack, and began levering the heavy Jeep higher. Her face grew hot, and her breathing puffed into the chill twilight quiet like a laboring engine.

It was Sunday, the day she tried valiantly to keep free from appointments. Technically, she had weekends off. Sometimes she managed an entire day away from the pueblo. Once in a great while she managed two.

Today she had driven to Gallup to celebrate her father's birthday, returning later than usual. Fifteen minutes from home her Jeep had blown a tire.

"I...hate...this," she gasped, almost out of breath. The flat tire came off the ground, turning a slow circle on the axle. Sighing with relief, she flexed her cramped shoulder muscles, then tugged the wheel free and propped it against the fender. Dirt streaked her skirt, and she grimaced.

"So much for chic," she muttered, opening the tailgate. To get to the spare tire she needed to remove nearly all of the supplies crammed into every nook and cranny of the rear compartment.

Just as she stuck her head into the back, a hawk screeched overhead. Looking up quickly, she scanned the surrounding emptiness, an uneasy feeling stealing over her. She was alone in the vastness—a bright spot of lilac silk in a brown landscape.

The sunset shimmer had faded into cinnamon. In another half hour or so the twilight shadows would disappear into the black emptiness of night. Until moonrise it would be too dark to see what she was doing.

The hawk screamed again, then streaked toward the ruins starkly outlined against the western sky.

Working as fast as she could, she removed the boxes one by one, stacking them haphazardly at her feet. Suddenly she heard a distant rumble of thunder. Slanting a worried glance toward the sky, she was surprised to see stars twinkling down at her, faint but clearly visible. That's funny, she thought. No clouds. So how could it storm?

It couldn't, she realized an instant later, her uneasiness growing. Holding her breath, she listened. The noise swelled, then grew more distinct. Hoofbeats, coming toward her fast. Her heart tripped, and her throat constricted.

Just last week two women students from Tucson had been assaulted and robbed near the ruins. By an Indian riding a brown horse, they had told Mary Two Skies who had been on patrol that night.

Shaken and close to collapse, neither woman had been able to provide a useful description. Just that the man had reeked of liquor and had spoken filthy obscenities in unaccented English.

"Calm down," she muttered, struggling to swallow her fear. No doubt it was John Olvera. His ranch was due east about six or seven miles. Aurora had often mentioned the solitary rides he took when his emotions piled up on him.

But John rode on a dun-colored stallion. The horse plunging toward her was dark—black, maybe, or brown. She narrowed her gaze, but the bareheaded rider sat forward in the saddle, his features blurred by the speed at which he rode.

Glancing around frantically, she spied the tire iron. Hand shaking, she retrieved it from the ground and hid it behind her back.

The horse grew larger, the rider's face now distinguishable. Susanna inhaled sharply. It was Mat.

He reined to a stop, gravel flying from the horse's hooves, dust rising in a shadowy cloud. He wore chaps over his jeans and a fleece-lined vest over a soft-looking flannel shirt open at the throat. His clothing and even his wind-tossed hair carried a light powdering of dust.

"Problems?" he asked, resting his gloved hands one on top of the other on the saddle horn. He slouched easily in the saddle, making Susanna immensely aware of her own rigid posture.

"Nothing I can't handle."

If her curt tone bothered him, he didn't show it. "You ever changed a tire before?"

"Yes, lots of times."

Why didn't he just leave? she thought irritably. Surely he didn't want to have anything more to do with a woman who made her dislike so obvious.

The mare sidestepped nervously, her iron shoes clattering against the gravel. Mat calmed her easily with the pressure of knees, his gaze never leaving Susanna's face.

"Want some help?"

"No, thank you." She flicked a glance at the sky. In a few minutes she would have to change the tire by touch. She managed to repress a shudder.

Mat saw the fleeting look of anxiety cross her face and muttered a curse under his breath. Most women would have been reduced to tears by a flat tire out in the middle of nowhere. But Susanna wasn't like most women. She had an obstinate determination that rivaled his own and the resiliency of a willow reed, easily bent but rarely broken.

Still, she *was* a woman, dressed more for candlelight and champagne than hard manual labor. He kicked his feet out of the stirrups and glanced toward the sky.

"If you have a flashlight, get it," he ordered as he swung down from the saddle and ground-tied the mare. Like it or not, Susanna would have to put up with him. No matter how much she detested him, he wasn't about to leave her here alone.

Susanna felt a frown cross her face. The man might be used to spitting out commands, but she wasn't used to obeying them.

"I don't need a flashlight," she stated in a flat tone. "And I don't need help."

"In other words, you don't have a flashlight."

Susanna ground her teeth at the note of masculine disapproval in his voice. "I have one," she admitted grudgingly. "But the batteries are run-down. I intended to replace them, but ..."

Mat swore succinctly. "Tomorrow, first thing, you get yourself to a hardware store and buy batteries."

Susanna bristled. "I'm perfectly capable of taking care of myself, thank you."

Mat spared her an impatient glance. "Maybe you haven't heard, Susanna. Two coeds from Arizona were attacked not too far from here the other night. They thought they could take care of themselves, too."

Susanna hesitated, then threw the tire iron to the ground and tilted her head at a defiant angle. "I heard," she said, trying not to notice the smile that played at the corners of his mouth.

Mat chuckled. "You've got guts, I'll say that for you, even if your common sense leaves a lot to be desired."

Even in the gathering dark, she could see the tiredness etched into his lean cheeks. When he moved, his limp was more pronounced than usual, as though he'd been riding for too many hours.

In the shadowed light he seemed larger than life and determined to have his way. Arguing would simply be a waste of time.

She gestured toward the open tailgate. "The spare's under the floorboard. You'll have to move the boxes." She knew she was behaving ungraciously, but she couldn't afford to let down her guard.

He nodded. Then, taking his time, he pulled off his gloves, tucking them into the narrow belt cinching the well-worn chaps. Unbuttoning his cuffs, he rolled one sleeve to the elbow, then did the same with the other, revealing thick wrists and powerful forearms corded with sinew and roped with prominent blue veins.

Two strides took him to the back of the dusty vehicle. "Looks like a twister struck in here," he said, angling a glance toward her stony face.

"I have my own system," she said in an affronted tone. "It works for me."

His mouth softened into the half-reckless, half-boyish grin she remembered. Suddenly she realized that this was the first time she had seen him grin that way since his return. "How do you know what's missing?"

She blinked, still caught up in the sensuous promise of that slanted white smile. "What?"

"The robbery. I still need the details." He began removing boxes, stacking them neatly in front of the haphazard pile she'd already started.

"I filed a report," she declared in a stubborn tone. She thrust her hands into the pockets of her jacket and walked to the front of the Jeep.

"Not with me."

As he worked, Mat watched her in the way of all cops, showing little, seeing everything. In her dress and heels she looked different. Softer, more approachable. Delicately feminine, like the purple wildflowers that could only bloom after the last thaw of winter.

He found himself wondering what it would be like to run his hand over the soft curves barely hidden by the simple design of her dress. Something shifted inside him, elusive and secret, like a sigh in the dark.

Without exercising his usual care, he grasped a heavy canvas bag with his left hand. He couldn't hold it, and it crashed to the ground. There was a tinkle of breaking glass, followed instantly by the cloying scent of strong antiseptic. Something wet spread rapidly over the tan canvas.

Mat fought down a vicious need to smash his half-useless hand into the Jeep's frame. "Sonofabitch," he grated, his jaw stiff, his frustration obvious.

Compassion softened the hard edges of Susanna's resolve, but she made herself ignore the insistent little voice that urged her to forgive this man.

She, more than most people, knew the terrible frustrations he faced every day as he struggled to compensate for the damage done to his brain and body.

But she had suffered damage, too, she reminded herself grimly. Giving up her son had left scars as angry and painful as those marking his face and scoring his body.

"Whatever it is, I'll replace it." His voice was tight, and his mouth was bitter with an inward-turning anger that hadn't been there before.

"Don't worry about it. It's only disinfectant," she said, stooping down to open the bag. "There must be cases and cases of it at the clinic."

"I'll clean up my own mess." His left hand clamped over hers, sending a quick spurt of adrenaline into her already overloaded system. Slowly he tugged on her arm, forcing her to stand.

"Will you give me a chance to clean things up, Susanna?" His voice was low, stiff, the voice of a man not used to asking for what he wanted. "Will you let me make it up to you for hurting you?"

Exerting only enough pressure to enforce his will, but not enough to bruise her delicate skin, he pulled her closer until her thighs brushed the smooth leather of his chaps. His chest was an immovable pillar of muscle and sinew, his breath warm on her face. His eyes, so intensely aware, so deeply masculine, held her immobile. Suddenly it was so quiet, she heard only the sound of their mingled breathing.

"Bury the past, Susanna. Concentrate on the future. Let me be your friend."

His fingers tightened only slightly, but enough to warn her of his superior strength. She felt the warmth of his touch spread up her arm. Because her pulse reacted immediately, she knew she had to be very careful with this man.

"You're not my friend, Mat. I'm not yours," she said, trying to pull away. "I'm not sure we were ever really friends."

His thumb moved against the pulse leaping in her wrist. "That doesn't mean we couldn't be."

"It's too late for that." She pulled her hand from his. Her skin still felt alive where his fingers had pressed.

"Only if you want it to be." He glanced toward the setting sun, his face as shadowed as the deepening night. Susanna had a sudden sensation of terrible loneliness. Were they his feelings she sensed? she wondered sadly. Or her own?

When his gaze returned to her face, it carried a new expression, one that made her catch her breath. Here was the man who had come back from the dead inch by tortuous inch. Here was a man who never gave up, no matter how terrible the odds against him.

"All I want is a second chance. I'll do all the work."

It was a mistake to look into those eyes. There were questions there she didn't want to answer, promises she didn't dare trust. "I don't believe in second chances."

His mouth moved, an ironic smile raising his scarred cheek. "But I do. And I promise I'll never hurt you."

I promise I'll never hurt you.

Her answering smile was tinged with bitterness. "You have a way of breaking your promises, Mat. I learned that the hard way."

"A lot of things have changed in ten years, Susanna," he told her in a husky tone. "Me, most of all. A man learns a lot about himself when he's flat on his back with nothing to do but think about things that hurt, things that make him ashamed. I was a lousy father and a worse husband. From what you tell me, I was a damn poor excuse for a man."

His voice roughened, and his face tightened until the bones seemed about to poke through the dark skin. "But that's history. I can't change that. All I can do is show you that *I've* changed, that I would rather die than hurt you again."

He stopped then, as though he'd said all that had to be said, all that was necessary. Perhaps for him that was true. But what about her? What did she want? It shook her to realize she didn't know.

Mat fingered a strand of hair as he had done that afternoon in her kitchen. He had declared unequivocally that they would be friends. But lovers was what he had meant. A small shiver passed through her, and he drew back his hand as though he had resolved to be patient with her.

"Have dinner with me tonight. You pick the place."

His mouth moved closer, sending her heart thundering like the hoofbeats that had brought him to her.

"I'm busy." Even as she said the words, she knew that she wanted his mouth pressed against hers, that she wanted to feel his body against hers. Involuntarily her lips parted, bringing quicksilver fire to his eyes. His head dipped another inch.

"Tomorrow night, then."

"No, Mat. Not tonight or tomorrow or any time." Desperation gave her voice a hurried quality. "I'm not interested in an affair with you."

The undamaged corner of his mouth slanted into a bone-shivering half smile. "My memory's pretty shaky, I admit, but for the life of me, I can't remember saying anything about an affair. Just dinner." The half smile became a grin that sent shock waves to her toes.

"However, it is an interesting suggestion," he added in a husky voice. "One I'll give some thought."

She already had. Too many times for her peace of mind. That realization added fuel to the always smoldering sexual awareness between them until it was like a hot flame inside her. She had to flee or be badly burned.

Bunching her fists, she said slowly and distinctly, "Stay out of my life. Don't try to be charming. Don't try to be nice. Don't even talk to me."

"Susanna—"

"I mean it, Mat." Once started, she couldn't seem to stop. Maybe she had held the words in too long, or maybe she needed them to prop up the defenses that he seemed determined to shove aside. "Whatever feelings I had for you died when…when I lost Bobby. As far as I'm concerned, you're just a man I wish I'd never met."

His eyes went still. His face seemed to change, and yet not a muscle moved. Whatever he was feeling, it was locked up tight behind that hard facade. Susanna wished she had that kind of control.

He nodded slowly, his eyes dangerously still. The lines in his face, etched there by hard experience, somehow seemed to deepen. "Whatever you want from me, you can have. Just be damn sure it's what you really want."

Was it? she asked herself hurriedly. Did she want this man to treat her as a stranger? To stop looking at her with those fierce obsidian eyes as though trying to see into her soul? To stop kissing her and holding her and flirting with her?

Maybe it wasn't what she wanted, but that was what she had to have in order to keep herself safe.

She drew breath. "Yes, that's what I really want."

Mat set his jaw. Surrender wasn't a word he counted in his vocabulary. A man never gave up, no matter what punishment he had to take in order to win. Retreated, yes. Rested if he had to, regrouped, rearmed, changed strategy if necessary, but he always fought until he won—or died.

A man also paid his debts, and he owed Susanna a big one, one that he knew now he would be paying for a long time.

"It's getting dark," he said in clipped tone. "I'd better get that tire changed." Without giving her a chance to answer, he turned away, his wide back straight and proud.

Susanna bent to retrieve the lug nuts scattered at her feet. She had gotten exactly what she wanted, so why did she feel so alone?

The ringing of the phone gradually penetrated Susanna's troubled sleep, jerking her from yet another dream of Mat. Feeling disoriented, she pressed her face into the pillow and groaned. He had been making love to her.

Her heart pounded, and her skin tingled. The dream had been so real. Too real. Her breasts were heavy and hot, and her lower body was tight with tension.

The phone shrilled again. "Okay, okay," she muttered, her voice thick. Eyes still tightly closed, she groped for the receiver by the bed, praying it wasn't another emergency.

Because Brad Greenleaf's surgical assistant was down with the flu and because Susanna was still qualified as a surgical nurse, she had helped him perform an emergency appendectomy during the early hours of the morning, returning home just as the sun was coming up over the mesa.

A quick look at the clock told her it was nearly five in the afternoon. She had slept nine hours. Thank goodness it was Sunday.

"'Lo."

"Susanna, it's Aurora. Did I wake you from a nap?"

Susanna fluttered her eyes, trying to clear her foggy brain. "No, I'm not awake yet," she said on a yawn.

She heard Aurora chuckle. "Want me to call back?"

"No, give me a minute." Susanna pressed the phone to her ear with her shoulder and used her hands to push herself upright. Her nightshirt slid sensuously over her skin, sending ripples deep into her sensitized body. She bit off a moan and tried to find a more comfortable position.

After years of living in the quiet, she had suddenly become hypersensitive to noise. She couldn't seem to breathe properly when Mat was next door. Sometimes, in the dead of night, she woke up to discover she was holding her breath, listening. Or was it waiting? She was never sure.

"Everything ready for the party?" Susanna said into the receiver when she was feeling coherent again. Tonight the Santa Ysabel Artists Cooperative was celebrating its first birthday with a party. As executive director, Aurora was acting as hostess.

"It better be. I had Grandfather do a blessing for us yesterday, and today my students have spent all day decorating and fixing the food. If something goes wrong, I'll blame it on the clay spirits."

Susanna smiled into the receiver. Afternoon sun streamed through the window to pattern the floor tiles, and the scent of wood smoke from the fire she'd built in the fireplace two nights ago still lingered in the air.

"Are you going to autograph copies of your book?"

"No, but maybe I should. I'll be lucky if it sells a dozen copies."

A former professor at the School of Fine Arts at SMU, Aurora had just published a textbook on pre-Columbian ceremonial vessels in which she showcased the rare and, until now, never publicly glimpsed Santa Ysabel polychrome bowls, both of which were considered virtually priceless by art appraisers worldwide.

Susanna stifled another yawn. "Hey, I bought one. It's wonderful. I love the way you make history seem so real. I can almost see those ancient potters you talk about."

"Don't laugh. I think they're still living in my house somewhere, haunting me."

Susanna heard a shout in the backyard, followed by a peal of little-boy laughter. Her gaze flew to the window. Cody and Mat were playing ball.

From the things Missy had told her during their almost daily chats, she knew that Mat worked ten-hour shifts during the week and every other weekend. When he wasn't working, he tried to spend time with his children. But all too frequently, it seemed, he came home so tired he fell asleep in his chair, with Cody in his lap and a storybook on his knee.

"Susanna? Are you there?"

"Sorry. I . . . What did you say?" She tried to drag her gaze away from the window, but she couldn't seem to stop watching the laughing little boy. And his father.

"I asked if you would do me a favor."

"Of course."

"Actually, the favor is for John." Aurora sounded apologetic. "He's been trying to reach Mat for over an hour about some kind of security problem for tonight, but his phone is always busy. It might be off the hook."

Outside the window Mat tossed the ball to Cody, his movements unusually awkward, as though his back were giving him trouble.

Cody missed the ball, and it bounced off his wide little chest. With an excited squeal, he toddled across the yard after it, his short legs pumping furiously.

Bobby would have been like that energetic little boy. She closed her eyes in an effort to block out the pain. It didn't help.

"What do you want me to tell him?" Sudden tension made her voice unusually husky.

Silence hummed over the wire. "Sue, if you'd rather not . . ."

"No problem," she said heartily, faking a laugh. "Mat and I aren't enemies, you know."

"How's it going? With the two of you, I mean." Aurora's tone was sympathetic.

Susanna tightened her grip on the phone. "It isn't. We nod politely when we meet. He goes his way, I go mine. It works just fine."

"He thinks you're pretty terrific."

Eyes opening wide, Susanna nearly dropped the phone. "What did you say?"

"He's been out here a lot, riding, mostly, or sometimes helping John for the exercise. He talks about you a lot, mostly about how good you are for his daughter." Susanna heard Aurora take a deep breath. "I've seen him ride. He reminds me of John before we got back together. I think he's in a lot of pain because of what he did."

Susanna shifted her gaze to the window again. She knew the feeling. "He'll get over it."

She heard a sigh. "You're really determined to punish him, aren't you?"

Susanna gasped. "That's not fair, Aurora. I thought you, of all people, would understand."

"I do. That's why I don't want you to make a bad mistake."

Susanna closed her eyes. "You sound like you're on his side."

There was a pause. "I nearly lost John because I couldn't let go of my pain. I don't want you to make the same mistake."

How could she lose what she'd never had? She took a tighter grip on the receiver. "I see Mat outside. I'll tell him to call John."

A sigh came over the line. "Lord, you're stubborn."

A smile tugged at Susanna's lips. "I'll see you tonight."

"Come early, before seven."

They exchanged goodbyes, and Susanna hung up, then returned her gaze to the scene beyond the dusty pane. This time Cody trapped the ball in his arms, his small mouth pursed in concentration.

Every time she saw Mat's son she thought about Bobby. Every time she saw Missy she wondered about the boy he had become. Was he tall, with his father's wide shoulders? Had he learned to handle his fierce temper? Did he still hate peas? Did he know he was adopted? If so, did he hate the woman who had given him up?

She took a ragged breath, pressing her hand to her lips to keep them from trembling. Oh, Bobby. I didn't want to do it. I *didn't*.

Ten minutes later, her composure still shaky but her eyes dry, she stepped off the small stoop into the backyard and walked resolutely toward the man and boy a few yards away.

She had exchanged her nightshirt for a thick warm sweater and pulled on a pair of soft corduroy slacks. Her hair was piled into a loose knot on top of her head. Her face was still scrubbed clean.

Mat saw her before she had taken more than a few steps.

"Afternoon," he said with a nod as curt as the tone of his voice. Surprise filtered through her for a moment before she realized he was keeping his promise to give her exactly what she wanted. So why did she feel so hurt all of a sudden?

"I have a message for you," she said, letting him know by the tone in her voice that she had sought him out for no other reason. He remained silent, watching her with eyes narrowed against the setting sun. Before she could continue, Cody caught sight of her.

"Zana," he shouted, his round face breaking into a toothy grin. "Come play ba'." He began to run toward her, his chubby arms outstretched, his scuffed sneakers raising puffs of dust with each step.

Unable to resist when he called her by the name only he used, she caught him under the arms and swung him around. He shouted in glee, his brown eyes shining with excitement.

Mat kicked a clod of dirt across the yard and settled his shoulders, trying to ease the tightness in his neck. Didn't the woman own clothes that fit? he thought irritably, stabbing the toe of his boot into the hard ground.

He'd never thought a sweater that was three sizes too big could be sexy, but damn it, this one was. Maybe because the soft folds outlined just enough of her breasts to send a man's imagination into overdrive. Or because the stretched-out ribbing drew the eye to the most sensuous part of her thigh.

Tired as he was, his body began to stir, making him grit his teeth. He jammed his fingers into the back pockets of his jeans and told himself he was a fool in words that would have impressed the devil himself.

"Up, up," Cody cried as Susanna lowered him to the cradle of her arms. She bent her head to blow a kiss into his tiny ear. He giggled, ducking his head against her shoulder to escape her teasing mouth.

Without seeming to, Mat watched them laughing together, their eyes lit with a sparkling happiness that made him ache in some private, rarely visited place deep inside himself. He had never felt that kind of uninhibited joy, not in the span of time he recalled, anyway. In his gut he had a feeling he had never experienced it.

Jealousy stabbed him hard enough to bring a scowl to his face. What kind of man was jealous of his two-year-old son, for God's sake? he thought, running his hand across his suddenly knotted belly. One who was frustrated, that was what kind.

Sensing Mat's impatience, Susanna set Cody on his feet, then gave him a little pat on his bottom. "Go find your ball, sweetheart."

Mat stopped his son with a firm hand on his chubby shoulder. "It's time to go in, now, scout. Grandmother will give you a cookie."

"Cookie," Cody repeated agreeably, toddling across the yard, arms akimbo, sneakers raising another cloud of dust. At the door he turned and waved bye-bye before banging his chubby fist on the door. It opened instantly to reveal the matronly form of Grandmother Ettaway.

"You said you had a message for me?"

"Yes, call John at the ranch," she said stiffly when Cody was safely inside. Was this the way it was going to be from now on? she wondered. The two of them exchanging stilted conversation when they happened to meet? Not quite looking at each other when they passed? "He's been trying to reach you, but your phone has been busy."

Mat muttered a few choice words. "Cody likes to talk to the dial tone. I've punished him, talked to him, bought him a toy phone of his own. I've even put the phone up where he can't reach it, but it looks like he found a way." His face softened as though he were going to smile, then closed up again, shutting her out. "Thanks for the message. I'll take care of it."

Susanna, fighting a smile of her own at his description of his son's exasperating naughtiness, felt as though he'd slapped her.

"You're welcome," she said stiffly as she started to walk past him, but he caught her hand, spinning her around to face him. Every time he thought about that damn letter he'd written, he wanted to punch a hole in the wall she'd put between them. Every time he remembered holding her in his arms and kissing her, his body tightened with the kind of raw need that drove a man with a hard lash. Two weeks of cold showers had put a rough edge on his temper.

"Is this the way you really want things to be between us?" he grated. *"Is it?"*

She heard the raw note in his voice, and the sound was like a knife piercing her heart. Her instinct for people told her that she had finally hurt him. Was Aurora right about her? Was she trying to cause him as much pain as he'd caused her?

She was suddenly ashamed of herself. "No," she admitted with a sigh. "Sooner or later the tension between us is going to hurt the children and I would...hate that very much."

He glanced toward the sky, his lean face more gaunt than usual, as though he'd lost weight. He jammed his hands into his back pockets and dropped his gaze to the ground between them for a beat before slowly raising it to her face.

"I was dead wrong, Susanna. Shamefully wrong, and that's something I'll have to live with for the rest of my life." It was a statement—unequivocal, steely, uttered in the flat cadence of a man who didn't make excuses or spare himself in any way.

Susanna stared at him, trying to reconcile this man with the image of the one who had used her, then discarded her like so much soiled laundry. She couldn't make the two merge. Like crude ore forged to tempered steel by the fiery heat of pain and suffering, Mat *had* changed, in his heart and in his soul.

If things were different, if they still had Bobby, maybe...

Mat moved closer. His skin exuded a musky heat that spiraled into her senses like potent wine.

"Start over with me," he urged in a low deep voice. "Let me take care of you this time." His scarred hand found the curve of her neck. His fingers rubbed the knotted muscles at the nape until they were as fluid as warmed honey.

The land around them had gone unnaturally still, as though the earth were holding its breath. She raised both hands and pushed against his shoulders. It was like trying to move one of the river oaks deeply rooted into the banks of the Wildcat.

"Is that what you really want, Susanna? For us to be strangers, two people who just happen to share a house?"

"Yes." Her voice caressed the word, giving it the opposite meaning.

With a husky groan Mat lowered his head and fitted his mouth to hers. He tasted her lips slowly, thoroughly, his hands cupping her shoulders as gently as he could manage.

She shivered, and he pulled her closer, his arms and his body offering protection from the wind. His body heat began seeping into her pores, warming her with a familiar excitement that made her feel good all over.

She slid her arms around his neck, burrowing her fingers into the thick shaggy hair covering his nape. He stiffened, and a hard shudder rippled across his shoulders.

He drew back, wiping his kiss from her mouth with the pad of his thumb. She fluttered her eyes open and looked up at him, her mouth still soft and full from his kiss. It took all of his control to keep from giving in to the hunger prowling inside him.

"See how good it can be between us," he whispered, fighting the need to kiss her again.

Clasped in his loose embrace, Susanna was intensely aware of him. In the hushed serenity of the afternoon, he seemed even more restless than ever. His sexuality was almost as powerful as his corded arms and well-muscled thighs. When she was in his arms, nothing mattered but the way he made her feel inside. When he kissed her, she wanted to beg him to take her higher and higher until she was lost in a dizzying whirl of sensation.

But what would happen when her needs were sated? Would he expect her to be his mistress? Would the women come to whisper about her the way they whispered about Lupe? Would she ultimately become an object of pity when Mat tired of her?

"It's late," she murmured, her voice unnaturally low. "I have to get ready for the party."

His grin was a slanted line of regret. "Yeah, and I'd better call John before he has second thoughts about the new Chief of Police." Mat raked a hand through his hair, leaving it even more untidy. "You mix up a man's priorities, Susanna Spencer."

"But I have mine in order, Mat," she said firmly, struggling to ignore the melting heat that still smoldered inside her. Her face tingled where his afternoon beard had rubbed. Her mouth, sensitized by his kiss, felt swollen. "A romance with you isn't on my list."

If she hadn't been watching his eyes, she would have missed the flash of emotion in his eyes, so quickly did he erase it.

"Why did you let me kiss you?"

"I shouldn't have." It wasn't the answer he wanted, but it was the only answer that was safe.

He let out a long ragged breath. "You wanted me. You still want me. I see it in your eyes."

Her innate honesty wouldn't allow her to lie. Besides, what good would it do? He was right. His kisses had burned all the way to the soft warm part of her. But there was more to life than drugging kisses and stolen nights of sexual fulfillment. Mat wasn't offering his love, only his body.

"Sex is easy, Mat. We proved that ten years ago. But it doesn't last, not like love."

His mouth jerked. "What's love? My wife swore she loved me, but that didn't keep her from cheating on me with damn near every guy who looked her way. If that's love, I don't need it.''

Susanna was suddenly very weary. There it was, the gut-deep essence of the man spelled out in seven short words. It was simple, straightforward, even honest.

She took a deep slow breath, fighting the need for him that still raced through her veins. ''But I do.''

She turned and walked away.

Chapter 9

Mat flipped up his collar and began tying the plain black tie. What once required a quick three or four seconds now took much longer.

He scowled at his reflection in the cracked mirror over the bathroom sink. Twenty minutes in a cold shower had cooled his ardor but done little to improve his mood.

He needed a drink. Hell, he needed a bottle, he amended savagely. And a woman. Any woman, as long as she was willing. He'd make sure she had a good time, wouldn't he? Damn straight he would. Mat Cruz knew how to take care of a woman.

Didn't he?

A muscle jumped at the edge of his hard jaw. Who the hell was he kidding? He didn't want just any woman, no matter how beautiful or willing or sexy. He wanted Susanna.

Impatiently he tugged the knot snug against his collar, then flipped down the starched collar points. One quick glance told him he was presentable enough.

Not that it mattered much, he thought, gripping the smooth sides of the sink and dropping his head. He would be working tonight, not making love.

He closed his eyes, summoning the image of her face just before his mouth took hers. He had been awestruck by the soft sheen of her eyes as she gazed up at him, her lips trembling slightly, her breath catching in her throat. Not even the threat of a slow painful death could have kept him from kissing her. He had intended to be patient with her, to prove that he wanted more from her than he had taken ten years ago. But when her mouth had softened under his, he hadn't been able to pull away.

He still felt her hands clinging to his neck, pulling him closer. His body still ached from the hot rush of blood her kiss had stirred in him.

Damn the woman, he thought, and then was ashamed of himself. She was right in everything she'd said. He didn't love her, and he wasn't about to pretend he did. According to her, that was exactly what he'd done ten years ago.

The hell of it was that he also couldn't pretend he didn't want her. Just being around her made him hurt in ways he hadn't known existed. Not just physically, but in some protected, half-forgotten part of his soul, where he longed to believe he deserved to be loved.

A familiar tightness ran up his spine to the muscles between his shoulders. His hand went to the back of his neck, working on the knot that always seemed to be there these days.

He'd come so close to putting a crack in that icy wall she had built around herself. He might be out of practice, but he wasn't dead. He knew when a woman was responding.

Yeah, she had wanted him sexually, all right. It was the rest of him she didn't want—unless he could prove that he loved her. Which was the one thing he *couldn't* do.

His mouth slanted into a cynical smile. God sure as hell knew how to make a man pay for his sins, he thought. Give him a glimpse of heaven and then tell him he can't have it—except in his dreams.

Admit it, Cruz, he demanded silently. God had nothing to do with this particular punishment. You put yourself in this purgatory. It would almost be funny—if it didn't hurt so damn much.

"Daddy?"

He glanced over his shoulder. Missy was hovering just inside the door, a worried look pinching her small face.

"What's wrong, baby? You don't look very happy."

She shuffled her pink bunny slippers nervously. "Are you gonna spank Cody 'cause he knocked over the phone so Mr. Olvera couldn't call us?"

Mat bit off a sigh. When he'd found the phone off the hook, he'd blown up. At the time Susanna's words were ringing in his ears and his body was still taut and aching. But that had been no reason to take it out on his kids.

"No, baby, I'm not. Cody didn't mean to be naughty. I know that now."

She fiddled with the sash of her robe. "You yelled at him," she said in a small voice. "Why did you yell at him if you weren't mad?"

Mat took a slow breath. How did a man explain to his nine-year-old daughter the violent need to lash out that had gripped him when he realized he didn't have a chance in hell of making things up to Susanna?

"Let's have a talk, you and me."

He took her hand and led her into his bedroom. He sat on the edge of the bed, then pulled her onto his knee. She sat stiffly, her hands pressed together between her legs, her eyes full of confusion.

"Daddy made a mistake, Missy," he said, smoothing her hair. "It's not the first one I've ever made, and it won't be the last. I shouldn't have yelled at Cody, and I shouldn't have blamed you for letting him play with the phone. But that doesn't mean I don't love you, because I do. And I need you very much." He dropped a kiss on her head. "Okay?"

She nodded, then circled his waist with her thin arms and rested her head against his chest.

"I wish you were staying home so we could play Chinese checkers."

The forlorn note in her voice made him flinch. He'd taught her to play because the doctors told him the movements necessary to manipulate the tiny marbles would be good therapy for his partially paralyzed hand.

For the past three nights he'd promised to play a game with her after dinner. One night he'd been called out to help Two Skies handle a domestic squabble that had threatened to escalate into a brawl. The other two nights he'd been so tired he'd nearly fallen asleep at the dinner table. He'd gone to his bed as soon as he'd tucked the children into theirs.

"I have all day off tomorrow," he told her gently. "We'll play as many games as you want." He rubbed her back, feeling the sharp little bones of her spine through the soft robe.

She sat up, her eyes bright again. "Promise?"

"Cross my heart." He touched the tiny cleft in her chin with his thumb. Her small features were a feminine version of his, with the exception of her chocolate-brown eyes. Those were her own.

"I have to warn you, though," he said with a grin. "This time I intend to win."

Missy's mouth took on a mischievous pout. "Uh-uh. I'm the champion of the world, remember? You even said so."

He chuckled. "Yeah, but I'm catching up."

She shook her head. "I'm the bestest."

"That you are, the bestest daughter a daddy can have." Mat kissed her, then slid her from his lap. "Baby, do me a favor and ask Grandmother Ettaway if she's going to spend the night or if I'm supposed to take her home when I get back. She told me at dinner, but I forgot."

"Okay. Be right back." Missy skipped out, her good humor restored. Mat envied her. A few soothing words, a few warm hugs, a kiss or two, and her world was in order again, he thought as he transferred his keys and wallet from the dresser to his pockets.

Missy returned, munching on a cookie. "Grandmother said she'll stay if it's real late when you get back. Otherwise, she needs a ride."

Mat pinned his badge to his shirt, then turned to face her.

"I doubt I'll be late, unless the parties here are wilder than I think they are."

He hated the nights he had to drag the children from their beds to accompany him while he drove the housekeeper across the pueblo to her apartment. But it couldn't be helped. He wouldn't leave them alone, not even with Susanna next door.

If things had been different, maybe, but...

Forget it, Cruz, he told himself with a biting anger. The woman is not about to let you into her life.

His teeth ground together. What was so damn great about love, anyway? Half the guys in his outfit had sworn they'd loved their wives, but that hadn't stopped most of them from fooling around when they got the chance.

Missy climbed onto his bed and sat cross-legged in the middle, watching him unlock the olive drab footlocker where he kept his weapon when it wasn't on his hip.

"Daddy, is Susanna going to be our new mommy?"

He nearly dropped the Colt. "What makes you ask that?" he asked as he strapped on the gun.

"You and her were kissing. I seen you when I was helping Cody wash his hands for supper."

Mat saw the hope in her eyes and felt sick inside. He didn't want to make her sad, but he couldn't let her go on hoping.

"Once, a long time ago, before you were born, Susanna and I met each other right here in this house. It was when your Grandmother Cruz died. Remember I told you I grew up here?"

Missy nodded solemnly, her eyes watching him intently.

"Well, I did something really bad to Susanna, something that made her feel sad inside. Because of that, she doesn't want to be my friend."

Her jaw took on a stubborn slant that reminded him of Susanna. "You could say you're sorry. And then she'd like you again."

He pulled Missy close and rested his chin on her head. If only it were that easy.

"That's just it, Missy. I said I was sorry, but it didn't make any difference. Sometimes, when you hurt someone very badly, saying you're sorry isn't enough."

He framed her small face with his hands and kissed her forehead. "Walk me to the car. Daddy needs a little tender loving care tonight."

Susanna's Jeep wouldn't start. She had forgotten to turn off her headlights when she'd returned at dawn, and the battery was dead.

She was already half an hour late for the party, and the studio was a good twenty minutes' drive from her house.

Calling herself a few choice names, she dropped her forehead to the steering wheel and closed her eyes. "This isn't happening," she mumbled. "Please tell me I'm still asleep."

"Having trouble?"

Susanna raised her head to find Mat standing between her Jeep and his Bronco. Missy was with him, dressed for bed in her robe and slippers.

"You might say that, yes," she told him with a disgusted look at her beloved Jeep. Why now? she wanted to mutter.

She had planned to be gone before he left his house. Now it seemed he was her only hope of getting to the party at all.

The thought made her grit her teeth. She opened the door and stepped out, just as Missy ran up to give her a hug.

Mat approached more slowly, his gaunt face wiped clean of expression. She had time to notice that he looked crisp and professional in his uniform—and dangerously sexy—before she returned Missy's hug.

"You look pretty," the little girl said when Susanna released her.

She managed a smile for the little girl. "Thank you, sweetie."

"Daddy's going to a party tonight, at the place where they make pots and things, but I can't go because he's working." Missy slanted a curious look toward Susanna's intricate silver earrings. "Are you going to the party, too?"

Susanna glanced toward the Jeep. "I was, until my car wouldn't start."

"Is it broken?" Missy asked.

"Not exactly." Conscious that Mat stood watching her from a few feet away, she forced a smile to her face. "I need one of those cars with a computer that talks. You know, like, 'Susanna, you've left your lights on again, dummy.'"

Missy giggled. "Cody has a teddy bear that talks. It's his favorite. Daddy says it's going to self-destruct some night."

Susanna thought about the rag doll in the cedar chest. It hadn't talked, but Bobby had loved it. The agency hadn't let him keep anything from his former life, not even his tattered blanket. Susanna would never forgive them for that.

She took a ragged breath. "How's school?" she asked, smoothing Missy's hair.

"Okay," Missy said with a noticeable lack of enthusiasm. "We have a new teacher. Miss Knifechief. She said she went to school with Daddy, but he can't remember her." She cast a quick glance toward her father. "Can you, Daddy?"

"No."

Mat shoved his hand into his pocket and watched Susanna without seeming to. Her blouse was the color of a cactus rose, and cut like a man's shirt, with full sleeves and tiny cuffs. Made of some soft material, it just begged to be touched. But not by him. The expression on her face told him as much.

He leaned against the Bronco and dropped his gaze to his dusty boots, listening absently to Missy's chatter. Was this the way he was going to feel every time he ran into Susanna—like a man locked out of the one place he wanted to be?

"I could use a push," Susanna told Mat when Missy ran out of things to tell her. Sometime during the past two hours she had decided that she would be friendly but distant when they met again. It was the only way the two of them could coexist in such a small place.

He glanced toward the lonely road leading to town. The light was almost gone. In another few minutes it would be dark.

"Your battery might be ruined, in which case your lights will go out on you before you get halfway to the studio. Be better if you rode with me."

Impatience was stamped on his face, along with another emotion she couldn't read.

"The battery's only a few months old. By the time I get to the studio it'll be charged again," she countered, trying not to notice the way his tailored trousers fit snugly over his lean hips and strong thighs.

"What if it isn't?" Arms folded, he leaned against the Bronco and crossed one ankle over the other. In spite of the relaxed pose, his lean body radiated a tightly coiled energy that sent darts of warning down her spine.

"Then I'll deal with it."

"Right." He dropped his gaze to her red huaraches. "How far do you think you'll get in those?"

Instead of answering, she turned her attention to the little girl at her side. Missy had enough problems without having her precariously balanced world upset by something she couldn't understand. "It's getting pretty chilly out here, sweetie. Maybe you should go on in now."

Missy's gaze shifted to her father, but unlike the last time the three of them had been together, she seemed much more comfortable with him. Susanna wondered if he had taken her advice to reassure the timid little girl. And then she knew that he had. Sadness settled like a hard lump in her stomach. Mat would have been a good father to Bobby.

"Susanna's right, baby," Mat said quietly. "Run on in now."

He moved away from the Bronco and bent to wrap his arms around Missy's small body for a good-night hug. Susanna moved away, but not before she remembered how safe she had once felt in those strong arms.

"Will you check on me when you get home?" Missy asked, clinging to his strong neck.

"First thing I do," he said, kissing her cheek.

"Bye, Daddy." She turned toward Susanna, suddenly looking shy. "Bye, Susanna."

She gave Melissa a hug. "Sleep well," she said, her heart tearing. All that she was cried out to love this darling child and her adorable brother. But she couldn't allow that to happen. Mat was bound to get married again. And the woman he chose would become the mother of his children. She wouldn't want Susanna interfering. Susanna understood that. The maternal instinct was fierce. In spite of all the years, she still considered herself Bobby's mother. The woman who was raising him was simply a surrogate.

Missy ran toward the house, then turned to wave before she opened the door. "Have a good time," she shouted before disappearing inside.

Now that she and Mat were alone, Susanna was even more aware of the tension between them.

"Will you give me a push? *Please?*" She had trouble keeping her vow to be polite. The man had a way of looking at her that made her forget a lot of things, things she needed to remember in order to keep from ending up in his bed.

"You hate having to ask me for anything, don't you?"

Was it a trick of the light that gave his face such a vulnerable expression? she wondered as he moved toward her. Or was it her own thoughts coloring her perception? "Does it matter?"

"No," he said in a tone she'd never heard before. "It doesn't matter."

He nodded toward her Jeep, his eyes opaque, as though he'd mastered the thoughts that had put shadows there. "Hop in, and I'll give you a push."

"Thanks."

She slid into the driver's seat and started to close the door. Mat stopped her with a hand on the frame. "I'll follow you. If this thing stops again, you're getting in with me. No arguments."

She opened her mouth to protest, but the rigid way he held his jaw stopped her. Mat was not a man a rational person deliberately crossed. He had given in this time, not because of anything she'd done or said, but because it suited him. If she pushed him too far, she just might find herself walking to town. She closed her mouth with a snap, sealing her words inside.

"Wise move, Susanna," he said, turning away. She thought she heard him chuckle.

The open house was winding down. Most of the families with small children had come and gone. Those that remained were in a festive mood, filling up on goodies from the two long tables covered with food and drink, talking buoyantly in a familiar mixture of Tewa and English. Susanna had done her share of both eating and talking, but after nearly three hours her feet hurt and her throat was dry.

She slipped through the crush to the drinks table, where she drew a cup of coffee from the large urn. Behind her, she heard a burst of laughter coming from the corner where John Olvera and the other members of the Council were entertaining guests from other pueblos throughout the state.

Mat stood alone a few feet from the group, his eyes moving restlessly over the throng. He rarely spoke to anyone, and when he did, it was only briefly. It was very clear that he was there to keep order, not to socialize.

The trip to town had been uneventful. The Bronco had stayed behind her the entire way, and Mat had been waiting for her when she'd climbed out of her Jeep in the makeshift parking lot. Without exchanging a word, they had walked into the party together. The People were too polite to stare, but they had been noticed nevertheless. For some reason, knowing that they were not really together made her terribly sad.

When she'd known him before, she hadn't really liked him, not in the way a woman should like the man she loves. Craved his lovemaking, loved him dearly, yes, but the arrogance he'd worn on his shoulders had put a wall between them. Now that the arrogance was gone, so was the wall.

If they had been meeting now, for the first time, she had a feeling she would like this man very much. She hated to admit it, but she was becoming more and more ambivalent about her feelings for him. And that was dangerous.

As though feeling her gaze on his face, Mat turned his head slightly, bringing his eyes in line with hers. The room was full of copper-skinned men with black eyes and dark hair. But his eyes had a dangerous glitter in them instead of humor, and his face was lean where most were broad.

It was a virile face, sculpted by a bold hand, without a hint of softness. Except when he smiled. And then the brutal lines eased and his mouth took on a vulnerable slant.

Her mouth started to relax, and then she realized he wasn't smiling. If anything, he looked as though he resented her glance.

A wave of embarrassment climbed up her neck. She jerked her gaze away so quickly that her hair tumbled over her forehead. Her hand smoothed it into order again. From the corner of her eyes, she watched him move into the crowd.

As he passed a group of teenage girls, they stopped chattering to direct veiled glances toward Santa Ysabel's new Police Chief. For many of the guests this was the first time they'd seen him. Had he heard the whispers of the women lamenting his lost good looks, or the subtle speculation about the ability of such a badly injured man to father more children?

Susanna bit her lip. He was probably the bravest man she had ever known, and maybe the strongest, not only physically, but inside, where it counted most. Not too many men had the grit to start over the way he'd had to do.

"I'm not sure which of you looks worse. Mat, I suppose, although he hides it better." Lost in thought, Susanna hadn't noticed Aurora arrive at her side.

Susanna poked a dent into the top of the white foam coffee cup with her fingernail. "Sometimes I think I should accept that offer from the women's clinic in Santa Fe. I'm a nervous wreck. I've overdosed on peanut butter cups so often lately I've gained seven pounds, and I keep misplacing things, like my stethoscope and other minor pieces of equipment like that."

Aurora gave her a sympathetic look. Even though she was only a little more than two months pregnant, her figure was fuller and her complexion glowed. Susanna envied her.

Two Council members, bedecked in silver and deep in conversation, approached, excusing themselves as they reached past Susanna for cups.

The women moved out of the way, finding a quiet spot near an open window. Susanna tugged the soft lapels of her shirt away from her throat, letting the fresh air cool her heated skin.

"It's got to be ninety in here."

"More like a hundred."

Susanna took a sip of coffee. "Yuck," she muttered, staring into the muddy liquid. It tasted as bitter as her mood. "Either John made this coffee or there's something dangerous growing in that pot."

Aurora laughed. "Poor John. His coffee has become infamous." Her expression softened. "He thinks it'll cure just about anything."

Susanna took another sip, then winced. "And I thought hospital coffee was bad." She sent a pointed glance toward the paper cup filled with orange juice in her friend's hand. "Why didn't you warn me?"

"Because you looked like you needed something strong to perk you up."

"That's true enough," she admitted with a sigh. "I can't seem to catch up on my sleep." Not when she lay awake night after night thinking about Mat.

She let her gaze drift toward the other side of the room, but instead of Mat, another man caught her eye. Stocky, with a bull neck, he had unusually short hair and mean-looking eyes.

His beefy shoulder was angled against the wall as he stood chatting with one of the young potters, a wispy-looking woman named Alice Comacho.

"Oh, my God," she said in a shocked whisper. "That looks like Buck Ruiz."

The brother of the former Tribal Chairman, Ruiz had been twice convicted of assault and battery. The last she'd heard, the man had been in prison in Santa Fe.

"It is Buck," Aurora answered in a disgusted voice. "He's out on parole. Again."

"What's John going to do about it?"

Aurora finished her orange juice, then crushed the cup in her strong potter's hand. "Nothing. As long as Buck doesn't break Tribal Law, he's entitled to live here." She hesitated, then added softy, "Actually, Buck is Mat's problem now. That's why John was trying to reach him, to tell him about Buck."

"I thought you said it was a security problem."

"It is. John wanted to make sure Mat knew about him before the party started. He was afraid Buck would show up drunk and cause trouble."

"He doesn't look drunk, but he certainly looks like trouble," Susanna muttered, noting Alice's flustered expression. Susanna didn't like the man. She never had. He seemed to swagger, even when he was standing still, but she had to admit he had a certain outlaw appeal. Maybe that was why Alice looked so smitten.

"I hope Alice knows what she's doing," Aurora said in a tight voice. "As I told John, it wouldn't surprise me to find out Buck was the one who accosted those two coeds."

Susanna went cold inside. "What did John say?"

"Not much. You know how he is. He never says anything until he's thought it through. But I had a feeling the same thing had occurred to him. I also think that's one of the things he wanted to talk with Mat about."

As the two women watched, Buck held out a hand and Alice took it. Together they started for the door.

Across the room, Mat watched Susanna shake her head at something Aurora Olvera said. The two women were the only non-Indians in the room. Both were striking women, but Susanna was the one who riled his blood.

He'd been a fool to walk away from a woman like her. So why had he? After a dozen operations and more painful procedures than he wanted to count, he'd sworn he would never let a doctor touch him again, but now he realized he would do anything to regain his memories of his time with Susanna, even let the damn surgeons slice open his head again.

But there was nothing more to be done. No more surgery, no more hypnosis sessions to dredge up buried images, nothing. The blackness in his head would always be with him, not as noticeable as the scars on his face, but just as difficult to accept.

Mat took a quick survey of the room. The party was still going strong. Everyone else seemed to be having a great time. Especially Susanna.

She hadn't been alone all evening. Damn near every eligible man in the room had talked to her at one time or another, especially that good-looking kid who ran the clinic. What was his name? Greenleaf?

Mat ran a hand down his left cheek, then glanced at the scars disappearing under the cuff of his shirt. Slowly his hand closed into a fist.

Every time she smiled at another man, he wanted to kill the guy. Every time she threw back her head and boomed out that wonderfully infectious laugh of hers, he felt a sharp prodding inside. It galled him to realize he was jealous.

Just the sight of her provocative thighs in those white jeans made him want to drag her off to his bed and make love to her until she forgot the past. But life didn't work that way.

Frustration knifed through him. Before the bombing he would have gone a few rounds with the barracks champ to ease the tension knotting his belly. Or ridden his vintage Harley to the limit of its power. Now he could only grit his teeth and wait it out.

"Chief?" Deputy Spruce stood at his elbow, a worried look on his pockmarked face.

"Problems?" Mat asked in low tone.

"No, sir. Well, not exactly. It's past eleven. Should I put in overtime tonight?"

Mat glanced at his watch, then shook his head. "Take off. Two Skies and I will handle things 'til the party breaks up."

"Thanks, Chief. I wouldn't ask, but my wife's been sick, and now my oldest boy's gone and caught what she had."

He and Mat exchanged a few more words, then Spruce left.

Mat shifted his gaze to the corner. Aurora was now talking to someone else. Susanna was gone.

It took him less than a second to determine that she was no longer in the studio.

He bit off a furious oath. She had promised to let him know when she left so that he could make sure her battery had recharged.

A scowl tightened his face as he hurried to the exit. Good thing he'd learned patience during his convalescence. Otherwise Susanna would find out what happened to a woman who pushed a man beyond his limit.

Chapter 10

"Please, Buck. Don't do that!"

Recognizing Alice's voice, Susanna stopped fumbling in her purse for her keys and sent an anxious glance in the direction of the shrill cry. The moon was nearly full, but the far end of the deserted parking lot where she stood was deeply shadowed. She saw nothing but pickup trucks and Jeeps.

Suddenly, from the same direction, to her left, she heard the harsh rasp of a man's laugh. "You know you want it, bitch. You been givin' me the eye all night."

"No! Don't, Buck. Please don't." The frightened voice stopped abruptly, muffled into silence.

Fear pounding in her head, Susanna half ran, half walked toward the sounds of scuffling feet, searching the shadowed spaces between vehicles. The studio was too far away for anyone to have heard. She was alone.

Heart pounding, Susanna pulled up short, her breath stopping. She heard the sound of a scuffle between two parked vehicles. Buck Ruiz had Alice pushed up against the door of a battered Chevy half-ton, his knee insinuated between her thighs. One hand was busy inside her blouse.

"Let her go, Buck," Susanna ordered, stepping forward until she was so close she could smell the rank odor of sweat and cheap whiskey coming from him.

His head snapped up, then swiveled toward her. A sense of danger ran down her spine, but she stood her ground. Over his shoulder, Alice's eyes sought hers beseechingly.

"This ain't your affair, lady," he growled. "Turn on around and git the hell outta here before you git hurt bad." In the shadowed light, his smile was an ugly slash in his dark face.

She took another step, and her foot kicked something hard, sending it flying. It landed with a clink against the front wheel of another truck to her left. A hasty glance told her it was a whiskey bottle. No doubt empty now.

"You heard Alice. She doesn't want you to kiss her," she told him quietly. Without seeming to, she gauged the distance to the bottle. It wasn't much of a weapon, but it was all she had.

"Help me, Susanna," Alice beseeched, her voice rising to the point of hysteria. "He's drunk and—" So quickly his hand seemed to come from nowhere, Ruiz backhanded her. Alice's head snapped back, and blood trickled down her chin. Cringing, she tried to wrench away.

Susanna ran toward the bottle, but before she reached it, Ruiz grabbed a handful of her long hair and jerked her backward. She fell heavily, sending a jolt of pain up her spinal column.

"Stay the hell out of my business," he warned, his voice a menacing growl. "Or the next time you'll get hurt worse'n that."

He opened the door to the truck. "Get in," he growled to Alice, his hand closing over her arm to force her to do as he ordered.

Susanna managed to drag air into her lungs, enough to bring life back into her frozen muscles. She lunged for Buck's legs, but he kicked her hand away. Her wrist began to throb where the toe of his boot had caught her.

"Hold it right there, Ruiz. You're under arrest."

Susanna exhaled in relief. Mat stood two feet away, his legs spread, his hand close to his gun. Thank God, she thought. Now that it was over, she began to shake.

Ruiz froze, then spat out a crude curse. He released Alice with a jerk of his hand, then drew himself up slowly, his smelly body exuding menace.

"You okay?" Mat asked Alice, who nodded, her hand pressed against her swelling cheek.

"He's drunk," she managed to gasp out in a strangled voice.

"Move away from her, Ruiz," he ordered in a tight cold voice. "Now."

"What'll you do if I don't, cop?"

"Don't try me." Mat's voice was glacial.

Susanna was afraid to move. From the corner of her eye she saw Alice huddled against the fender of the pickup, looking equally frozen.

Seconds ticked by. Neither man moved, each measuring the other. Finally Ruiz shrugged, his mouth twisting in derision. "Hell, no woman is worth a bullet," he muttered, glaring at Alice. "'Sides, she's too damn bony for my taste."

Mat watched him in silence for several counts, then his gaze flashed toward Susanna. "Are you hurt?"

"Just my dignity," she said with a shaky laugh.

She thought he smiled, but the light was too poor to be certain. "That'll heal."

"I heard her screaming, so I tried to stop him," she explained, her voice still slightly breathless. "I didn't know what else to do."

"Next time, come get me or one of my deputies."

"Don't worry, I will." She inhaled slowly, still slightly dazed. Her backside felt bruised, and her scalp ached, but two aspirin and a hot bath would take care of that.

She started to get up, but a muscle in her back crimped into a painful knot, and she cried out. Mat shot her a quick glance. At the same moment, Ruiz lunged forward.

Before Mat could react, the other man's knuckles caught him in the face, breaking his nose. Pain exploded in his head, temporarily stunning him. Blood spurted in a hot sticky rush, covering his cheeks and dripping onto his shirt.

Shaking his head to clear his vision, he fought back instinctively, landing a quick blow to Buck's gut. His hand stung, then went dead. He connected with his right to the jaw, sending a jarring pain through his wrist.

Buck's head snapped back, his lip split. He roared out an obscenity; then, with a maddened bellow, he attacked with an alcohol-fueled frenzy, his shoulder catching Mat in the groin. Pain exploded in a blinding flash in Mat's gut. Doubled over in agony, he slowly sank to his knees, his head swimming. He fought to remain conscious, refusing to give in to the blessed oblivion that waited.

"Ain't no cripple gonna arrest me," Ruiz spat out, his voice twisted with scorn. "Remember that next time you think about spoilin' a man's fun, *Chief*."

The toe of his boot caught Mat in the side. This time the pain set off skyrockets in his head. Through a bloody haze Mat was dimly aware of the slam of a truck door, followed by the roar of an unmuffled engine and the spinning of tires. Gravel sprayed over him, and exhaust fumes fouled the air.

"Mat! Oh my God, Mat." Susanna was shaking so hard she had trouble scrambling to her feet. Everything had happened so quickly, and yet she still had seen every blow Mat had absorbed.

With that kind of battering, he had to be badly hurt. She had to get him to the clinic.

Hands trembling uncontrollably, she fumbled in her purse for a tissue, then used it to wipe away the worst of the blood streaming down his face. A gash like a jagged comma split the corner of his mouth. One eye was already starting to swell shut. The other was slit in pain.

Mat opened his eyes to see the worry twisting Susanna's face. He was supposed to be taking care of her, not the other way around. Fury at his helplessness roared through him as he shook off her hands and staggered to his feet.

With stinging eyes, Susanna watched him fight to keep on his feet. The blood on his shirt looked black in the moonlight, and his face was drawn and shadowed. Praying that her shaky knees would support them both, she slipped an arm around his waist and said urgently, "Mat, put your arm around my shoulder. Your ribs may be broken. We have to get you to the clinic."

He heard the urgency in Susanna's voice, and something more. Pity. His gut twisted until the pain was worse than the agony in his side. "Leave me alone," he muttered. "Don't need your help."

Digging deep into the last of his strength, he shook her off. He wasn't going to another damn hospital. Not ever. He'd had enough of needles and bedpans and cloying sympathy.

"Alice, go get John Olvera," Susanna ordered in a low voice. "Tell him to hurry."

"No," Mat managed to rasp out, each word an effort. "No one...don't need an audience." Blood from his fractured nose ran down to the back of his throat, and he began to cough, each wracking movement sending the pain deeper.

Alice looked at Susanna, her eyes wide with horror. "What should I do?" she asked in a broken voice.

Susanna glanced at the stiff line of Mat's shoulders. His breathing didn't sound as painful, and he seemed to be gathering strength. Intuition told her that he would feel unbearably humiliated if the entire community knew of this incident. She couldn't let that happen.

"Don't do anything, yet," Susanna told Alice. "And for heaven's sake, don't tell anyone what happened."

Mat's strength returned in stages. The red tide receded from his head. The hot iron stopped stabbing his side, leaving a throbbing ache that was bearable. His stomach stopped churning, and some of the numbness left his legs.

Susanna watched him with stony eyes. The man was impossible, she thought angrily. Stubborn, intractable, reckless, bullheaded—she piled up the adjectives, telling herself she was glad she was smart enough not to fall for him all over again.

He took one step, then another. Somehow he made it to his Bronco without passing out. His left hand closed around the handle. Icy cold, it kept slipping away from him. He had to try twice before he could get the door open.

Susanna watched helplessly as he climbed in, closed the door and started the engine. "Lord save me from macho men," she muttered, feeling helpless and frustrated. All her protective instincts told her that Mat needed her, but he would rather injure himself more severely than admit it.

"I feel awful, Susanna," Alice whispered next to her. "Like . . . like it's all my fault, him getting beat up and all. My sister's always telling me I'll get myself into trouble, flirtin' the way I do and all." Her voice broke. "She's gonna throw me out of her place when she finds out, I just know she will."

Susanna tried to comfort the distraught girl as best she could, but her attention was on Mat. The Bronco was moving slowly, but in the right direction. The road's deep ruts had to be torture for his bruised body.

What if he passed out at the wheel? Or started to bleed internally? She glanced at her Jeep.

"Do me a favor, Alice. Find John Olvera and talk to him privately—and I mean *privately*. Tell him exactly what happened, and be sure to tell him that Buck has taken off somewhere, and Mat's in no shape to go after him. Ask him to call me in an hour or so, okay?"

The girl nodded, her expression bleak. Her hand clutched the torn remnants of her blouse together at the neck. "And don't tell anyone else but your family," Susanna warned in a low tone. "It won't help Chief Cruz if this gets around, and it won't help you, either."

At the moment Buck was John's problem. Whatever he did about it, she only prayed he wouldn't embarrass Mat.

As soon as Alice was on her way, Susanna hurried to her Jeep.

Thirty minutes later she pulled into the carport and shut off the motor. Mat had pulled the Bronco into the circle of light near his front door.

Susanna snapped off her headlights, then hurried to him. As she approached the driver's door, she slowed her steps, expecting him to emerge, but the door remained closed.

Through the window she saw that he had slumped over the steering wheel, apparently unconscious.

She took a deep breath, then opened the door on the driver's side. His cheek rested on the hand that still gripped the wheel, his face turned toward her. Sweat glistened on his skin. His hair was plastered to his forehead and the back of his neck. His eyes were closed.

A gust of chill wind caught her in the face, and she shivered. He couldn't remain here, she realized. Somehow she had to get him inside.

Hand shaking, she touched his cheek. His skin was clammy. "Mat, wake up. You made it. You're home."

He groaned, then stirred. The eye that wasn't swollen opened slowly, closed, then opened again as he gathered strength.

"Enjoying the view?" he muttered, his voice thick with sarcasm.

Susanna reminded herself that he was a proud man who wouldn't take well to defeat and managed to hang onto her temper. "Not particularly. It's cold out here, and I'm tired."

"So go on inside."

"That *is* the plan. Now, if you'll just let me help you—"

Mat's control snapped. He couldn't take much more of her pity. "Stop mothering me," he ground out. "That's the last thing I want from you."

"I'm not mothering you. I'm a nurse, remember?"

"Fine. Go nurse someone else."

At the hoarse note of frustration in his voice, Susanna drew back, the hand she'd stretched toward him knotting into a fist. "Have it your way," she threw at him stiffly. "Pass out in the dirt. Let Missy or Grandmother Ettaway find you in the morning."

She stepped backward two paces and crossed her arms over her chest. Go ahead, kill yourself, her attitude seemed to say.

Mat glared at her, his pride and his battered body in direct conflict. A man protected his woman. He was the strong one, the one she depended on to do the hard jobs, the tough, dirty jobs, the one she turned to to keep her safe from bullying bastards like Ruiz.

At the moment, however, he wasn't sure he could stand on his own two feet, let alone help anyone else.

Holding his breath against the burning in his ribs, he climbed out of the Bronco and slammed the door behind him. Hand clutched to his side, he walked stiffly toward the door to his half of the duplex.

"Mat, wait," Susanna called, hurrying to his side and grabbing his forearm. "You can't go in there. Not like this. What if Missy wakes up and sees you? She would be terrified."

Mat glanced down at his ruined uniform, then dragged a hand down his stinging face. It came away bloody. One glimpse of him like this and Missy would start screaming. He couldn't let that happen.

"You're right. She can't see me like this," he muttered, each word taxing his strength. He turned his back to the side of the house and slumped against the rough adobe. He was about at the end of his string. Another few minutes and he would be out cold.

Rousing himself, he gave Susanna as much of a smile as he could manage. "Give me time to get out of sight, then go get her and take her to your place for the rest of the night. Ask Grandmother to stay with Cody."

Susanna shook her head. "It makes more sense for *you* to stay at my place tonight. In the morning I'll explain to Missy that you've been in an accident but you're fine. If she wants to see you, I'll tell her you're sleeping." A ghost of a smile flitted across her face. "By the time she gets back from school you'll be your old self again."

He wanted to argue, but he knew Susanna's plan made sense. Much as he hated to let her see how bad off he really was, he couldn't risk hurting Missy.

The wind whistling over the mesa stung his cheek, and he shuddered, feeling cold to his bones. He shuddered again.

"Come on," Susanna said in a low voice. "I'll make us some hot coffee, and then I'll slip next door and tell Grandmother that you won't be home tonight."

"Sounds promising," he managed with a lopsided grin that hurt his mouth. "What do you have in mind?"

"Forget it, Cruz," she said around the lump in her throat. The man was half dead, and yet he was flirting with her. She should be outraged that he refused to take no for an answer. Instead, she was unbearably touched by his grit in the face of defeat.

Defeat? No, she thought instantly. Mat might have been beaten, but he wasn't defeated. Mat would always fight back, no matter how slim his chance of winning. He would find Buck Ruiz and arrest him.

Things she didn't dare feel threatened her composure. She didn't want to admire his courage. She didn't want to love him.

Her breath stopped. Something twisted inside, then tore lose, releasing an emotion that stunned her.

It couldn't be. She couldn't have fallen in love with him again.

But . . . but that was exactly what she had done.

The thought stunned her, until she grew as still as Mat. If he reached for her, if he let himself need her, she would be lost. All she'd ever wanted was to be needed, to be the one person in the world who mattered to someone, mattered more than anything else.

Please hold me, she told him silently. Show me I matter to you more than your stubborn macho pride. Show me nothing else is as important to you as I am. Show me you love me.

She held her breath, watching as Mat opened his eyes and pushed himself away from the wall, then groaned as his bruised gut protested the movement.

He swayed toward her, and she felt herself reaching out to help him, but at the last moment he jerked away from her as though her touch pained him more than his wounds.

The disappointment went deep, so deep Susanna had to bite her lip to keep from crying out. In silence, her heart bruised and sore, she led the way inside, watching him without seeming to. "Can you make it to the kitchen? The—"

"The light's better there," he finished for her, reminding them both of the day he'd brought Cody to her for first aid.

"Yes," she said woodenly, leading the way. She pulled out a chair and indicated that he should sit.

Too tired to argue, Mat did as he was told, feeling like a damn fool. Five years ago—hell, a year ago—he could have taken a pounding like this and still licked the bastard with enough energy left to haul Susanna off to the bedroom to celebrate. Now he could barely make a fist, and the chances of seeing her bedroom were somewhere between none and none.

Sighing, he let his weight rest against the chair back. The rungs hurt him where the marks from the lash were still tender.

"I'll get my kit," she said without looking at him.

Mat watched her walk toward the hall, then disappear into the room that was no doubt her bedroom. His mind followed her there, tried to picture the place she slept, the *way* she slept. More than anything he wanted her to be sleeping in his arms, her head pillowed trustingly on his shoulder. More than anything he wanted to be the man she loved.

He folded his arms on the table, cradling his aching head, and gave in to the bottomless weariness clawing at him.

Two minutes later, when Susanna returned, she found him out cold.

A heavy silence blanketed the house, broken only by the click of the bathroom door as Mat walked into the hall. He moved cautiously, carrying his boots, his bare feet making no sound on the tile.

It was early—a few minutes past six. He'd wakened at first light, his body stiff and sore, his face a mass of painful bruises. He'd been disoriented and surprised to find himself in a strange bed, until recollections of the night before had come crashing back. He'd been coldcocked by Buck Ruiz, and Susanna had taken him in so that Missy wouldn't be upset.

His ego had taken a beating, too, especially when she'd had to help him out of his bloody clothes. There he'd been, in her bed at last, stripped nearly to the buff, and there hadn't been a damn thing he could do about it.

The last thing he remembered was the soothing sound of her voice as she urged him to take a couple of aspirin. When he woke up, he'd been alone—and depressed as hell.

A hot shower had helped. The clean clothes Susanna had fetched for him last night had made him feel presentable again, but there was nothing he could do about the marks Ruiz's fist had left on his face.

What're a few more scars? he thought. Once he had taken his good looks for granted, even traded on them. Men had envied him. Women had looked at him with smiles instead of that half-fascinated, half-pitying look he'd come to dread.

His mouth tightened. Susanna had been the only woman who hadn't looked at him that way. He almost wished she had.

He paused at the entrance to the small living room, his gaze going unerringly to the woman lying on the couch. Sometime during the night the heavy woolen blanket had slipped to the floor, leaving her small body vulnerable to the chilly night air.

She slept on her back, her face turned toward him, a small frown between her sleek brows, as though her dreams troubled her. She was breathing deeply, her mouth slightly parted, her cheeks faintly pink. One hand rested just below the swell of her breasts; the other curled into an open fist near her cheek. She was wearing a faded blue football jersey that had somehow become bunched above her hips, revealing silky bikini panties almost the same color as her skin.

His heart rate kicked into high, and his body began to swell. Battered as he was, he still wanted her.

But it was more than a physical ache tormenting him. He wanted to be her friend. To be there when she needed him. To offer advice when she asked for it, unspoken support when she was too proud to ask.

Slowly he crossed the room, trying to ignore the need that grew more insistent with each step. Putting down his boots, he used both hands to pull the blanket over her.

Holding his breath against the pain, he bent to brush her mouth with his.

She stirred, her gold-edged lashes fluttering. She muttered something he didn't catch against his mouth, then sighed his name. Her lashes settled on her cheeks again, casting sensuous shadows against her creamy skin. With the sunlight in her hair and gentleness in her eyes, she was irresistible.

Mat drew back, knowing he should leave, yet unable to make himself move. The house surrounded them with a soft silence, and the morning sun bathed the room in glistening amber light. He had a sense of serenity, of peace, as though time had stopped.

The craving to touch her, to share himself with her one more time, was overpowering, beyond his ability to resist. He dropped carefully to one knee, then the other. His hand slid beneath the blanket to flatten gently against the swell of her thigh, his fingers resting on the lacy edge of her panties.

Her skin was smooth, heating his palm. A few inches to the right and he would find the hot, moist essence of her. Higher and he would discover the sleek rounded contours of her breasts. The need prowling his gut sharpened, dug in deep, sending hot flames of desire racing along his veins.

Still trapped in a dream of Mat, Susanna felt her breathing quicken and her heart rate tumble into a more rapid rhythm. Sensations ran up her leg, into her belly, rising to her warm full breasts. She stirred restlessly against the hard cushions beneath her, feeling small tugs of desire surrounding her nipples. Was she asleep? Or was Mat really there, his warm palm resting on her hip?

Sighing through parted lips that still felt the pressure of his, she opened her eyes to find him watching her with expressionless eyes.

A helpless pleasure shot through her. He was there—the man she loved.

"It's early," he murmured. Beneath his slanted eyebrows a V had formed and was deepening. "Go back to sleep."

His fingers tugged her nightshirt lower, covering her thigh. Small flutters of pleasure followed the whisper-soft pressure of his hand.

"All you all right?" she asked, her drowsy gaze skimming the bruises staining his jaw.

"I'll survive."

She'd checked on him at two and again at four. He'd been restless, but sleeping deeply, his rangy body stretched across her bed, clad only in his shorts.

Heat spread along her cheekbones as she remembered the feel of his corded legs as she slid his trousers from his powerful legs. He'd been furious when he'd been forced to accept her help. He'd been even more furious when he had become noticeably aroused at her touch.

Slowly her hand came up to touch the swollen gash by his mouth. Mat flinched, not from pain, but because her touch was unexpected.

Susanna frowned. "I didn't mean to hurt you."

"You didn't."

He cupped her hand in his, turning the palm inward and drawing it to his mouth. His breath rasped against her skin, hot and moist.

Susanna inhaled swiftly, feeling the insistent heat of desire kindle inside her. She lay perfectly still, afraid he would leave, more afraid that he would stay.

Using his finger, he traced the fullness of her mouth so softly he scarcely felt it himself. Her lips trembled into a smile.

Mat wanted to kiss her so badly that he had trouble thinking about anything else. "Did you know that Hopis consider a smile to be sacred?" he asked, his voice rasping deep.

She blinked up at him, her eyes going wider. "No, but I think I agree with them."

"Your smile is sacred to me, Susanna. Someday I want you to smile for me and really mean it."

He wanted to tell her that he forgot the things he could no longer manage when he was with her, that he felt like a whole man when she was in his arms. He wanted to tell her that her smile blunted the hard edges of the guilt and pain that were always with him, that he needed her the way he'd never needed anyone in his life.

But she didn't want to hear those things from him. She only wanted to hear that he loved her. But love was something he would never feel again.

"The morning suits you," he said instead. He loosened her hair, combing the long thick strands with his fingers until they cascaded over her pillow in glossy fragrant waves. "Did we ever make love at dawn?"

She shook her head. "You were afraid someone would notice that I was gone."

The breath he drew in slowly was ragged. "I wish I could remember, Susanna. I've tried, but that time is like a black hole in my head."

Slowly, knowing she shouldn't, but impelled by the need to take away some of the raw pain she felt radiating from his tense body, she raised her arms to his strong neck and drew him down to her.

"Kiss me," she whispered against the hard firm contours of his mouth.

His groan shuddered against her parted lips. His kiss wasn't gentle, but Mat wasn't a gentle man. His world had been the world of hard men and even harder duties to perform. She didn't expect tenderness from him. She didn't expect anything from him but pleasure, the kind that was softening her muscles to sweet, warm silk.

Driven beyond his control by weeks of denial, Mat slid the blanket from her body, replacing it with his hands. Susanna arched toward him, eager to feel his callused hands on her skin again.

With an absorption that consumed him, his blunt fingers explored, touched, grew warm with the need to know more of her skin. He felt her strain toward him, her small body taut with the same need, taxing his control.

His hand trembled as it sought her breast. She filled his palm, firm and round. He felt her warmth through the smooth knit of her shirt, and he wanted more of her. All of her.

Susanna pressed against the large hand cupping her breast. She didn't want to love him, had tried not to love him, but she did. And loving him as she did, she also wanted him desperately. Nothing mattered but the demanding touch of his hand and the soft pressure of his mouth against her throat.

His hand skimmed down her side, found the hem of her shirt, moved beneath the soft material to the even softer skin it covered. Her belly quivered under his touch, and she whimpered deep in her throat.

A rush greater than any drug shot through him, sizzling through his veins. He couldn't get enough of her. His fingers moved lower, slipping inside the thin scrap of silk. His fingers rubbed the downy hair beneath, sending ever-deepening sensations along her skin.

His fingers followed the sensations, dipping into the waiting heat. He felt her body contract, heard the ragged intake of her breath. He slid his mouth to her earlobe, nipping gently, savoring the helpless trembling of the hand clutching his shoulder.

Her breath warmed his neck as she gave small eager sighs of pleasure. He wanted to bathe himself in her warmth, to drown in the pleasure he felt touching her and kissing her and tasting her.

His mouth moved lower, to the small pointed nipple beneath the thin cloth. His tongue touched the hard tip, wetting the material in a ragged circle.

Susanna arched toward him, rubbing her breast against his hard mouth. She felt a shudder travel the length of him, heard a harsh moan escape his corded throat.

Mat lifted his head, his breathing taking on a tortured edge. His swollen body throbbed against the straining buttons of his fly. Another minute, a few more seconds, and he would be beyond the point of stopping.

It wouldn't take much more to have her clinging to him helplessly, as desperate for him as he was for her. But this time things had to be honest between them. Clean. He wouldn't dishonor her again.

"I want you, Susanna," he whispered hoarsely when her lashes fluttered and her drowsy gaze sought his face. "But I need to know you want me as I am, without promises, without the words of love that neither of us means."

No words of love.

Susanna heard the warning in his voice. Mat was offering to make love to her, but not to love her.

Sliding her arms from his neck, she angled her body into the corner of the couch and drew her knees to her chest. He hadn't lied this time. At least that much had changed.

"You'd better go," she said with as much dignity as she could manage, her body still burning from the touch of his hard fingers. Somehow she made herself ignore the small ripples of need that continued to run like a slow-moving current down her thighs.

Mat saw the glow of desire fade from her eyes, leaving him feeling as cold as drenched ashes inside. He brought her hand to his mouth and kissed the place on her wrist where her pulse jerked in small angry beats.

Desire clawed at him, urging him to pull her into his arms, to use his mouth and his hands to convince her that she was wrong, that she didn't need love.

But she seemed so small and fragile in the gentle morning light, like a dew-washed bud. And so easily trampled.

He would rather ache forever than hurt her again.

"I'll always be sorry I couldn't give you what you wanted," he said as he let her hand slip from his.

He grabbed his boots and walked away from her—while he still had the strength to go.

Chapter 11

The door to John Olvera's office was half open. Mat rapped once with his knuckles, then pushed it wide and walked in without waiting for an invitation.

John looked up from his desk, his eyebrows arching in surprise. "You look like a man spoiling for a fight, but not with me, I hope."

"No, not with you." Mat tossed an envelope onto the desk, then realized he was standing at attention and made himself relax. During the weeks since they'd begun working together, John had become more friend than superior.

John picked up the letter but didn't open it. "What's this?"

"My resignation."

John tore the envelope in half. "Not accepted," he said, dropping the two halves into the trash basket by the cluttered rolltop desk. "Anything else you need?"

Mat ran a hand over his jaw. His bruised skin was raw where the electric razor had scraped off his whiskers. "Maybe you don't know what happened last night."

"I know. Alice told me. She said Buck took off like Spirit Stealer was chasing him."

"You go after him?"

John smiled. "No way, Chief. I'm just a rancher, re-member? I figured I'd only mess things up if I tried to do your job."

Mat knew exactly how much he owed this man. First, a chance to start over, and now, his self-respect. If John had roused the other men last night, Mat Cruz would always be considered no better than a woman in their eyes.

He balled his fist and beat it softly against the desk. "You need to know, John. I blew it. I'm rusty as hell. I should have read that guy better. That doesn't say much for me as an example for Spruce and Two Skies."

John laced his fingers behind his head and leaned back until the old swivel chair creaked. "That's a crock, and you know it."

Mat's head snapped up and he started to interrupt, but John held up a hand.

"There's no defense against a sucker punch," he said in a matter-of-fact tone. "I ought to know. Ruiz came at me with a knife once, a year or so ago. I would be dead now if Aurora hadn't warned me."

Mat felt some of the tension ease from his bruised gut. Among the young men of the tribe, John's courage was legendary. It meant a lot to know that John still believed in him.

"Looks like you might be right about Ruiz being the number one suspect in that incident with the college girls." Mat shoved his hat to the back of his head and lowered himself into a vacant chair. His muscles were sore and stiff, and his broken ribs made it difficult to breathe properly.

"Looks like. He was sent up for half killing a hooker in Gallup."

"Any idea where he might have gone?"

John rocked back and forth, his thoughts focused inward. "His brother Diego has the spread next to mine. Buck stays there, mostly."

"Do you know when he got out of prison?"

John shook his head.

Mat took off his hat and ran his hand through his hair. "I'll make some calls, talk to his parole officer. If he was free when the assault took place, I'll send for a mug shot and show it to the victims, along with others. If we get a match, I'll swear out a local warrant and ask for help from other local jurisdictions."

"Then what?"

Mat managed a stiff smile. "I've done some research on our ancestors. Seems Wind Warrior advised Cadiz to dig a deep pit and bury the lawbreaker up to his neck, then spread honey on the man's head and wait for scavengers to mete out justice. According to Grandfather Horse Herder, it was most effective at keeping the crime rate down."

John threw back his head and laughed. "It is tempting, isn't it?"

Mat ran two fingers over the swollen bump that used to be the bridge of his nose. "Very tempting. I have a feeling we wouldn't lack volunteers to dig the pit."

John agreed. "I might even be first in line."

Mat remembered the humiliation he'd felt when Buck's boot had crashed into his side. "I'll flip you for it," he muttered.

John grinned. "Sounds good to me." His grin faded suddenly. "All joking aside, if you hadn't shown up when you did, Alice and Susanna could have been hurt badly."

Mat didn't want to think about that. His defeat at the hands of a worthless man like Ruiz still felt raw.

"Actually, Susanna was putting up a damn good battle. When I arrived, she was trying to pull him down by his legs." He thought about the fiery look of determination on her face when she'd been fighting Ruiz. Her feelings went deep, probably deeper than he could imagine. If she loved a man...

"She still has a hook into you, doesn't she?"

"You might say that, yeah. For all the good it does me."

Mat realized he'd fallen silent, and that John had been watching him in that thoughtful way of his. Before he'd asked John to be his sponsor for the Healing Way, he had told him the whole story. As much as he knew, anyway.

He stood abruptly, then sucked in against the pain. "Since I'm still drawing a paycheck, I'd better get busy and earn it."

John slanted him a meditative look. "You're going after Buck, aren't you?"

"With everything I've got."

The Bronco bounced from side to side. Dust billowed behind like a long red wake. The steering wheel jerked violently under Mat's hands, requiring all of his strength to keep it steady.

He cursed steadily over the whine of the engine, praying at the same time that the vehicle wouldn't snap an axle. The trip from his office to this remote part of the pueblo normally took sixty minutes under the best of conditions. He'd done it in a little over forty, fighting a brisk headwind all the way.

But he didn't dare slow down. Susanna needed him. Her message had said it was urgent.

"Come as soon as you can," she'd said into the machine in his office. Because he'd been following up a lead on Buck Ruiz in another part of the pueblo, he had gotten her message several hours after she'd left it.

"Hell of a police force without radios in their patrol vehicles," he muttered, downshifting a split second before making the sharp turn to the Comacho leasehold.

Susanna's Jeep was parked in front of the largest of the sagging adobe buildings. He pulled in next to the dusty Jeep, twisted the ignition, and was out of the truck before the engine stopped turning over.

Favoring his still tender ribs, he ran as fast as he could toward the pale blue door. It opened before he reached the sagging stoop, and Susanna stepped into the stinging wind.

Dust swirled around them, and the air smelled of rain. Susanna squinted against the gusts, her face stark white, making the purple shadows under her eyes even more noticeable.

"What's wrong?" he asked without preamble. She looked so exhausted that he wanted to sweep her into his arms and hold her until she regained her strength. But that would only make it harder when he had to let her go.

In the two weeks since they had almost made love he had done his best to avoid her. Or maybe she had been the one doing the avoiding. Either way, he hadn't seen much of her.

Her mouth began to tremble, but she managed to compose herself. "Buck Ruiz came looking for Alice early this morning, just after the men went out to tend the sheep. When . . . when he didn't find her, he beat up her sister, Rebecca, trying to make her tell him where Alice was."

Mat swore steadily and viciously, then asked in a low voice, "How is she?"

"She's badly hurt, but she'll survive." Her voice choked, and her teeth gnawed at her lower lip. "The . . . the baby she was carrying wasn't so lucky. The attack brought on premature labor. I . . . I tried everything, but I couldn't save him."

Her voice broke, but she held on to her control. She had to. If she started crying, she might never be able to stop.

She glanced around, feeling as lonely as the empty land surrounding them. For the first time in years she felt terribly helpless—and alone.

"This is the second child she's lost," she murmured in a sad voice. "The first was right before I came here. When she got pregnant, I promised her everything would be all right."

The wind caught her words, drawing them out like the lonely notes of a bugle playing taps. Mat curled his hands into fists to keep from reaching for her.

"Sometimes things happen that are beyond your control. All you can do is fight it through the best way you can, the way you did when you took on Buck Ruiz with nothing but grit as a weapon."

His voice was surprisingly gentle, so gentle she wouldn't let herself trust the feelings the husky sound evoked in her.

Her shoulders slumped, and she huddled into her heavy sweater. She was so tired. "I'd better get back to Becca," she said, gathering herself together.

She started to turn away, but he stopped her with a brief touch on her arm. "I'll find him for you, Susanna," he vowed in a hard cold voice that she knew came from an even colder anger. "I'll make sure he never hurts anyone else again."

He bent his head and brushed her lips with his. This time there was no passion in his kiss, no hard-driven demand, only a healing tenderness. "I won't ever let anyone hurt you again," he murmured, flattening his hand against her cheek. "Not even me."

He turned and walked away. Without looking back, he climbed into the Bronco, backed around expertly and sped away. Frozen in place, her own hands replacing his on her cheeks, Susanna watched him until he was only a black speck in the distance.

Then she burst into tears.

Susanna pulled into the carport and killed the engine. The clock on the dash said 12:20. Her aching back told her that she should have been in bed hours ago.

She'd been in the operating room since nine, helping Brad deliver twins by cesarean section. Before that, she'd been with the mother-to-be while she had tried to deliver her baby naturally. Complications beyond her control had made that impossible, and she'd called Brad to do the surgery.

Yawning, she fumbled in the seat next to her for her bag. The moon was past full, its glow dimmed to a faint silver shadow against the black sky, but the light she routinely kept burning over her door shone like a welcoming beacon.

Leaving her keys in the ignition, she shoved open the door and started to step out. Lights, reminded a weary voice inside her head.

Grimacing, she snapped off the headlights and rolled up the window before getting out. Mindful of the dark windows in the other half of the duplex, she closed the door with a soft thunk instead of her customary slam, then made her way with dragging steps to her front door.

She reached for the knob, then froze. Someone had opened the door next door. Her spine shivered, and her breath quickened. Mat was up late.

She had seen only glimpses of him in the past week since their conversation at the Comacho leasehold. From Aurora, she'd learned that he'd put out a warrant for Buck's arrest and that he'd contacted the authorities in the surrounding area, but Buck appeared to have gone to ground somewhere. Like a rattler in high summer, she thought, veering toward his door. Maybe Mat had some information for her.

But it was Melissa who stood there, blinking like a frightened little rabbit.

"Missy, darling, you should be in bed," she chided gently, brushing back the child's sleep-tumbled hair.

Melissa huddled against the door frame, looking far younger than her years. "I've been waiting and waiting for you to come home," she said in a small scared voice.

"I'm here, honey. What's wrong?" Susanna dropped her bag by the door and looped an arm over Missy's trembling shoulders.

"Daddy's awful sick, Susanna. I'm scared he's going to d-die." Her thin voice ended in a sob.

"Where is he?" Susanna stared through the inky living room to the dim light spilling into the hall from the smaller of the two bedrooms.

"He's in bed." Missy began to cry, her thin body shaking with frightened sobs that wrenched at Susanna's heart. "Oh, Susanna, I don't want anything to happen to my daddy."

Comforting the child as best she could without knowing what was wrong, Susanna hurried to the master bedroom. There was enough light from the hall to throw the room into a silvery grayness.

Mat lay on his back, his body stretched diagonally across the double bed. Bathed in shadows, his face looked more gaunt than usual. His eyes were closed, his teeth bared against a terrible pain. His hands were wrapped around two rungs of the brass headboard, which he had bent out of shape in his agony. The covers were twisted around his waist, as though he'd been thrashing for hours.

Susanna approached the bed, quickly scanning his face
and bare chest for signs of injury. None were apparent, only
a network of jagged intersecting scars that had only half-
faded. "Mat, can you hear me? Are you awake?"

He groaned, then tossed his head from side to side, his
breath coming in rasps. His hair was wet, plastered to his
head. The pillow beneath him was soaked with the sweat
that poured from his body.

"My God," she whispered. "What is it?" She shot a
quick glance at the child hovering in the doorway. "Missy?
Do you know what happened?"

The terrified little girl hung back, her lower lip clamped
between her teeth to stop the sobs.

"He gets headaches, sometimes," she choked out. "I
don't know what to do, Susanna. Sometimes he says things
I can't understand."

Susanna heard the edge of hysteria in the child's voice.
"I'm a nurse, Missy," she reminded her in a calm voice. "I
won't let anything happen to your daddy."

Missy wrung her hands. "He said not to bother you. He
said he could handle it all by himself."

Susanna glanced over her shoulder. Mat groaned again,
then began to mumble incoherently. The muscles of his arms
bulged, raising ropes of straining sinew against his coppery
skin. The bed shook with his struggles.

"Missy, try to remember. Does your daddy have medi-
cation for his headaches? Pills, maybe?"

"Yes, big yellow pills."

Susanna snapped on the light, wincing at the sudden
glare. Fighting the fear that constricted her throat, she
searched the table by the bed. She saw a clock, a paperback
book, Mat's watch, but no pill bottle.

"Missy, help me, okay?" she asked, turning back to the
little girl. Missy nodded, her eyes trained on her father.

"Check the medicine chest in the bathroom and see if you
can find the yellow pills."

Without a word Melissa turned and ran from the room.
A second later, Susanna heard the medicine chest open.

"No, no, God, no," Mat mumbled indistinctly, then groaned. With a sudden violent movement he rolled over to his stomach and buried his face in the pillow. His big hands clutched the damp foam rubber, the long powerful muscles of his back bunching from the strain.

Susanna sat on the edge of the bed and used the sheet to wipe the beaded sweat from his thickly muscled shoulders. More scars lined his back, different from the others.

"This is all I could find, Susanna," Missy stood by the bed, a small plastic vial clutched in one hand, a glass of water in the other.

Susanna took the bottle and scanned the label. Percodan. Relief poured through her, and she allowed herself to relax slightly.

"That's it, honey, thanks." She took the glass from Missy and placed it on the nightstand next to the lamp. Opening the vial, she shook out two tablets, which she placed within reach.

She hesitated, then took Missy's cold hands into hers. "You go on back to bed before you catch a chill," she whispered, brushing the tears from the little girl's white face. "I'll take care of Daddy."

"Promise?" Missy asked tremulously, her brown eyes beseeching. She looked so small and fragile that Susanna wanted to wrap her in love and tell her nothing would ever hurt her again. But that was a promise no one could make. Not even someone who wanted to love her as much as Susanna did.

"Promise," Susanna said solemnly, crossing her heart with two fingers the way she used to do when she was Missy's age.

Missy hesitated, then threw her arms around Susanna's neck. "Tuck me in, please, Susanna," she begged in a small voice.

Susanna hesitated, then realized that Missy needed her as much as Mat did. "Okay." Susanna took her hand and led her across the hall. The bedroom was lit by a small lamp, in the shape of a gingerbread house, that sat on the dresser.

Two beds sat side by side. Cody lay curled in the center of his, his thumb in his mouth, his breathing slow and even, a ratty teddy bear with a chewed ear clutched under one chubby arm.

A sad little smile formed in Susanna's mind. He looked so much like Bobby it hurt to look at him. And then she remembered that Bobby would be almost ten now, with features so changed that she might not even recognize him if they chanced to meet on a crowded street somewhere.

Somehow tearing her gaze away from the peacefully slumbering little boy, she bit her lip to keep from moaning at the pain that tore at her.

Missy climbed into her bed and slid down against the pillow. Her face seemed very small and lonely against the colorful pillowcase. Wishing desperately that she could do this every night, Susanna carefully tucked the sheet and blanket around her, then bent to kiss her forehead.

"Night-night, honey," she whispered in an unsteady voice. "Try not to worry about your daddy."

"I won't. Not if you're here."

Susanna felt tears well in her eyes. Missy was so special to her, and yet she dared not think of her as anything but a friend.

Swallowing her anguish, she hesitated, then turned toward the other bed. Smoothing the woolly blue cover closer to Cody's stubborn little chin, she kissed him gently, then hurried to the door, closing it behind her.

In the master bedroom, Mat groaned again, turning his face away from the sound of her footsteps. The first thing she had to do was get the pills down his throat, she told herself with a calm that threatened to shatter any moment.

Touching him gently on the shoulder, she bent low to say in a soothing voice, "I need you to turn over, Mat. Now."

She pushed against his hard shoulder, trying to ease him onto his back. His muscles flinched at her touch. She made herself tighten her grip. If she could get his shoulder over, the rest of him would follow, but his body was too heavy.

Through a haze of pain, Mat heard a voice, felt a touch. Gentle hands, he thought. Warm. Nice. She smelled nice, too. Like flowers. A shadow of thought, not even solid enough to be considered a memory, passed over his mind, then sank into the black void.

"Mat, listen to me," Susanna urged, keeping her voice low in order not to hurt his head. "You have to turn over so I can help you. Please, Mat." He bit off a groan, but allowed her to shove him to his back.

"Help me, Mat. Sit up." He opened his eyes and looked at her. Pain dulled his black eyes and furrowed his brow. He struggled to focus, his face contorted into harsh lines.

"Susanna?" His voice was hoarse.

Susanna saw the unfocused look in his eyes and realized he was only semiconscious. She had seen men in the throes of pain like this try to smash their heads against the nearest wall in order to find relief.

She bent lower so that he could hear her. "Yes, it's Susanna," she said, letting her hand linger against his damp jaw. "I want you to swallow these pills."

He blinked up at her, his dark eyes slitted against the light. Murmuring encouragement, she slipped her hand under his neck, raising him enough so that he could swallow the potent painkiller.

His eyes closed. "Damn head," he muttered when she eased him back onto the pillow. His breathing was labored and his skin clammy. He rubbed his cheek against the damp pillowcase. A shiver ran through him, and he muttered a curse before turning on to his stomach again.

It was cold in the room. She had to keep him warm. Taking care not to jostle him, she untangled the sheet wrapping his lower body, uncovering lean, sinewy legs covered with soft-looking black hair and tight, muscular buttocks.

Susanna felt desire begin to flow through her like flame-warmed brandy. As a blushing nineteen-year-old, she had mapped that body with her hands and her mouth, touching and tasting, filled with the giddy power she'd held over him whenever she touched him.

God, Susanna. No one has ever loved me the way you can. Don't stop. Don't ever stop.

Gritting her teeth, she pulled the sheet over his restless body, then added the blanket she'd found bunched against the brass footboard.

She hesitated, then slipped the sodden pillow from beneath his beard-shadowed cheek. Casting a quick glance around the room, she found its mate on the floor, as though flung there. Retrieving it quickly, she settled him against it.

When, inadvertently, her hand squeezed his shoulder, he flinched, flinging out his arm and dragging her against him. For an instant she lay there stunned, her cheek pressed against his thundering heart.

"So sorry," he mumbled, moving restlessly beneath her. His hand slid down her back to her bottom, holding her firmly in place. Instinct told her there was nothing erotic in his actions. He was simply seeking human comfort the way people in excruciating pain often did.

"Don't leave me," he muttered. "Susanna? Where are you?"

"Here, Mat. I'm here."

His arms relaxed, and she edged away. He muttered a few words that she couldn't understand, then sighed heavily, his big hand groping for hers. His fingers curled around hers, imprisoning her hand completely. His eyes fluttered closed.

The clock ticked off the minutes until ten had passed. Susanna's shoulder began to cramp.

Uncurling from her uncomfortable position on the edge of the hard mattress, she tried to pull her hand from his warm, possessive grasp.

He stirred, his brows sliding into a fierce frown. His fingers tightened until she nearly cried out from the pain. Gritting her teeth, she huddled into a ball, her knees pulled to her chest. The narcotic would hit him soon, and then she would slip away to her own bed.

Closing her eyes, she tried to ignore the feel of Mat's callused hand against hers. "I love you," she whispered into the silence. So very much, she added silently. And I can never tell you.

Heartsick and weary, she closed her eyes and drifted into a doze, taking with her the memory of Mat's tormented, almost-handsome face.

Chapter 12

Mat woke at first light, his mouth as dry as Deadman's Arroyo, his head full of cobwebs. Running his tongue over his bottom lip, he tasted the salty tang of sweat. His muscles ached, and his face felt battered, as though he'd just gone three falls with the heavyweight champion—and lost.

He groaned and closed his eyes, letting the room settle around him. His hand had gone numb again, and some sadistic sonofabitch was pounding a chisel through his temple. Without moving his head, he passed his hand over his morning stubble. He needed a shower and a shave before he would begin to feel human again.

Sighing heavily, he tried to sort through his vague memories of the previous night. He'd been thinking about Susanna, hadn't he? But then, he'd done that a lot lately.

Driven by the unslaked desire that was always in him, he had tried to remember, to know what it had been like to feel her soft, welcoming body beneath his, but all he'd managed was another headache, the kind that invariably had him praying for unconsciousness.

He started to stretch out the kinks in his legs, then realized the numbness in his hand was caused by a warm weight pressing against his forearm. A frown pushed through the lethargy holding him.

He opened his eyes and turned his head. Shock took the blood from his face. Susanna was lying against his chest, her head pillowed on his shoulder. Her hair was a tumble of brown and gold against her cheek, a thick luxuriant mane that invited him to bury his face in its softness and breathe in the fresh soapy scent of her.

Shock turned to disbelief as he realized she was holding his hand, her small hand curled around his palm, as warm and trusting as a child's.

His throat felt raw, and the throbbing in his head increased. No one had held his hand in the hospital. Instead they'd simply tied him down to keep him from hurting himself.

He rubbed hard fingers across his brow. Lord, he must really have been out of it. Sometimes it got that way when he couldn't get to his pills in time. When that happened, he went a little wild, trying to escape the pain.

Damn it! Missy must have been terrified, he thought with a worried glance in the direction of the children's room. The door to his bedroom was shut. No doubt Susanna had closed it to keep the kids from hearing his groans.

Had Missy gone for Susanna, turning instinctively to the one person she knew wouldn't let her down?

He knew without having to think about it that Susanna had been there for his daughter, just as, it seemed, she'd been there for him.

But why was she still here?

She stirred, and a sigh parted her lips. Her lashes fluttered, then settled against her tanned cheeks, tempting him to trace the feathery tips with his mouth.

She was sleeping heavily, her chest rising and falling in a slow even rhythm. Each breath outlined the curve of her breasts against the soft material of her sweatshirt.

The vague feeling of longing inside him sharpened to raw male need. He clenched his thighs against the hot spur digging deep into his groin. Somehow he kept his hand relaxed against hers.

Slowly he raised his head to bunch the pillow under his neck, gritting his teeth against the hollow feeling in the pit of his stomach.

He let his gaze linger on her soft mouth, his own mouth drawn into a hard line. He should wake her. But he couldn't make himself do it.

Not yet.

He'd been alone for so long. He needed her warmth and her trust just a little longer.

As though sensing his thoughts, Susanna mumbled something in her sleep before nuzzling her cheek against the sensitive scar tissue stretched over his shoulder. But instead of pain, he felt a heightening of the need tearing at him. His pulse rocketed, and his body threatened to explode. Compressing his jaw, he made himself lie perfectly still, every muscle straining to keep from reaching for her.

Slowly, like a kitten waking from a nap in the sun, she stretched languidly, her bare feet sliding down his shin with maddening slowness. The inner part of her thigh was like slow moving heat across the top of his, and her breasts slid against his side. This time he couldn't stifle the groan that shook him.

Susanna knew before she opened her eyes that she was in Mat's bed. She felt the length of his heavily muscled legs pressed against hers. She heard the ragged sound of his breathing and felt the strength of his fingers holding hers.

His heart beat against her cheek where it lay pressed against the hard musculature of his chest, as though in the unconsciousness of sleep she had tried to get as close to him as she could.

Her pulse rate doubled. How could she have let herself fall asleep? she raged silently. She had intended to wait until he slid into a drugged sleep, then leave.

Chagrin spread through her, as hot as the blood racing up her neck and into her face. My God, she thought, squeezing her brows together in a frown, what would Missy think if she walked in on them now? What would Mat think if he woke to find her sprawled all over him? That she wanted him to make love to her, that was what. And that was exactly what she *did* want, what she would want for the rest of her life.

Taking a careful breath, she opened her eyes and began to ease away from him. Even though she was fully clothed and the sheet covered him to the waist, she could feel his thigh muscle contract into a hard knot beneath her.

Holding her breath, Susanna slowly lifted her gaze to his face. He was watching her through narrowed lids, a half-amused, half-pained look on his face. Her mouth suddenly filled with cotton wool.

"Good morning." His deep voice was rusty from sleep, and oddly tense. The tangle of black hair falling over his forehead and the dark shadow on his chin gave him a rumpled look that softened some of the hard edges of his damaged face.

"Good . . . good morning."

Feeling as though she were moving in slow motion, she tugged her hand from his and sat up. Her sweatshirt twisted around her torso, baring several inches of creamy skin.

As her hands fumbled to make herself tidy, she felt his gaze. Trying not to shiver in the chilly air, she crossed her arms over her breasts and hunched her shoulders. Her eyelids were still heavy from sleep, and her back was stiff from lying in one place for too long.

"How's the head?" she asked, trying without much success to crawl behind the impersonal facade of a professional. She was too aware of his body only inches from hers, and even more aware of the liquid desire slowly warming just below her skin.

"I'm okay." He glanced at the pill bottle on the nightstand. "Did you take care of me?"

"I got the pills down your throat. They did the rest."

His gaze dropped to the small hand curled into a half fist against her stomach. "Do you always hold hands with your patients?"

"Not always, no." She tried to ignore the reddened place on his heavily muscled shoulder where her head had rested. She had never woken up next to a man before, not even

Mat. It gave her a funny feeling to know that she had been completely vulnerable to Mat while she slept.

"Why didn't you just walk away and let me fight through it alone?"

She dismissed his pointed question with a shrug. "Missy was terrified. I had to keep you quiet so she wouldn't panic."

He eased himself higher on the pillow, trying not to flinch at the dull throbbing in his groin. The sheet slipped to his waist, drawing her gaze. He raised his knee in an attempt to hide the powerfully swollen evidence of his need, but he wasn't quick enough.

She jerked her gaze toward the door. "I'd better go—"

Mat's hand caught her wrist. "Not yet. I haven't thanked you yet."

Pain shot up her forearm, making her wince.

He frowned. "What—?" Her skin was discolored and sore where his fingers had clutched hers during the night.

His jaw whitened. "Damn, I'm sorry." His mouth twisted with inner pain. His grip eased until her hand was balanced on his wide square palm. "I swore I'd never hurt you, and that's all I seem to do."

She felt him tremble, and something tore inside. "This wasn't your fault, Mat. I'm glad I could be here for you." With each word, her voice grew huskier.

Mat's expression changed, something that might be hope replacing the regret in his eyes. "Why are you glad, Susanna?" he asked slowly, his voice as rough as his morning beard.

"Because I don't want you to hurt anymore."

Emotion ripped his face. "When you're with me, nothing hurts anymore, not even the pity in the faces of people who meet me for the first time. When I have you in my arms..."

He gave up trying to speak and pulled her toward him. Burying his face against her hair, he held her in his arms.

"Oh, Mat," she whispered against his neck, her voice shivering because she had moved him so.

From someplace outside she heard the cheerful sound of bird song. Sunlight coming through the window warmed her cheeks.

Closing her eyes, she tried to think, but the rational part of her mind seemed somehow short-circuited. Or perhaps she was simply too tired to make sense of all the things that were happening. Whatever the reason, she had somehow allowed Mat to get much closer than she had thought possible. Now she couldn't make herself push him away.

Was that because he was determined to make amends, or because she was tired of fighting the ghosts of the past?

She relaxed against him, allowing the heat of his body to soothe away her doubts. Whatever he offered, it was more than she'd had these last ten years without him. Whatever happened later, she would have this moment, this brief time of warmth and safety. For these moments he would be hers and she would be his, the way it had been in her dreams.

He whispered her name, or maybe she only heard the husky sound in her imagination. He drew her closer, his big hand gentle but insistent on her back. Lifting his head, he searched her face.

"Smile for me, Susanna," he ordered in a raspy voice. "Make me believe you've forgiven me." His thumb touched the corner of her mouth.

Susanna thought about the things he'd told her about the Hopis. Did he, too, believe that a smile was sacred?

For the first time since she'd seen him again, she allowed her feelings to show in her eyes. In her smile.

His breath caught. "Sweetheart," he whispered. He couldn't say more. It seemed incredible to him that she was really there, that she was accepting him as he was, without the promises he couldn't yet make, without the words he might never be able to say.

Tenderness shuddered through him, filling him with a need to give her all that he had inside him. He kissed her, silently sealing his promise never to hurt her.

As his mouth reluctantly left hers, a slow shiver climbed her spine, and her mouth went dry. It couldn't be love she saw in those dark depths, she reminded herself urgently.

"Indians aren't supposed to have heavy beards," she murmured, touching his scratchy face.

"I'm only half-Indian," he reminded her, an unfamiliar look of indulgent humor softening his smile. "Or so it said in my records."

He drew his finger down her nose. His touch was teasing, even affectionate, and she felt warm all over. She had never seen him so relaxed, and it gave her a quiet feeling of satisfaction to know she had done this for him.

Sighing in contentment, she rubbed her cheek against his, and his arms tightened. "Susanna?" His breath was warm on her face.

"Hmm?"

"Did I tell you anything about my father? Who he was or what he was like?"

Susanna thought about the hurt on his face in the canyon when he'd told her about his mother and her suffering at the hands of the man who had ruined her life. The man who had taught Mat not to believe in love.

Fury at that nameless, faceless man rose in her, but she kept her features composed. "All you told me is what you already know, that he was white."

He sighed. "It's like a big chunk of me is missing."

Susanna smiled into his eyes. "You know the important things. Who you are now, who your kids are."

Mat heard the quiet reassurance in her voice and could almost feel the calluses over his heart crack open, exposing him to thoughts and feelings he'd never had before, things like a real marriage and love.

He lifted his head and looked at her face. Her eyes were soft, her long lashes tipped with gold from the morning sun, her lips still parted and rosy from the pressure of his mouth.

His senses began a slow spiral that penetrated deep, exciting him almost beyond his control. He had to kiss her again, to feel her lips part for him, to taste her sweetness against his tongue. Maybe love didn't always smother a man. Maybe, with Susanna, he could learn what it was like to be a part of another person instead of lonely and separate.

"You're so warm," he whispered in a husky voice. "I've been cold so long."

"Me, too. I just didn't know it."

Mat groaned, his mouth fitting over hers with warm demand.

Her body responded as though it had a will of its own, her thighs softening and straining against the corded hardness of his, her breasts full and aching where they pressed against the impenetrable wall of his chest.

She ran her hands over his ropy muscles, surprised at the tiny tremors she felt under her palms. The same tremors began inside her.

Mat knew he was close to losing control. But he had promised himself to go slowly. Wrapping her in his arms, he rolled until she was lying beneath him.

She gave a low moan, but it wasn't protest he heard in the throaty sound. It was desire. For him.

"Easy, sweetheart, let me make this good for you." Holding both her hands above her head with one of his, he lowered his head and began exploring the satin smoothness of her neck. His hands stroked her softness; his tongue traced the trembling curve of her mouth. With the tip of his tongue he parted her lips, leaving them wet and soft; then, with shivering slowness, he filled her mouth. She tasted warm and intoxicating, like mulled wine.

His tongue explored, tasted, caressed the tender recesses. When he had satisfied his craving there, he withdrew to taste her lips again.

Her soft moan was warm against his mouth, and he began to shake with a need to feel more of her. He drew back far enough to allow his hands to push the sweatshirt higher. His fingertip traced the pale blue wisp of lace covering her smooth white breasts.

His heart tripped to find evidence of the deeply feminine sensuality she kept so carefully guarded. As eager as a nineteen-year-old, he fumbled with the tiny hook. Somehow he managed to work it free.

He moved to his knees, then lifted her toward him. Awkwardly, long-denied hunger for her making him clumsy, he rid her of her sweatshirt and bra.

"I can't believe I forgot," he whispered, easing her to the pillow again. He kissed the satiny roundness of each perfect breast, then followed the line marking her tan with his tongue.

His hands skimmed her waist until they found the elastic waistband of her sweatpants. "Help me, sweetheart," he whispered, slipping his hands beneath her to lift her hips. Obediently, she arched upward, allowing him to slip the pants from her.

His knee parted hers, then slid upward to rub against the V between her thighs. Ripples of hot sensation spread outward, downward, filling her. Her moan whispered between them, sending an insistent demand deep into him.

He found her breast again, his mouth leaving an exquisite brand on her skin, his hands moving beneath her to lift her toward him so that he could suck one nipple, then the other, deep into his mouth.

Susanna tumbled helplessly on a wave of desperate desire. She writhed under his hands, needing to ease the sweet tension driving her.

Ignoring his own needs, he took his time with her, using his mouth with a thoroughness that spoke of a desire to please her. With each touch of his hard hands, each kiss from his sensuous mouth, her body came more alive until she felt only Mat and the love she had for him.

She whispered his name, sending a shudder through his powerful body.

"Sweetheart, I don't want to make you pregnant again," he whispered in a strident voice that spoke of his terrible restraint. "Is it safe?"

At first, almost drowning in need, Susanna didn't understand his words.

"Are you on the Pill?" he asked, when he saw the confusion settle over her flushed face.

This time Susanna understood. She wished she hadn't. "No," she cried hoarsely, burying her face in his neck, nearly sobbing in disappointment.

Mat groaned silently, cursing his own stupidity. He had nothing in the house. In all of his fantasies he had never once thought about protecting her.

"I'll take care of you, I promise," he said in a hoarse voice. In this way, at least, he would show her that he'd changed.

Desperately she clung to him, moving her thighs over the rumpled sheet, trying to find relief from the swirling sensation of heat between her legs.

"Do you want me, honey?"

A moan whispered past her lips. "Yes, oh, yes. Now, Mat. Please, now."

Mat's hand shook as he made her ready for him. She was hot and wet and so very sweet. He eased into her, exercising every ounce of control to keep from plunging deep.

He clamped his lower lip between his teeth to keep from groaning, and the cords on his neck stood out from the effort he was expending. She tossed her head from side to side, her hands clutching his forearms. Her eyes were closed, her lips parted, her face flushed.

He thrust slowly, feeling her body expand to take him fully inside her. His breath was coming in gasps, and his blood pounded through his veins.

The tiny spasms of her body pulled him deeper. Each thrust took her closer to climax. Each movement strained his control. He fought to contain the raw hunger tearing at him. He had been without a woman too long. His body screamed for release.

Susanna felt herself rising, rising, her body moving in rhythm with his. Her muscles strained; her blood pounded.

Mat heard her soft whimpers and gritted his teeth. His gaze fixed on her face, he thrust deep, straining to the point of pain.

Exquisite tension ripped through her, exciting her, driving her. She arched toward him, desperate to ease the delicious torment.

Susanna felt the explosion start deep inside her, spreading upward and outward until she was awash in feeling. Joy pulsed through her, followed by a pleasure so profound that she lost all sense of thought, becoming the sensations filling her.

Mat felt the hot tremors surround him, and he groaned, driven to the brink by his desperate hunger. His body throbbed, still hot and engorged with blood.

Digging his fingers into the blanket, he rocked back and forth, easing her down from the peak. His muscles strained; his breathing became tortured from the savage effort he was making to hold back.

Gradually her breathing slowed, became easy. She muttered a gentle, contented sound that made him smile.

Slowly, unwilling to leave her, he bent to kiss her softly parted mouth. Her lips curved against his, and he felt a rush of satisfaction. He buried his face in the warm hollow of her neck, tasting the salty sheen moistening her skin.

He relaxed against the warm, silky body beneath him, careful to keep most of his weight on his forearms. Love me again, he wanted to beg her. Teach me how you want me to love you.

But he was afraid to say anything, afraid to break the almost mystical feeling between them, afraid to send her diving into the past again.

Adrift on a warm, wonderful ocean, Susanna stroked his back with slow lazy movements. She was floating, her body filled with a delightful lassitude. For the first time in weeks, months even, her mind was at rest. She felt nothing but sweet sensations of safety and security. She couldn't have moved if she'd wanted to.

Mat caressed her arm, feeling little tremors run under his hand. The sun from the window was warm and pleasurable on his bare back, but her skin was even warmer. He liked the touch of her and the delicate fragrance that rose from her skin.

He enjoyed sex, making sure he gave as much pleasure as he received. Not once in his memory had he made love without finding his own release.

In spite of the sharp ache in his loins, he hadn't felt this good in years. Hell, maybe he'd never felt this good. Or maybe he'd just forgotten. He sighed contentedly, savoring the exquisite feeling that being joined with her gave him.

"Was this the way it always was between us?" he asked, slipping his hand under hers to entwine their fingers. His other hand rested heavily against her breast.

Susanna's eyes fluttered open. Awareness came slowly, in stages. She was aware that she was in Mat's bedroom, in his bed. She realized that her fingers were threaded into his thick damp hair, and that he was lying on top of her, their bodies still joined. She had never felt so well loved.

"This was better," she managed to get out, her voice low and still filled with passion. Her face tingled where his morning beard had rubbed. Her mouth, sensitized by his kiss, felt swollen.

He sighed against her breast, then raised his head and kissed her. The clock said 6:15. His children would be waking soon.

He took a deep breath, trying to ignore the tension stringing him out as badly as an addict craving a fix. He had promised to take care of her, and he would keep his promise.

"I don't want to let you go, but it's getting late," he said in a voice deepened by the need that was still strong in him. "My kids get up early."

Susanna stopped breathing, straining to hear a sound from the children's room. But the silence was broken only by Mat's ragged breathing.

Clutching the blanket to her, she sat up. The light in the room had grown far brighter. Beyond the window the sky was a deep morning blue. The night was over.

She cleared her throat. "You're right. I'd better leave. The last thing we need are ... awkward explanations."

"Stay," he said in a husky voice. "Have breakfast with us."

He began caressing her breast. Even muted by the blanket, his touch had the power to shake her to the core. Tiny pulses of excitement began building again, and her body quickened, eager to feel him inside her once more.

Susanna shook her head. "I have appointments."

The morning light touched her gently, streaking her hair with gold. She seemed young and delicate, and so lovely he didn't know how he could let her go.

"Dinner, then," he proposed. "Here with the kids. Missy's crazy about you, and you care for her. I've seen your face when you're with her. She's special to you." He traced the veins in her hand with his finger. Her hand curled into a fist.

His gaze lifted to her face. "You do care for my kids, don't you, Susanna?"

She sighed. "Of course I do. They're wonderful children, bright and affectionate, especially little Cody. He's such a little snuggle bunny."

Like Bobby, she wanted to add. But what would be the point? Talking about him only sharpened the sense of loss.

"So spend time with them. If you want, you can cuddle Cody all evening long."

For an instant the temptation was nearly overpowering, but common sense intervened before she could accept. "I don't think that's a good idea." She tried not to remember the feel of Cody's sturdy little body nestled against hers. She tried not to think about his gurgling little laugh when she teased him, or the wonderful sweetness of his hand patting her cheek.

Mat watched the yearning darken her eyes, and his throat burned. Susanna loved Cody and Missy. And she had loved their son.

Did she want another child? His child?

He could search forever and not find a better mother for his children. She claimed to have loved him once. Maybe, when she had come to love his children, she could come to care for him again.

Once he had her in his life and in his bed, he would convince her that love didn't matter. Not when they had everything else.

"Everyone likes to be cuddled now and then," he said persuasively, running his hand over her silken thigh. Her skin was still warmer than usual. From his lovemaking.

"Even you?" she asked softly.

His eyes kindled into a fierce glow. "Especially me. Come back tonight and I'll show you just how much."

His finger traced the hollow between her breasts. Instantly, her body began to respond. He only had to touch her and she came alive.

Sometimes she thought he knew her body better than she did. And that gave him power over her, power that could maim and scar.

Once he had used her as a substitute for the woman he really loved. Was he making love to her now to acquire a surrogate mother for his children? Or had he come to care for her? Could she really trust the soft look she saw in his eyes when he looked at her now?

This time she had to be sure.

"I won't sleep with you again, Mat. If . . . if I accept your invitation, that has to be understood."

His face closed up. "Why not, if it's what we both want?"

He sat up, and the sheet slipped down to his waist, drawing her attention to the bulge of his arousal stretching the material. Heat climbed her neck and tinged her cheek, growing hotter and hotter. So that was how he had protected her, by denying himself release.

A shiver of doubt passed through her. He'd kept his word. Didn't that mean he wanted more than sex from her?

He took her hand, the left one, and touched the bare ring finger. "I want you. I can't very well hide that. But I promise I won't do anything you don't want me to do. Okay?"

Susanna shifted her gaze to the window. The thought of being a mother again, even a surrogate one, was more than she could resist.

A mother.

No, she could never be their mother. She had to keep that firmly in her mind. But she could be their friend.

But could she be Mat's? Without expectations, without promises? Without love?

Chewing on her lower lip, she shifted her gaze to his face. The bruises had faded. His nose had healed, leaving him with yet another scar across the bridge.

He was no longer that brash young soldier who had seduced her with such fire and charm. He had aged, inside, where only he knew how much. Any man who'd had his life blasted apart the way he had couldn't help but change.

"Okay?" he repeated, his hand sliding up her arm. Tiny shivers followed his touch, and she fought the need to press against him.

"Okay."

For an instant she saw a raw flame flicker in his eyes and knew that he was going to kiss her. Her pulse leaped and her lips parted. His head moved closer. Her lashes drooped, and she held her breath.

His kiss was gentle. "Six o'clock," he said in a husky whisper against her mouth. "You bring the dessert."

Chapter 13

"Wait, Daddy, I forgot my book bag." Missy turned and sprinted toward her bedroom, reminding Mat of a small pink dust devil. Ever since she'd heard that Susanna was coming to dinner she'd been a bundle of energy, smiling and laughing and chattering all through breakfast. Mat wanted to warn her not to get her hopes up, but he didn't have the heart. Besides, he felt pretty hopeful himself.

He pushed his chair back from the table, then stood and bent over to kiss Cody on his forehead, the only place on his son's face not covered with oatmeal. "Be good for Grandmother, okay?" he admonished gently.

Cody gave him a toothy grin. "'Kay. Play ba'"

Grandmother Ettaway looked up from the potatoes she was peeling. She was a short woman, less than five feet tall, with a squat body and long gray braids. Kindness was written in every weathered line of her face, and wisdom shone in her eyes.

As soon as she'd arrived at seven, Mat had asked her to fix his favorite mutton stew for dinner. When the old lady had found out the reason, she'd beamed with pleasure and her black eyes had sparkled. They were still sparkling.

"No ball, Cody," she said firmly. "Grandmother's feet hurt today. I will tell you a new story instead, about the Wind Walker and his adventures in the Great Sky."

Cody's lower lip drooped into a pout, but Grandmother went on calmly. "After lunch, my daughter will take us into town so that we may wash the clothes. If you are good, Grandmother will buy you ice cream."

"'I' cream," Cody repeated, filling up his spoon, then turning it over so the oatmeal plopped back into the bowl.

Mat crossed his arms and watched the old woman handle his stubborn son. She had her own way—far more subtle and much more effective than his do-it-or-else parenting. He had a feeling Susanna's way was a great deal like Grandmother's. For a time he hadn't been sure he would ever find out. But tonight, if all went well, he would start winning her over.

She didn't know it yet, but the lady was in for the fight of her life, one he intended to win. It didn't matter how long it took or how hard he had to work. One of these days Susanna Spencer was going to welcome him back into her life—and her bed.

"Ready, Daddy." Missy came bounding into the room, her ponytail swinging against her neck. She wore the new sweater he'd bought her last week, and the soft golden color reminded him of Susanna's eyes right after he'd made love to her.

"Okay, let's move out," he told Missy with a grin. He said goodbye to Grandmother, then ruffled Cody's hair. "Remember, Zana's coming to dinner tonight. Grandmother needs your help to make everything nice."

"Zana nice," Cody agreed with a messy grin.

Mat couldn't have agreed more.

Grandmother stopped what she was doing and followed him to the door. "You sure you don't want me to wash and iron the yellow shirt instead?" she asked in a wheedling voice. "My bones tell me Woman Who Delivers Babies would like that one better."

"No, the blue one. It's newer."

He didn't have many clothes—only the things he'd bought when he got out of the hospital and a few shirts he'd picked up in Gallup. His civvies were packed away in the boxes that were due to arrive any day now. Or so the army had promised him when he'd made a few calls, trying to speed things up.

A part of him, however, hoped they never came. When they did, he would be faced with a tough decision. Packed away with his personal papers were the journals he had kept for so many years. In their pages he was sure to find a record of his time with Susanna. The answers he'd sought, his feelings for her then, his reason for denying their son, those things would be written there.

As he and Missy hurried through the cold morning toward the Bronco, Mat glanced at the curtained windows in the front of Susanna's apartment.

What if he found he was a worse bastard than Susanna thought? What then? Would he tell her? Or would he try to bury it in the black void with his other memories?

The sun glinted off the windows, sparkling bright. And the air smelled fresh. He had a new start here, a priceless chance at a new life where he could feel useful and needed again.

He wanted a place to belong, where he was respected for his integrity and strength and ability. He wanted to feel invincible again. But most of all he wanted Susanna. With her in his life, he would find the courage to fight for those things. Without her...

He jerked open the door of the Bronco and slid behind the wheel. He would do whatever was necessary to win this battle. He had to. His survival depended on it.

"That's bull and you know it," Mat told Diego Ruiz in a low growl. "Two witnesses have already told me they saw your brother heading this way after he beat up the Comacho woman."

"They's lying," Ruiz said around the toothpick clamped between his yellow teeth. "Buck ain't been around since he put you in the dirt."

Mat saw the gleam of derision in the other man's eyes and fought down an urge to wipe it away with his fist. He'd taken a few such verbal hits since the night outside the studio. Two Skies had told him of other remarks, most of them expressing polite concern in the way of The People about his ability to protect them from a violent man like Buck.

He understood their concerns. But he still went cold at the thought of failing them again. Of failing Susanna.

"You tell your brother I put in a call to his parole officer in Gallup."

"So what? Buck ain't done nothin' wrong."

Mat rested his boot on the sagging board that served as a front stoop and studied the look in Diego's flat eyes. The man was lying. He was also stubbornly loyal to his brother.

"Last I heard, assault was against the law, Diego. Funny thing, the P.O. thinks so, too. So Buck has a choice. He can have his parole revoked and go back to state prison to finish his sentence, or he can surrender to me and take his chances with the Tribal Court."

Diego grunted an obscenity. "Ain't no way Buck'll surrender to anyone, let alone a wimp like you, Cruz."

Rage didn't quite describe the feeling that went through Mat at that moment. In fact, he wasn't sure he could give it a name. Maybe it was better that he didn't.

"Give him the message," he repeated in a curt tone that brought a look of hatred to Diego's small eyes. "Oh, and Ruiz, if I find out you've been hiding him, I'll throw you in that cell with him."

Mat turned and walked toward the Bronco. He was shaking, and his mouth was dry. This wasn't the first time he'd been humiliated because of his physical condition. His experiences in the hospital had been humbling, to say the least. But he'd been the only one hurt then.

This time there was more at stake than his pride. If Buck Ruiz thought he had the upper hand, he might try to hurt someone else. Alice, maybe, or Susanna.

As he climbed into the truck, Mat's jaw set into a hard dangerous line. He had promised Susanna to make Ruiz pay. And that was exactly what he intended to do. One way or another.

Susanna was in the bathtub when she heard the muffled sound of Mat's boot heels on the floor next door, followed almost immediately by the gush of water running through the pipes.

Mat was taking a shower, his naked body just beyond their common wall.

Her senses quickening, she scooped bubbles into her palm and inhaled the delicate scent. Slowly they evaporated, until only a thin layer remained on her skin.

In her mind she saw these same filmy suds sliding sensuously down Mat's chest, moving in slow motion over the hard contours, wetting his skin until it was slick and warm, becoming a thin rivulet as they approached his navel.

Susanna moved restlessly, causing the water to splash against her breasts. She moved lower until her nipples were covered by the soapy water. The warm silkiness felt wonderfully erotic against her skin, like the touch of Mat's hand. Instantly, her breasts began to grow hotter and hotter until her skin felt tight and tingly.

Flattening her palms, she thought about the feel of his chest against her fingers. His skin had been resilient, warm. A fascinating mixture of rough and smooth. Her fingertips tingled, eager to explore the intimate, supremely masculine parts of him, to feel that same hardness against her hand that she'd felt sliding into her.

Her breathing grew shallow, more rapid, louder. The tub seemed too small all of a sudden, the water too cool. Her skin was hot.

Suddenly the sound of running water ceased. She held her breath, hearing only silence next door. And then suddenly she heard the squeal of Cody's voice, followed by laughter.

Daddy's home, she thought. All's right with the world. She smiled, and for a moment allowed herself to imagine what it would be like to be a part of Mat's family.

Because he loved his children, he had tried hard to make himself into a good father. But what kind of a husband would he make? In bed, he was all a woman could want.

But the passion would fade after a time. What happened then? Would they end up like those people in restaurants, staring past each other without talking, never sharing their hopes or their dreams or their fears? Never sharing themselves?

She sank lower into the fragrant bubbles and closed her eyes. Mat would never be an easy man to know. He kept too much of himself inside. Nor would he be an easy man to love, especially when he didn't want her love.

But she had no choice. Like the dawn, her day started with thoughts of Mat and ended with them when she closed her eyes to sleep. Loving him was as much a part of her as her smile and her laugh.

Sighing, she lifted her hand to drizzle water on her belly. Mat had been careful this morning. Most likely she wasn't pregnant, but as a nurse, she knew that nothing but complete abstinence was one hundred percent foolproof. She might even now be carrying his child.

Susanna's mouth curved into a tender smile. A baby, she breathed silently, rubbing her belly as though to caress the small life there. Mat's baby. Maybe a son like Bobby...

"No!" Her voice echoed loudly in the tile-lined room.

She sat up so quickly that water sloshed over onto the floor. Her skin was suddenly ice-cold, in spite of the steamy heat in the bathroom.

Crossing her arms over her chest, she stared at the vapor that had collected on the mirror over the sink, trying to summon the beloved image of her son's small dear face. But instead of Bobby she saw Cody. Instead of Bobby's voice she heard Missy's.

Alarm shuddered through her. What was wrong with her? How could she forget the fact of her son, the sound of his voice? How could she even think about replacing him in her heart, as though he had never existed?

Guilt stole through her, leaving her chilled inside. No matter how much she cared for Mat's children, she could never allow them to replace Bobby in her heart. It would be like losing him all over again.

"I mean it, Cody. No more fooling around. Finish your applesauce so I can get you into the tub before Susanna gets here."

Cody gave his father an impish grin. "Zana," he said loudly, banging his spoon on the tray of his high chair.

Mat's patience began to thin. He should have asked Grandmother to stay until Susanna arrived, but the old woman had looked almost as hassled as he was.

Gritting his teeth, he pried Cody's spoon from his chubby fingers and scraped the last of the applesauce from the plate. "Open your mouth," he ordered in a deceptively calm voice. "One last bite for Daddy."

Cody eyed him solemnly. "No, no," he shouted, knocking the spoon from Mat's hand. Applesauce splattered the front of Mat's crisply pressed shirt and plopped onto the neatly set table.

"That does it," Mat muttered in a furious voice. He stood, jerked his son from his chair and carried him kicking and laughing to the bathroom.

"Sit," he ordered, depositing the grinning toddler on the closed lid of the commode. He glanced at his watch. Eighteen minutes before Susanna was to arrive.

According to his carefully thought-out battle plan, Cody should be scrubbed and combed and looking adorable in his teddy bear pajamas. Missy should be in her best dress, her hair brushed, her face shining with anticipation. As for him...

He ran his hand through the thick hair he'd had trimmed in Chamisa on his lunch hour. It was still damp from his shower and impossible to tame. The nurses who used to cut it claimed he had sexy hair. Right now, however, it felt about as sexy as the rain-slicked coat of a very angry grizzly.

Mat groaned and glanced down at his soiled shirt. It was the only one Grandmother had had time to iron. He groaned again, then turned off the water and hurriedly began to strip his son. Haste made him clumsy, and he muttered a few well-chosen words that made his son giggle.

"Stop wiggling, Cody," he ordered. "Your old dad has had a bitch of a day. Help him out, okay?"

"'Kay," Cody said solemnly. But as soon as Mat tried to untie his little sneakers, he began kicking. Five precious minutes passed while Mat captured his bicycling legs, then struggled with a stubborn knot in one of the shoelaces. He finally broke the damn thing.

By the time he had bathed Cody and washed the applesauce from the little boy's hair, he was nearly as wet as his son. He would have to change before Susanna arrived.

"There. Don't get dirty," he told Cody as he set him on his feet and gave him a hug.

The little boy clutched his bear to his chest, plopped his thumb in his mouth and ambled toward the living room, his tiger slippers making little scuffing noises on the tile.

Now he gets sleepy, Mat thought, hurrying into the bathroom to mop up the wet floor with the nearest towel. He hesitated, then tossed the sopping cloth into the tub.

A quick glance at his watch told him that he had five minutes. He could still make it if he hurried. He stripped off the wet shirt and threw it on top of the towel. Frowning, he glanced down at the damp spots over his crotch where he had leaned against the tub. His only pair of tailored trousers were a sodden mess. His hand went to his belt just as Missy came to the door, a furious scowl on her face.

"Daddy, Cody took my new red banana clip, and he won't tell me where it is," she wailed.

"What's a banana clip?" He hesitated, then dragged the shower curtain closed and headed toward his room, Missy following.

"You know, the thing I use for my hair." She tugged at the floppy sleeve of her sweater. "It's this exact color."

Mat frowned. "Did you look in your room?"

She gave him a pained look. "It's not there. I know Cody's been messing with it, just like he messes with all my things."

Mat bit off a sigh. He didn't have time to be exasperated. "You look through his toy chest. I'll look in his hiding places in the living room."

"Make Cody leave my things alone," she said in a grumpy voice before she returned to her room.

As soon as Mat walked into the hall he could smell smoke. Biting off an oath, he hurried to the kitchen. Grandmother had told him twice to take the casserole out at five-thirty, but he'd been so preoccupied with Cody that he'd forgotten.

Calling himself a rude name, he jerked open the oven door. Smoke immediately engulfed him, bringing tears to his eyes. "Damn it to hell. What else can go wrong?"

Without thinking, he grabbed the casserole, then let out a roar of pain. The earthenware pot crashed to the floor, shattering on impact. The scorched stew coated his boots and spread in a grayish river across the worn pine flooring. Mat sucked his singed fingers, too angry for obscenities.

"Daddy, you ruined our dinner."

That did it, he thought, his patience gone. "Me!" he bellowed indignantly, turning toward the sound of his daughter's reproachful voice. "The hell I did!"

He stopped, his heart giving an extra kick against his ribs. Susanna stood next to Missy, her eyes wide, her hand pressed to her mouth. She had on the same dress she'd been wearing that night when he'd changed her tire. Silk, he thought. Soft looking. Sexy.

"You're here," he said, and then cringed. Great start, Cruz, he thought. Witty, intelligent, charming. She's sure to be impressed.

"Missy let me in," she said, setting the pie she'd brought on the counter. "I hope you don't mind." She wasn't sure if she wanted to laugh or commiserate. Probably both.

Mat heard the odd note in her voice and knew that she was trying not to laugh. More than ever, he was acutely aware of his bare chest and drenched trousers. Feeling too damn much like a character in a slapstick movie, he glared down at the gooey gravy rapidly eating through the spit shine he'd just put on his best boots. So much for dinner, he thought with a scowl. Now what was he supposed to do?

He shifted his gaze to her face, his eyes narrowing in warning. "This is not funny," he ground out in his best command voice.

It didn't phase her.

"Of course not," she said in that same odd tone. She kept her gaze fixed resolutely on his scowling face, but in her mind she saw the distinctive outline of his sex beneath the charcoal wool of his trousers.

"Accidents happen."

"Absolutely."

His brows drew together over ebony eyes that glittered dangerously. He looked rumpled, frustrated, and so sexy her breath caught in her throat.

"Cody wouldn't eat his applesauce and Missy lost her banana peel—"

"Oh, Daddy, it's a banana *clip*." Missy sounded affronted.

"Clip," he repeated in a deceptively calm tone. "And the oven started smoking—"

"Burnt offerings," Susanna offered solemnly, waving her hand in front of her face. Her cheeks had turned from pink to red, and her bottom lip was clamped between her teeth.

Mat threw up his hands. It was either that or haul her into his arms and kiss her. "Go ahead and laugh, but that was your dinner I just splattered all over the floor."

"So I see." She began to laugh, great booming peals of unrestrained mirth. It was an infectious sound, one he found hard to resist.

"Enough, woman," he said with mock menace, coming toward her. "Or I'll make you clean this up."

"Oh no, I'm the guest, remember? You're the cook."

"The hell I am. I'm the host."

She made a point of looking him up and down. Only he knew what he was doing to her equilibrium.

"Hmm, is that the latest attire for elegant dinner parties?" she asked with a pointed look at his bare chest. Almost of its own volition, her gaze traced the path her imagination had assigned to a cluster of tiny sensuous bubbles. When she reached his open belt buckle, she stopped, jerking her gaze upward to his face.

A rueful grin slashed white against dark skin. "No, this is what a harried father looks like after his son decides to play Moby Dick in the bathtub."

"I . . . Next time wear an apron," she said, loving him so much at the moment that she wanted to melt into his arms and stay there forever.

"I'll remember that."

An awkward silence fell between them. Mat began to feel like a damn fool, standing there half-naked with a beautiful woman trying not to stare at his drenched fly. He glanced toward the door. "If you'll excuse me, I'll—"

"Zana!"

Susanna whirled at the shrill cry, just in time to catch Cody as he threw himself at her. "Hi there, Scout!" she exclaimed, unconsciously adopting Mat's pet name for his son. Did that mean she had accepted everything else? Mat wondered. Him included?

"Up, up," the little boy shouted, flapping his chubby arms. Laughing, Susanna lifted him into her arms and twirled around, her skirt flaring to reveal a glimpse of slender thighs sheathed in sheerest nylon.

Mat sucked in against the sudden throbbing of his unruly sex. Had it been only that morning that he'd stroked her smooth tanned skin? Had it been only a few hours ago that he'd thrust into her soft welcoming body?

Mindful of his daughter's sharp eyes, he kept his gaze on the unadorned neckline of Susanna's dress. But even as he watched the tiny pulse flickering in the hollow of her throat, he was remembering the feel of her silken thighs sheathing him.

A silent groan shuddered through him. How in the name of all the spirits was he going to get through the evening without making love to her?

"Looks like you're in good hands," he said when she finished whirling Cody around and around.

Dizzy all of a sudden, she swayed toward him, the room moving around her. Mat reached out to steady her, his forearm sliding around her slim waist, silk against skin.

"Whoa, there," he said, his laugh almost as unrestrained as his son's. "We don't need another disaster."

For several seconds they looked at each other over Cody's silky head, her generous mouth parted in an exuberant smile, laughter still in her eyes. Emotion stirred in him, the kind that made a man lose his reason.

Was this what had happened ten years ago? Had he felt this same desperate need to make love to her? Had he wanted her so much that he'd ignored everything but the burning need in his gut?

He withdrew his arm so quickly that she staggered, but she somehow managed to keep her balance. "Uh, I'll just go see if I can find a clean shirt." He glanced at Missy. "Maybe Susanna can help you find your banana peel."

Missy giggled. "Oh, *Daddy*," she protested indignantly. "You're being silly."

"Yeah, I know," he said as he turned away. "And it feels damn good."

"Black, one sugar," Mat said as he set the cup of coffee on the low table in front of the couch where she sat curled into one corner.

"Thanks. It smells good."

"It's strong, anyway," he said with a grin as he settled himself into the other corner.

While she had helped Missy find her barrette, he had changed into a plaid cotton shirt that was clean, but needed ironing. His sleeves were rolled, his collar open. His jeans were snug, the newness worn to a faded softness by his hours in the saddle.

Susanna's glance slid past him toward the fire crackling in the grate. Light from the flames danced across the walls, giving the dimly lit room a cozy feel.

"Missy all tucked in?" she asked, angling her chin to let the fire warm her face. It was nearly ten. Mat's daughter had been allowed to stay up an extra hour, in honor of Susanna's visit.

"Yes, tucked in and probably asleep by the time I walked out of the room."

After the rocky beginning, dinner had turned out to be fun. While Mat cleaned up the mess, she and Missy had made chorizo omelets and fry bread. Cody had sat on her lap during most of the meal, licking the honey from the bread.

After dinner, Mat had asked her if she wanted to put the sleepy little boy to bed, but she had declined. The memories of another little boy, another silky black head on the pillow, would have been more than she could bear.

When it had been time for his daughter to go to bed, Mat, with a sensitivity that touched Susanna deeply, hadn't repeated his invitation. She had been grateful, but oddly disappointed that Missy hadn't asked for her.

"I'm glad you could come tonight. I was afraid you might change your mind." Mat took a sip of coffee, then stretched and rested his cup on his belt buckle. He sat in the way she had come to expect, his shoulders relaxed but straight, his knees apart and bent, his injured leg stretched out a few inches more than the other to ease the pressure on his knee.

Susanna dropped her gaze to her cup. "I nearly did."

Half a dozen times she had picked up the phone in her office to cancel this date that wasn't really a date. And then she would remember the peace she had felt in his arms and change her mind.

"What made you decide to come?" he asked.

"I knew Missy would be disappointed."

Mat angled his shoulders against the lumpy cushions and stretched his long torso, much too aware of the slender legs outlined under the silk skirt. For an instant he thought about those perfect legs entwined with his, and the tightness returned to his loins.

"What about Missy's old man? Didn't you care that he'd be disappointed, too?" His voice was low, intimate. The firelight etched shadows into his lean face, giving him the rugged look of a man used to hard times.

She slid her fingers around the smooth hard handle of her mug and brought it to her lips. The coffee was potent and hot.

"Yes, I cared. That's why I didn't call."

Did she know how irresistible she was at that moment? Mat wondered, watching the fire turn her hair to sable. Did she know how he ached to pull her into his arms and beg her to take him just as he was, without demanding any more atonement for his mistakes, without needing the words of love he wasn't sure he could give any woman?

He shifted his weight, trying to find a comfortable spot on the hard cushion. "Tonight was difficult for you, wasn't it?" he said quietly, surprising her. "Holding Cody, feeding him, I mean."

"A little, yes. He's very much like Bobby."

He reached for her hand and placed it on his thigh, his hard fingers curling around hers. In comfort? she wondered. Or understanding? She didn't try to pull her hand away, but she didn't turn her hand to accept his, either.

Mat took a deep breath, then asked in a gruff voice, "Tell me about my son, Susanna. About . . . Bobby."

Stunned by his quiet request, she dropped her gaze to the strong masculine hand covering hers. Bobby's hands had been square, like his daddy's. "I don't want to talk about him. It hurts."

"Please. I'd like to know."

She wanted to refuse, but she couldn't. In spite of the problems between the two of them, he was still Bobby's father. He deserved to know something of his son.

"He was a lot like Cody," she told him in a still voice. "Sturdy as a little tree, and so curious I knew he had to be a scientist someday."

Mat smiled. "He didn't get that from me. According to my school records, I barely made it through twelfth grade."

She pulled her hand free and concentrated on the flames devouring the logs in the grate. "He got his smile from you, and his personality. I never knew which was worse, his temper or his stubborn need to master every new skill he tackled in one day."

Her soft tone nearly undid him. He wanted to hold her, to tell her how grateful he was that she had loved his son enough to give him life, even if for a short time. But the nervous way she played with the sash of her dress told him she was ready to bolt.

"Did he talk?"

She nodded. "The first word he learned was 'no.' He used it a lot." Her voice softened, and a gentle smile played over her lips. "And then he would look up at me and grin, like he was daring me to make him change his mind."

His spontaneous laugh touched her. "What else did he say?"

She inhaled slowly. "Mama and bye-bye and bankie." Her fingers tightened convulsively on the silk. "He was very smart and . . . and I loved him so much."

"Was he sick long?" His voice was stiff, as though asking hurt him.

It was a mistake to look into his eyes. She saw terrible grief there, and questions. Too many questions.

Tell him, urged a little voice. Don't let him go on suffering because he believes Bobby is dead.

"It's late," she mumbled, getting to her feet. "I should go."

She turned blindly toward the door, only to be pulled against a hard warm chest. His arms were protective and strong, his body sheltering. His aftershave reminded her of sagebrush and wind.

"Thank you," he said, his breath warm against her temple.

Confusion made her blink. "For what?" She tried to resist the warmth of his body, tried to keep herself stiff and distant, but the gentle stroke of his hand against her spine was so soothing.

"For having my son. For loving him. For all the things you did to make him safe and happy before he died."

Susanna heard a note of admiration in his deep voice, and she couldn't breathe. She didn't deserve to be admired, not for what she'd done.

"Please, I . . ."

Mat said softly, his hand brushing her cheek. "I understand. It hurts. But some things you just have to accept."

How? she wanted to shout. Tell me what to do and I'll do it. Willingly, gladly. She choked, and her shoulders jerked under the weight of a pain that had never completely left her.

Mat drew her into a loose embrace. "I told you the other day that I didn't need love. But I was wrong. Dead wrong. I need your love, Susanna, more than I've ever needed anything. And I intend to work harder for it than I've ever worked."

He framed her face with his hands. "Can you love me again, Susanna?"

I already do, she wanted to tell him, but she couldn't. Because if she told him that, she would have to tell him everything. About the adoption, about the contract she'd signed, promising never to try to find the little boy who was legally no longer hers, about her terrible failure as a mother.

If he blamed her, if he hated her, she would start hating herself all over again. She wasn't sure she would survive if that happened.

"You're thinking about the past, aren't you?" he asked in a low husky tone. "You're wondering if you can trust me."

"I have to be sure," she whispered truthfully.

"Then I'll just have to convince you." Mat pulled her into his arms. She closed her eyes and let herself luxuriate in his strong, warm embrace. His big scarred hand was gentle on her back, making her feel safe and cherished. Her arms stole around his lean hard waist, and he smiled against her temple, as though that small gesture pleased him.

They stood that way for a long time without speaking, without moving, warmed by the flickering fire and lulled by its muted crackle. Susanna felt a slow, heavy lethargy enter her body. She wanted to stay there forever. But that was impossible. Nothing was forever. Except the pain of giving up her son.

"Stay here tonight," he said quietly. "I need you, Susanna. I'm tired of waking up alone."

She sighed, then raised her gaze to his face. She found him watching her, his face still.

"I can't, Mat. It's too soon."

Or, she wondered as he walked her to her door and gently kissed her good-night, was it really too late? For both of them.

Chapter 14

Susanna sat in a rocking chair that had been shipped from Brazil, Cody's warm body curled in her lap. A fire burned in the grate, providing a crackling accompaniment to the story she was reading to the sleepy toddler.

It was Saturday, the last day of November. Mat had spent the afternoon unpacking the boxes that had arrived on Friday. Because she'd had to work, she had arrived late, just in time to fix *carne asada* and sopapillas for dinner, while Mat drove Missy to a friend's house for a birthday slumber party.

Now, dressed in jeans and a faded army sweatshirt that had been packed in one of the boxes, he lay on the couch, his feet propped on the arm, a book open on his flat belly. His eyes were closed, his features relaxed and vulnerable, his mouth gentle. Just looking at him made her senses tumble and whirl as though she were on a giddy carnival ride.

Tonight, she told herself. After Cody was in bed, she would tell him about his son. About Bobby. And then she would tell him that she loved him.

"One more, peeze," Cody murmured when Susanna closed the book. His long lashes drooped over sleepy brown eyes, but he refused to give up.

"How about it, Daddy?" Susanna asked, her gaze lingering on Mat's face.

His eyes opened slowly, his expression matching his son's. His grin was lazy. "You're spoiling him," he protested, but his tone was indulgent, even affectionate.

"Do you mind?"

"Nope, not a bit." The muscles of his torso rippled, then tightened as he sat up and swung his legs to the ground. "I just wish you'd spoil me just a little, too."

Susanna's heartbeat accelerated. "What about the cookies I made for you last week?"

His sooty eyebrows arched in gentle reproach. "You made me share."

"Hmm, that's true." She pretended to think. "I fixed your favorite for dinner tonight."

His sigh was exaggerated, lifting his broad shoulders in a way that emphasized the incredible strength hidden under the soft olive drab material. "Yeah, but last week you made me eat liver."

"It's good for you," she protested softly, a smile hovering over her lips. Each day she spent with Mat she fell more inexorably in love with him. She couldn't help admiring the way he disciplined himself to endure a daily hour of grueling exercises, even after the most exhausting day, or the way he worried about Missy's continuing fear of losing him, or the way he tried every day to show Susanna how much he valued her presence in his life.

He seemed to know exactly when to tease her, when to brush a tender kiss across her cheek, when to remain silent. It was a seduction of her spirit, of her soul, instead of her body, and far more difficult to resist.

But, true to his promise, he hadn't pushed her to sleep with him. Kissed her, yes. Petted her until she was a quivering collection of nerve endings, absolutely. Every night when he left her at her door, she felt the powerful arousal he made no effort to hide.

But maybe tonight, maybe after all the barriers between them had been torn down . . .

"Zana. One more." Cody began bouncing up and down in her lap, drawing an amused smile from his father.

Mat glanced at his watch. "It's already half an hour past his bedtime. Five more minutes and he'll be too wired to sleep. I'd better tuck him in."

Susanna heard the sigh in his voice and knew that he was achingly tired. Every day for the past week he and his deputies had borrowed horses from John Olvera and scoured the remote canyons, searching for Buck Ruiz. So far they'd found traces of a camp fire and a butchered sheep, but nothing to prove that Ruiz had been the one who'd left the signs behind.

Mat stood and stretched, then came to take his son from her arms. His hand brushed hers, and their eyes met. Hers soft and vulnerable, his glinting with a promise and a hunger that thrilled her.

"Shall we give Susanna a night-night kiss?" Mat asked his son, his gaze dropping to her mouth.

"Kiss," Cody agreed amiably around his thumb.

"Daddy first," Mat declared, bringing his head closer.

"It's not your bedtime," Susanna murmured, her heart fluttering.

"Say the word and it will be," he said, his tone as serious as hers had been teasing.

His mouth brushed hers, warm and seeking. One hand cupped her jaw, his fingers stiff with restraint. Heat burst into flame, traveling through her in a rush.

"Don't go away," he murmured against lips that wanted to cling to his. "Give me five minutes." Susanna heard the sensuous promise throbbing in his deep voice, and her fluttering heart faltered.

Five minutes, she thought. And then she would keep her promise to tell him the truth. After that . . . after that . . .

He'll understand, she told herself firmly, letting her gaze slide to Cody's small dark face. He won't hate me. She took a deep breath, her stomach suddenly filled with nervous jitters she could no longer repress.

"Night-night, sweetie," she said, kissing Cody's silky head. "Don't let the bedbugs bite."

Cody gave her a sloppy kiss on the mouth, his fat hand patting her cheek contentedly. "Night-night, mama."

Mama.

From a distance she heard another voice, saw another pair of chubby arms. Bobby hadn't understood why another woman was holding him, why his mama was leaving him. He had struggled to get down, to get to her. Over and over he had cried out for her.

Mama, Mama.

The soft smile froze on her lips. Her eyes widened until she saw only a blur. Her body seemed to shut down. Dimly she heard a voice calling her name. It was a deep voice, strong, resonant, yet agonized, like the pain slicing into the place where her heart should be.

"No," she whispered. "Don't take my baby." She crossed her arms over her midriff and tried to hold the pain inside.

"What is it, sweetheart? What's wrong? Are you talking about Bobby?"

She felt a hand on her cold face, its steady strength forcing her head up until she saw only the man she loved. The sorrow in his eyes nearly undid her. "There's something you should know," she said in trembling voice. "Something I have to tell you."

Mat kissed her gently, then shifted Cody to the other arm. "I'll put him down, and we'll talk," he commanded, his brows drawn. "Promise me you won't leave."

She shook her head. Where would she go?

Mat tightened his left arm around his son and walked down the hall. Cody stirred in his arm, muttering something Mat didn't catch. His ear still hadn't become completely attuned to his son's toddler jargon.

"Good night, son," he whispered, lowering Cody to the bed nearest the wall. "Daddy loves you." He hesitated, then added in a voice made rough by the emotion churning in him, "Susanna loves you, too, even though she won't let herself admit it."

The little boy frowned, then curled into a little ball and tucked his teddy bear under his arm. Mat pressed a kiss to his forehead, then turned on the night-light and left the door slightly ajar before returning to the living room.

Susanna stood in front of the fire, her features drawn and white. For a long silent moment Mat looked at the shadows darkening her golden eyes.

His gut pulled taut. Somehow he had to find a way to replace the hurt with so much happiness that she would gradually forget the bad times.

The hell of it was, he didn't know how. Nothing he tried seemed to reach past the walls she kept putting up as fast as he could tear them down.

Seeing the questions in his eyes, Susanna made herself smile. "I'm sorry," she whispered, trying to gather her courage to say the words. "I guess I'm not ready for . . . for another family."

Exhaustion made her voice paper-thin. Her body seemed disconnected, heavy. The air in the room was thick and smelled cloyingly of piñon smoke.

She raised her hand, then noticed that she seemed to be moving in slow motion. Her fingers touched his face, lingered on the harsh remnants of his own private nightmare, caressed.

"I'm sorry," she repeated numbly. Sorry he had suffered, sorry she hadn't been able to keep their son safe, sorry they might never have a chance to make things right.

She heard a voice, the low mutter of a curse. She dragged air into her lungs. She had to tell him.

"Mat, about . . . about Bobby—"

Strong hands lifted her; even stronger arms cradled her against a warm chest. "Shh, sweetheart," Mat ordered in a gruff rumble close to her ear. "Don't talk. You're dead on your feet. You need sleep. Whatever it is, it'll keep until morning."

Susanna let her head fall to his shoulder. His skin smelled of soap and sunshine. His arms were protective and hard. She closed her eyes and tried to blot out the pain tearing at her. But she kept hearing Bobby's voice, full of hurt and confusion, calling out to her as she walked out of his life forever. She shuddered, her defenses ripped away, her body numb. When Mat carried her into his bedroom, she didn't protest.

Matt kicked the door closed, then crossed to the bed. With one hand, he stripped back the covers, pushed the pillows against the brass headboard, then lowered himself until he sat with his back against the pillows. He pulled her into his arms.

Her small body was limp, hardly any weight in his arms, nearly as fragile as his daughter's. But Susanna wasn't a child. She was a woman in every sense, and stronger than most men he'd met. Right now, however, she had reached her own personal limit, the place where her strength was finally gone, her grief over Bobby's death alive and twisting.

Mat knew all about death and the pain it left behind. He'd seen his best friend cut in two by machine-gun rounds. He'd lost his wife in the worst way he could imagine, but he'd never felt this kind of crippling pain. He buried his face in her hair, his own pain an ache deep in his gut.

"Go ahead and cry, sweetheart," he whispered hoarsely. "Let it out."

Susanna clutched his shirt between trembling fingers and swallowed the sobs that wanted to escape. "I can't, I...I..."

"Yes, you can. Sometimes it's the only thing that helps."

"You don't cry."

Mat thought about that day in the canyon. "I've cried," he said. "When I found out I had a son I would never see."

The last of the scar tissue tore deep inside her, leaving her defenseless against the grief that had always been there, waiting.

"I want my baby," she whispered. Tears collected in her eyes and spilled over onto her cheeks. A sob escaped. Then another.

Harsh, wracking sobs shook her. She pressed her face to his shoulder and let them come. Years ago she hadn't allowed herself to grieve. The pain had gone too deep. Allowing it expression would have killed her. Now it only ripped her heart and soul with razor claws.

Mat felt the shudders shaking her, heard the muffled cries that seemed torn from her lungs. Hot tears born of a fiery agony bathed the still-tender scars on his neck.

Trapped in her grief, Susanna heard the deep rumble of a man's voice murmuring her name with a rough tenderness that soothed instead of threatened.

Beneath her cheek his heart throbbed with a hard tumbling rhythm that pounded through her until it felt like her own heartbeat.

She was dimly aware that his hand, the one bearing the terrible scars of his own agony, was stroking her hair so lightly that she felt no fear, only a wonderful feeling of safety. The tremors that shook her grew less violent. The sobs that threatened to choke off her gasping breath lessened, grew less savage.

Mat held her close, letting his body offer the comfort he couldn't put into words. Gradually she relaxed against him, her strong, slender arms wrapped tightly around his waist. Her breathing gentled. The trembling stopped.

Mat felt some of the tension leave her body, but her face was buried in the curve of his neck, and her hands still clung. His leg began to cramp, but he was afraid to move, afraid to disturb the fragile peace she seemed to have forged with the demons driving her. Gritting his teeth against the searing knot of pain in his thigh, he made himself wait it out. Sweat broke out on his brow, and his stomach roiled.

Finally, just when he knew he had to move, she stirred, like a drowsy child awakening from a long, deadening sleep. Her soft, damp cheek rubbed against his collarbone, and her breasts pressed his cheek.

Mat felt an instant response in his belly. It spread to his loins in a hot stabbing rush. He groaned silently. In another minute his body was going to send a message to hers that would shatter the frail peace between them. Now was no time to let Susanna know how much he wanted her.

"Sweetheart," he began, then stopped to clear the sudden huskiness from his throat. "Stay with me tonight. Let me take care of you."

Still trapped in her own thoughts, she looked up at him with wide, uncomprehending eyes. Teardrops glistened on her lashes, and a small V stretched between her gently arching brows.

"I don't want to be alone," she whispered, her lashes rising and falling in small fluttering jerks. "Not…not yet." Just for tonight she needed to believe that he loved her.

He wiped the tears from her face with his long fingers, then moved so that she was lying against the pillow his back had warmed.

Slowly, murmuring soothing words, he removed her loafers and long socks. "Such small feet," he said, kissing her ankle. "Soft skin. Nice legs."

Susanna smiled, sinking into the weariness cocooning her. His deep voice soothed, saying words she didn't really hear. His hands were gentle, caressing without seducing, as they worked the buttons of her flannel shirt, then lifted her to slide the soft material from her pliant body.

In the subdued light of the moon, his eyes were very dark, his hair even darker against his muscular neck. His hand moved to the waistband of her jeans, found the metal button. With one twist, the denim parted.

She heard the sound of a zipper, felt the cool air in the room touch her bare thighs as he slid the jeans down her legs, his callused palms wonderfully rough and caressing.

Mat tossed her jeans over the brass rail at the foot of the bed, his gaze devouring the satin smoothness of her skin. Her panties and bra were sheer lace, hiding nothing.

Not that it mattered.

The image of her ripe body, warm and rosy from his kiss and his touch, was burned into his brain. For weeks he had been in torment, watching her, wanting her, dreaming of her in ways that were definitely X-rated.

Each time he was with her, he silently coveted her. Each time he touched her, he remembered the way it had felt to love her. Kissing her had made him come alive inside in a way he'd thought was gone forever. Making love to her had left him hungry for more. Lying beside her, his body still entwined with hers, he'd felt at peace with himself.

More than anything he wanted to feel that way again. He wanted her to love him. He wanted to love her and protect her and give her all the babies she wanted.

But right now she needed rest.

Gently he bent to press a kiss into the tousled bangs that smelled of flowers. Her eyes were closed, the thick lashes casting delicate crescents on her cheeks. Tiny freckles burnished her cheeks with gold, and her mouth was pink and full.

With a gentleness only his children had seen in him, Mat traced the sensuous line of her lower lip with his thumb. When her mouth began to curve into an invitation, his heart stopped.

His hand clenched, his jaw tightened, and his belly burned as he struggled to keep his distance.

"Mat?" she whispered, her voice made husky by the tears she had shed.

Her lashes fluttered, then lifted, revealing eyes as golden as summer grass kissed by the dew. "Don't leave me."

"Not a chance," he whispered gruffly.

"I feel funny. Woozy." Her words were slurred, as though she were sedated. Mat had seen the same reaction in men who had suffered violent trauma during combat.

"I know, sweetheart." Gritting his teeth against the hard throbbing of his need, he sat down on the edge of the bed and pulled off his boots. She needed to rest, and he intended to hold her until she felt safe enough to give in to the drowsiness hovering behind her eyes.

Susanna felt the mattress dip under his weight, and she turned toward him, her knees flexed, her cheek half-buried in the pillow. A strange languor held her in its grip, giving everything a surreal quality, like a dream played out in soft focus.

She watched while he undressed, marveling at the long, clean lines of his back. His torso, defined by sinew and bone, was packed with hard-edged muscle, the kind built slowly through tortuous effort and punishing determination.

His shoulders, bare now that he'd tugged off the khaki sweatshirt, spoke of power and strength in their wide span, strength that she longed to pull over her like a protective shell.

Her heart, pounding slowly, began to accelerate. Her skin, shivered slightly by the cool air, tightened until she felt as though the blood raced just below the surface, every beat of her heart speeding it faster and faster.

She needed him tonight, needed his courage and strength to replace her own. Tomorrow she would tell him everything. Tomorrow would be real.

Tonight was a dream. Her dream. Tonight they were man and wife, the way they should have been years ago. Tonight they would help each other, be strong for each other, love each other.

If these next hours were all that they would have, she wanted to spend them in his arms. "Make love to me, Mat," she whispered, her hand sliding gently over his hip. "Please."

Mat's fingers, busy working the buttons of his jeans, stilled. Slowly he turned to look at her. "Are you sure?" he asked, his voice so husky it seemed to abrade his throat.

Her long thick lashes fluttered, then raised. "Make me forget," she pleaded softly. "I don't need the words, only your body in mine."

Impatient to be in his arms again, she watched as he stood and tugged off his jeans and briefs. Then he returned to the bed where Susanna waited, walking toward her with a loose-hipped stride that suggested fluid, coiled power.

Her eyes devoured the hard muscular length of him. His skin was a variety of textures, smooth where his body had escaped damage, corrugated like hard steel where the scars had formed, covering the terrible wounds. A light dusting of hair covered his legs and arms, but his chest was bare, a broad expanse of burnished copper. A soft black triangle surrounded the potent shaft that was already partially engorged.

In the shadowy light his face seemed too angular, the hollows below his arrogant cheekbones too pronounced.

The uncompromising line of his jaw matched the corded strength of his neck and the startling width of his shoulders. Unlike most powerful men she had met, he wore his masculinity easily, without bravado or macho posturing. Her man, she thought. The man she loved.

She moved to give him room, her bare thighs sliding across the crisp sheets like a whisper in the dark. He eased in beside her, taking her into his arms with a rough male dominance that drove darts of sweet anticipation deep into her core.

"You're beautiful when you cry," he murmured, his fingers wiping the last of the drops from her lashes. "And when you laugh. Even when you're glaring at me."

He spoke softly, without inflection, the way a wrangler gentled a nervous filly. He drew her to him, his hands horny with calluses, but gentle where they touched.

His kisses were sweet, tender, healing even as they excited her. Nothing was hurried, in spite of the tension radiating from his corded muscles. Susanna forgot everything but the symphony of sensations swirling through her body, raising her higher and higher.

When his mouth left hers, she whispered a protest that turned to a soft gasp as his teeth nipped her earlobe. His tongue probed the recesses of her ear, trailed moist heat over the delicate whorls, then retreated. She arched her neck, giving him free access to the sensitive skin there.

Her hands moved over his shoulders, his chest, his arms, absorbing the masculine heat, memorizing the various textures. Her desire was born of need and loneliness, tempered to a hot hunger by the potent male energy he projected.

Mat trembled at the possessive way her hands explored him. It had been so long since he'd been touched with gentleness and caring, so long he had no memory of the feelings it had aroused in him.

He kissed her again, more deeply this time, using his tongue to explore the sweetness of her mouth. Her hair tumbled over her shoulders, rich dark silk touched with flame. His fingers threaded through the luxuriant length, releasing the warm, fresh scent of roses.

He slid his mouth along the strong line of her jaw, kissing her, tasting the slight tang of her skin, remembering the set of her small chin even as he touched the tiny dent in the center with his tongue.

His finger traced the lacy edge of her bra, pausing between her breasts. His warm mouth followed his touch, leaving her trembling in its wake.

Another touch, a twist of his wrist, and her bra was loose. With the same slow concentration, he slid one strap, then the other, over her shoulders and down her arms, enjoying the milky perfection of her skin.

He felt her strain toward him, her small body taut with the same need that was taxing his control. He nuzzled her breasts, inhaling the sweet, delicate scent trapped between them.

Had she nursed his child? he wondered, his throat clogging with words he couldn't say, words of admiration and reverence and love, words she wouldn't believe even if he had the skill to utter them.

His mouth did what his voice could not, celebrating the ripeness of each breast with his tongue, while his hands slid under the filmy panties. Slowly, each movement conveying his caring, he slipped them free.

Outside the wind blew against the windowpanes and whistled through the trees. Susanna closed her eyes, sinking into the golden velvet behind her lids, blocking out reality until only Mat's kiss, Mat's strong body and Mat's clean masculine scent were surrounding her.

But that wasn't enough. She needed to be closer, a part of him, with him a part of her. She needed to give herself to him in the same elemental way that she longed to be taken.

The yearning rose in her like a hot wave, erupting in a moan. She arched her back, trying to ease the exquisite tension his fingers were spreading between her legs.

"Soon, sweetheart," he murmured, his hand making slow, sweet circles over the small mound between her legs. Susanna gasped, a long shuddering sound that traveled the length of her body. Her hands burrowed into his soft clean hair, closing and opening in the same spasm of need building deep inside her.

Mat moved lower, his control stretched nearly to the limit. And yet he held back, wanting to make this night, this moment, last.

He levered himself up, parting her thighs with his hand. His fingers found the soft delta, pressing, caressing, enjoying the spun silk that warmed his palm.

A small sobbing sound escaped her throat, and she moved from side to side, stunned by the sensations Mat was arousing in her. She whispered his name, her eyes half-open and kindling with golden fire.

His hand caressed the tender flesh of her inner thigh, arousing small tremors beneath her skin. His fingers curved downward, dipping into the moist heat sheltered there.

Susanna gasped, her every sense exploding into a starburst of sensuality that held her captive. She resisted nothing, exciting him even more, even as it humbled him. Susanna was light and sweetness and beauty—all the things he had missed in his dark, lonely life.

The need to bury himself in her sweetness raged like a fever in his blood as his hands moved to cup her soft round bottom, lifting her toward him. His tongue thrust into her, hot and caressing. Like brandy, her feminine nectar was best savored slowly.

His thumb followed his tongue, pressuring the small bud between her legs until she cried out, her voice hoarse, her breath coming in short gasps.

She was at his mercy, her own will overridden by the wild firestorm of pleasure he was slowly, inexorably fanning with his hands, his mouth, his tongue.

Mat withdrew and took the precautions that would protect her, his body hard and hot and ready.

Through a silky veil of desire, she heard the unspoken plea in his voice. To forgive him, to accept him as he was now, to love him as he would always be. The raw vulnerability around his mouth told her that he would never express those needs, but they were there, inside him, where they hurt most.

Tenderness welled up inside her, even more powerful than the desire shaking her. Shaking with love, she slowly opened her legs, offering all that she was.

His hoarse groan began in the deepest part of him and shook his entire body like a fevered tremor. With a slowness that tested him severely, he eased himself inside her, feeling her body mold around his in a hot, slick welcome. She clung to him, her neck arched backward, her breasts thrusting against his chest.

He held himself rigid, his muscles straining against the savage need to move, absorbing the tremors convulsing deep within her.

Susanna cried out, twisting and turning wildly against his hard body, desperate to be filled by him. Mat lifted her, plunged more deeply until he became a part of her, possessing her with a driving force until she was half-maddened, crying out his name in need and love.

Absorbing her desperate cry, Mat began to move inside her, one slow thrust leading to another and another until the hot friction sent her spiraling into a realm of ecstasy she hadn't known existed.

Mat felt the explosion rip through her. With a hoarse cry, he thrust once, again, his body convulsing with a violence that matched hers, pulse after pulse of hot release flowing from him until he knew only Susanna, only this hot wild need to be a part of her.

He was hers, his heart, his soul, his future held in her small hand. Only she had the power to hurt him beyond his ability to endure. Only she had the power to heal the agony that twisted inside.

"Don't ever leave me," he whispered into the moist shadow between her breasts.

"Never," she vowed on a drowsy sigh.

Her eyes fluttered closed. She was asleep.

Chapter 15

The baby was crying. Susanna struggled to reach him. The room was filled with a thick fog filling her throat, choking off her breath. Her legs burned, but she was running as fast as she could.

The cry came again, louder. She ran faster, her hands searching desperately, her eyes filling with stinging tears.

Suddenly the mist cleared. Ahead was a large white room. Icy white, sterile, brutally cold. A cradle, tiny and empty, stood in the middle of the blinding whiteness, rocking back and forth.

A man with a cruel smile stood next to the cradle, her baby held easily in his powerful arms. His features had been stamped by a kinder hand on the small face nestled in the soft blanket. Father and son.

No! she screamed. *Don't take him. Please don't take my baby.*

She struggled to reach him, but the floor was quicksand, clawing and tugging her back. *Please,* she begged piteously, her eyes pleading with him.

The man turned away, his brutal mouth edged with derision. Before she could reach him, he'd been swallowed by the mist. Gone forever.

"No, no, no."

"It's all right, sweetheart. I'm here. It was just a dream."

Susanna jerked awake, the sound of her cries still hanging in the dark. Her heart pounded erratically. Her mouth was cotton dry.

Mat held her in his arms, his hand stroking her back. He whispered reassurance over and over until the tremors shaking her began to ease. With an unsteady hand he wiped the tears from her cheeks. Susanna huddled close to his solid chest, her heart still beating unnaturally fast.

The room was shrouded in predawn gloom. Everything was gray, except the sheets on the bed, which seemed ghostly white. During the night Mat must have covered them with the blankets that now lay heavily over them.

Had he held her the entire night? she wondered, feeling the weight of his thigh between hers and the warmth of his hand wrapped around hers. In spite of the musky heat cocooning her, she was so cold inside. She shuddered, hiding her face in the curve of his neck.

"Easy, sweetheart. You're safe now." He pulled the blanket close to her neck, then began combing his fingers through her hair, spreading it over her shoulders. His body supported hers, his warmth seeping into her until she felt it begin to absorb some of the chill.

"Were you dreaming about our baby?" His voice carried a rough texture that she now identified as pain.

She nodded, and his arms tightened. Another shiver took her. She had to tell him now, before her courage failed her.

"There's something I have to tell you, something I should have told you weeks ago," she said in a voice trembling with sorrow and regret. She dropped her gaze, shaken by the hope in his eyes. "Something I have to...to confess."

His mouth jerked. "If it's about other men, I don't want to know."

Susanna smiled sadly. If only it were that simple. "There have been no other men, Mat. Only you."

Only when she felt relief travel through his powerful body did she realize how tense he'd been. He started to grin, but she stopped him with a kiss. Before his mouth could soften under hers, she buried her face in his neck, her hand curving around his neck to hold him close.

Tears flooded her eyes, and sobs shook her. She clung to him, desperately afraid that this would be the last time she would feel his strong arms holding her with such tenderness.

"Shh," he whispered over and over, trying to absorb her obvious anguish. "Everything will be all right, I promise. There's nothing you can tell me that will make any difference to the way I feel about you."

He'd been awake for hours, staring at the ceiling, Susanna's body nestled against his chest, trying to deal with feelings he hadn't even known existed in him.

More than anything he wanted to cherish this woman, to share his hopes with her, and his triumphs. But more than that, for the first time he knew what it was like to trust a woman enough to share his hurt with her, his insecurity.

For as long as he could remember he had made himself be strong—for the country he loved, the men he was charged with leading, his family. He fought alone, cried alone, even grieved alone. But now, with Susanna, he didn't have to be alone ever again.

He brushed the hair away from her face, then kissed her. In the shadowed light his eyes glittered with an emotion that frightened her. "Did you mean it when you said you wouldn't leave me?"

Her finger traced the vulnerable slant of his hard mouth. "Yes, I meant it."

"That's all that's important, Susanna," he said in a thick voice. "Nothing else."

Slowly, feeling as though she were leaving a part of her behind, she moved out of his arms. The blanket slipped away, exposing her skin to the cold morning air.

Quickly she clutched it to her chin. She had never felt more exposed or more breakable. But this time her pain was self-inflicted. She was responsible for the terrible feelings knotting her throat, not Mat.

"Bobby isn't dead," she said in a torn voice, fighting to keep her chin up.

The shock started in his eyes, then spread like a lightning bolt to his jaw, which tightened until it was edged in white. His son was alive, he thought with numbed happiness. He had another son—a boy Missy's age. He felt hot tears come to his eyes. He sat up, his bare chest dark against the white wall.

Relief shot through him like a rifle slug, leaving him shaken. But on the heels of relief came an explosion of shrapnel-sharp questions.

"You said he died when he was nine months old." Mat tried to make sense of her words, but it was the expression on her face that held him. She looked devastated, like a victim of war who had suddenly lost everything of value.

"It seemed . . . easier that way." She was clutching the blanket so tightly her fingers hurt.

"Easier? I don't understand how it could be easier, believing that my son was dead when he isn't." With an aggressive gesture that spoke volumes about the things he *wasn't* saying, he raked his hand through his hair.

"Why isn't he here? When can I see him?"

Susanna felt as though she were being sliced to shreds inside. "You . . . you can't."

Mat heard the bleak note in her voice, and fear twisted his belly. But he ignored it, just as he had been trained to do. First he had to know what he was fighting.

"There isn't anything I can't do if I want it badly enough, Susanna. And I *want* my son."

Shivering more from dread than chill, Susanna climbed from the bed and looked around for her clothes. She saw his, but not hers. Grabbing his sweatshirt, she quickly pulled it over her head. The shirt smelled like Mat, and the soft material molded to her body, covering her in all the places where his body had warmed her in the night.

"He's not yours anymore. Or . . . or mine. Not legally, anyway." She swallowed the terrible taste that pushed at her throat. "I . . . put him up for adoption."

Mat went stiff inside. Was this his punishment? To live with the fact that he had a son somewhere he would never know? To know that Susanna had hated him so much she had rejected his son?

"Tell me," he said with a deceptive calm.

Susanna laced her fingers together to keep them from reaching out beseechingly. She rushed into the facts to keep from begging him to understand.

"When Bobby was born, I had to leave nursing school. I was unskilled, with only enough training to qualify as a nurse's aide. The only shift available was from eleven at night to seven in the morning. Still, things were fine for a while. The nurses on staff felt sorry for me, so they let me keep Bobby in one of the empty rooms. My supervisor arranged for me to work weekends, too, and vacations."

She stopped, her breath failing her. Resting both hands on the hard brass rail at the foot of the mattress, she dropped her head, trying to fill her lungs with air. But the band constricting her chest made it hurt to inhale.

Mat clenched his fists against his thighs to keep from reaching for her. He should have been the one working to support his child, not her. He should have been there protecting her, loving her. No wonder she had looked at him with such revulsion when they met again.

"What happened?" he asked, wanting to take the burden of the telling from her, yet knowing he couldn't.

"There was a layoff at the hospital. My supervisor tried, but there were people with more seniority who also had families to support. I got a job as a waitress, but the only way I could make enough money was to work two shifts. That meant child care."

Slowly, as though reciting a story about someone else, she told him about her illness and the social worker who had tried to take Bobby from her. Tears ran down her face, but she let them fall. She had to finish before grief overtook her again.

"I tried, Mat," she said in a sad, small voice when she was done. "But in the end I ... I couldn't stand seeing him grow up never knowing if there would be enough food in the house or enough money for clothes so that the other kids wouldn't make fun of him or ... or ..." She couldn't say more. She had no more strength.

In silence Mat climbed from the bed and pulled on his jeans, knowing for the first time what it was like to hate. But it wasn't fate he hated, or even the woman who had convinced Susanna that she was a bad mother, although he wanted to make the woman pay for what she'd done. No, the lash of his hatred was directed toward the person responsible for Susanna's pain. Mateo Cruz.

Yeah, he'd been some stud, all right, he thought, watching her small face get whiter and whiter. Seducing an innocent nineteen-year-old who had only wanted to comfort and love him. Leaving her to have his child alone. To struggle to take care of him.

He straightened his shoulders and turned to face her. Only a few inches separated them—yet Mat didn't know how to bring them closer.

He'd been so sure he could make her forget what he had done to her. But now, seeing the scars he had inflicted on her soul, he realized that he had no words strong enough or eloquent enough to convince her to forgive him.

"Now ... now you know it all," she said, twisting her fingers together. Tell me you understand, she pleaded silently. Tell me you still want me.

"Yes," he said in a voice she had never heard before. "Now I know."

Mat was a man who prided himself on his control. He'd spent more nights than he wanted to count ticking off the seconds until the next pain shot, sometimes biting through his lip to keep from screaming. But he'd never once broken. Never once begged.

But this instant, face-to-face with the man he'd been, the man who had done a terrible wrong, he felt like falling to his knees and begging her to forgive him.

"Susanna, I—"

The phone shrilled, startling them both. Adrenaline flooded Susanna's veins, making her go hot all over.

Mat muttered a succinct curse before snatching up the receiver. "This better be important," he barked into the phone, raking his hair with his hand.

The indistinct rumble of an excited voice filled the air.

"When?" Mat asked when silence fell again.

As he listened, the annoyance on his face turned to a stony look that brought Susanna's hand to her throat in an unconscious gesture of fear.

"Give me ten minutes," he ordered in the coldest voice she'd ever heard. "Find Two Skies and tell her to bring her rifle."

"What is it?" Susanna asked when he hung up.

"A few hours ago Buck Ruiz went back to the Comacho place and threatened to kill Rebecca if she testified against him. Her husband just brought word. Spruce said Ruiz was just sighted near his brother's ranch. I'm going after him."

Susanna heard the savage anger in his voice, and her blood turned icy. "Promise you won't go alone," she pleaded urgently, her mind filled with the image of his battered face.

Mat ground his teeth, the memory of Ruiz's knee smashing into his gut burning like acid in his soul. "Call Grandmother," he said, turning away. "She'll stay with Cody."

Susanna sat slumped over the kitchen table, staring into a cup of tea that had grown cold long before. Mat had been gone over four hours.

She had spent that time trying not to think of the look on his face when he'd left. That was the reason she hadn't done as he'd ordered and gone for Grandmother. When he returned, she wanted to be able to talk with him privately—if he gave her the chance, she thought, pushing away her cup.

When Cody woke up at seven she'd given the little boy his breakfast, each bite he'd taken making her stomach roil. After she'd cleaned away his mess, she'd read him as many stories as he could stand, holding him for what might be the last time. With each hour that passed, each minute, each second, she had grown more anxious.

Her anxiety was worse now that Cody was napping. The house mocked her with its silence. The rooms, filled with Mat's clothes and books and masculine clutter, taunted her with his absence.

Suddenly the front door opened with a whoosh of cold air, startling her from her seat. "Mat?" she cried eagerly, her heart going to her throat as she sped into the other room.

"No, it's me," Missy said with a sunny smile as she flung her overnight case into the nearest chair and closed the door. "Where's Daddy?"

Susanna hung on to the door frame, disappointment making her weak. "He's...out on a call. I'm baby-sitting."

Missy's expression brightened. "Oh boy! Can we play Chinese checkers after I get something to eat?"

"Sure." Susanna's voice came out in a hoarse thread, and she cleared her throat.

She followed Missy into the kitchen and opened the refrigerator. Her hands were shaking so badly she had trouble removing the bread and sandwich makings.

As Susanna worked, Missy perched on a kitchen chair and chattered gaily about the party. With each word she uttered, Susanna hurt more. Was this the last time she would be a part of Missy's life? Of Cody's? Of Mat's?

The ache inside her sharpened until she nearly cried out. "Sounds like you've made a lot of new friends," she managed when she realized Missy had stopped talking and was looking at her curiously.

"Yeah, they're really neat, even if they don't have TV or VCRs or lots of the things my other friends had."

Susanna set the food in front of the little girl, then turned back to the counter to pour a glass of milk.

"Susanna?" Suddenly Missy sounded unsure.

"What, sweetie?"

"Are you going to be here for always now?"

The carton in her hand jerked, splashing milk on the counter. "Would . . . would you like that?"

"I sure would, lots and lots."

Susanna dashed away the tears that spilled from her eyes. During the past few weeks she had begun to think that, in his own way, Mat was coming to love her. But that hadn't been love she had seen on his face when he had left her this morning. In fact, he had looked as though he had wanted to put his fist through the wall. Or her.

With a heavy sigh, she threw the damp towel into the sink. Taking a tighter grip on the milk carton, she poured out a glassful. She was halfway to the sink when the kitchen door slammed open. Buck Ruiz stood there, a knife with a ten-inch blade held ready in front of him.

The glass fell from Susanna's hand, shattering on impact. Jagged fragments flew in all directions, slicing Susanna's bare ankle.

"Don't nobody move," he snarled into the frozen silence. His ratlike eyes darted around the room, then returned to Susanna's face. "Where's Cruz?"

"At the office," Susanna managed calmly, resting both hands on Missy's shoulders. The little girl was shaking so hard her teeth chattered.

"No, he ain't. I checked there."

He advanced into the room, his boot heels clicking loudly on the tile. He was unshaven, and his eyes were bloodshot. Susanna smelled the stench of bad liquor on his breath.

"I heard Cruz had a couple of brats," he said, running his finger along Missy's cheek. The little girl cringed, trying to escape.

"Stop it," Susanna ordered, pulling the little girl closer. "Leave her alone."

His eyes narrowed, and a look of calculation came into the flat black pupils. "Man thinks he can run me off my own land, does he? Sic them parole people on me to do what he ain't got the guts to do. Well, the man's got another think comin'. No one messes with Buck Ruiz and gets away with it."

A drop of spittle formed at the corner of his mouth. "I come to teach him a lesson in respect for his betters before I go, but maybe there's another way to make him remember me." He grabbed Melissa's chin and jerked her toward him. "Cute kid, even if she is a mongrel, like her old man."

Nausea boiled in Susanna's stomach. She couldn't let this animal hurt Missy. "Leave her alone!" she cried, her voice rising. "I know where Mat is. I'll take you to him."

His fingers tightened on Missy's chin, making her cry out in pain. "If you're lying to me, bitch, I'll kill the kid, sure as I'm standing here."

"I'm not lying. I swear." So frightened she could barely breathe, Susanna forced herself to meet his malignant gaze, putting every bit of guilelessness she could manage into that steady look. Make him believe me, she prayed silently. Please.

For what seemed like forever he stared at her, his body radiating menace. Finally, with a sneer he dropped his hand. "The kid comes with us."

Panic shot through Susanna, settling in her throat. Her insides were jumping violently, and her hands were icy. She took a deep breath. Whatever happened, she had to get Buck away from the children. She had to keep them safe.

"She doesn't know where her father is. I'm the only one who does. But I won't tell you unless the child is safe." She lied with a smoothness that surprised her. Even her smile felt convincing on her stiff lips.

She edged between Buck and the girl. "If it's a hostage you want, you've got me. A terrified child would only be in the way."

Missy began to whimper. Susanna longed to comfort her, but she couldn't afford to draw Buck's attention to the child's helplessness.

An oily look of confidence came into his face. "That's true enough. Maybe you and me'll have us a party before I kill Cruz."

Before she could react, he clutched her upper arm in a viselike grip. "Take me to him, and no tricks. I ain't got much time." He began dragging her to the front door. "We'll take your Jeep. I come by horseback." So that was why she hadn't heard him arrive, Susanna thought as she half walked, half ran at his side.

"Lock the door," she called out to Missy as Ruiz pulled her over the threshold. The child sat frozen in her chair, her eyes so frightened the whites showed all the way around the dark brown centers.

Outside, the sunlight was blinding, making Susanna squint. The air was chilled, and smelled of dust. As Ruiz hustled her toward her Jeep, a jay screeched a warning overhead.

"You drive," he ordered, wrenching open the door on the driver's side.

As she eased into the seat, Susanna desperately searched her mind for a plan. She had to take him away from here, as far as possible. What then? she thought, staring at the knife in his grimy fingers. Wreck the Jeep? Hope that the impact would knock him cold? It wasn't much of a plan, but it was all she had.

"Don't try nothing stupid—" Buck broke off at the sound of a powerful engine. Mat's Bronco was making the turn into the short driveway. Half-hidden by the aspen next to the carport, Susanna watched helplessly as he drew closer.

Ruiz muttered a vicious Tewa curse. "This must be my lucky day," he added in English. His hand grabbed her collar, jerking her from the seat. Holding her in front of him, he waited until the Bronco braked to a halt.

Lost in his own thoughts, Mat didn't see Ruiz and Susanna until they stepped into the open from behind the Jeep. Ruiz was using her as a shield, one meaty arm encircling her waist, the other holding a knife to her throat. It took Mat less than a second to assess the situation. Ruiz had come for him. He'd taken Susanna instead.

An icy calm, more deadly than the most violent rage, came over him. Years of tough army discipline had given him an edge he didn't intend to waste. He knew how to fight, clean or dirty. And he was willing to die to keep Susanna safe. It was all he had left to give her.

Slowly Mat opened the door, keeping both hands where the other man could see them. There was a rifle slung across the back window and a loaded shotgun attached to the dash.

Neither would do him a bit of good as long as Ruiz had Susanna in front of him.

He stepped out into the glare, grateful that the sun was at his back. Keeping his hands away from his revolver, he stood perfectly still, letting Ruiz's nerves settle.

All Mat's senses were heightened, his concentration complete. He blotted everything from his mind but the need to keep this man from taking out his revenge on Susanna.

Without seeming to, he tried to gauge the man's mental state. Ruiz seemed jittery, but in control. So far, so good. A man in a panic did crazy things.

"Let her go, Buck," he said easily, ambling toward the Jeep with deceptively lazy strides. Susanna's face was pale, and her eyes radiated a desperate helplessness. Hang on, sweetheart, he told her silently. I won't let you down. Not this time.

"No way, Cruz. You think I'm crazy or what? This bitch is my ticket out of here."

"I won't give you any trouble," Mat said with a shrug. "You have my word."

Buck's arm tightened, pulling Susanna to her toes. She choked, fighting for air. With each step Mat took, the terror inside her grew. Buck had said he had come to kill Mat, and she believed him.

Please don't die, she pleaded silently, helplessly. Don't leave me.

"That's far enough, Cruz," Ruiz called out when Mat was still a good ten feet away. "Unbuckle your gun belt and toss it over here."

"Don't—" Susanna cried out, her words cut off suddenly by the pressure of the knife against her windpipe. Pain seared her throat, followed by the slow trickle of warm blood.

Fury flashed in Mat's eyes, but it was gone so quickly that she wondered if she had imagined it. His hands went to the buckle of the gun belt. Slowly, every movement causing her unbearable pain, he released the belt, holding it out to the side with his weakened left hand.

"Toss it here," Ruiz shouted, his stinking breath hot on her cheek.

Mat kept his gaze riveted on Ruiz's face. The man's cheeks were mottled, his eyes blinking nervously, his lips curled into a triumphant grin.

"Let her go first."

Ruiz tightened his grip on Susanna's midriff, making her cry out in pain. "You got two seconds, Cruz. Then she's a dead woman."

Mat cast a meaningful glance toward the .38 dangling from his hand. "You kill her, I'll kill you."

"Don't give me that. The bitch was in your house. Hell, everyone knows she's your personal whore."

Nothing showed on Mat's face, but inside he went rigid. "What's one woman more or less?" He held his breath. The bastard had to believe he didn't care.

Seconds ticked by while Ruiz calculated his chances. Sweat beaded on Mat's brow and trickled down his back. His thigh began to cramp, but he remained motionless.

"Maybe I won't kill her," Ruiz said, pushing his knee between Susanna's thighs. "Maybe I'll just cut her some so she's as ugly as you are." His laugh snarled between them. "What do you think of that, Cruz?"

Mat eyed him with open contempt. "I think you're as cowardly as the old women who hide in their hogans when the coyotes prowl. Come to think of it, you're not even that brave. You're so yellow you have to hide behind a woman's skirts to feel safe."

Ruiz spat out a curse, the veins in his neck bulging. "Shut up," he snarled, his rage nearly palpable. "I ain't hiding behind no one."

"Then why do you need her? It's me you want." He smiled. "Here I am. Or are you afraid to take on a cripple in a fair fight?" With a violent motion of his arm, Mat flung the gun belt toward the horizon. It landed in a shower of dust in the chaparral, too far for Ruiz to retrieve it easily.

Susanna shut her eyes in a spasm of pain. Mat had made himself completely vulnerable.

"Let's see how tough you really are, Ruiz," Mat challenged. "You think you're man enough to take me, let's see you do it."

Ruiz had the advantage of youth and brute strength, but he was also a bully. Mat knew his only chance lay in goading the man into a fight. Even if he didn't win, Susanna would have time to get the kids and escape.

"Don't do it, Mat," Susanna shouted, knowing exactly what Mat was doing, even if Ruiz didn't. She kicked out wildly, desperate to get to Mat to stop him from sacrificing himself.

With an enraged curse, Ruiz flung her aside. Losing her footing, she slammed into the Jeep, her head smashing against the rear window. Crying out in pain, she crumbled to the ground, reality whirling around her.

Before she came to her senses, Ruiz had landed the first blow.

Chapter 16

"Mat, the knife!" Susanna screamed, trying to get to her feet.

Mat saw the flash of steel in Ruiz's hand and jumped backward, knocking Buck's arm to the side. The knife fell between them, and Mat kicked it under the Bronco. Then, with every ounce of his strength, he slammed his right fist into the other man's mouth. His knuckles split, spattering Buck's face with blood.

Buck staggered, but his bull-like strength kept him on his feet. Lowering his head, he charged, knocking Mat backward and driving the air from his lungs. Pain exploded in his midsection, doubling him over. Ruiz crashed a knee into his jaw, sending him flying backward to fall on one knee.

With a mad bellow, Ruiz came at him again, but Mat rolled away from him, coming to his feet in a move he'd practiced countless times during hand-to-hand combat exercises.

He crouched low, making Ruiz come to him, absorbing the blows he couldn't dodge. His right hand had gone numb with the first punch, but he used his left with a force that sent a stinging shock wave up his arm.

Ruiz refused to go down. He was a brawler, using his fists like clubs, using brute force instead of finesse. His body was strong, but the alcohol he'd drunk made him reckless.

Knowing his endurance was limited, Mat hoarded his strength, trying to make every blow count. His muscles burned, and his head pounded with a pain that sent jagged starbursts of light shooting across his field of vision.

A blow to the stomach drove the breath from his lungs, sending searing agony rippling through him. Sensing victory, Ruiz hammered him, one blow after another.

Mat sank to his knees, his strength nearly spent. But he couldn't give in to the numbness waiting beyond the pain. He wouldn't break his word to Susanna.

Slowly, weaving like a drunken man, he managed to get one foot under him, only to have Ruiz slam the sharp toe of his boot into his side, sending him to the ground. Pain clawed at his ribs, telling him that they had been broken again. Dust filled his mouth, nearly choking him. His breath rasped through his bruised lips. Blood covered his face and ran into his eyes. He shook his head, trying to clear his vision.

Eyes riveted on the battling men, Susanna ran toward the Bronco. Lying flat, she stretched her arm toward the knife, but it lay just out of reach. Tears of frustration and fear rolled down her cheeks. She edged closer, tasting the dust that rose. Suddenly she heard Missy scream her name from the doorway. "Get back inside. Lock the door!" she screamed back.

From a distance Mat heard a woman's voice shouting something. Susanna. Through his pain he saw her white face. Her beautiful golden eyes. Her smile.

A feeling more powerful than the coldest rage, more powerful than lifesaving adrenaline, more powerful than anything he'd ever known, surged through him.

She was his, his woman. His life meant nothing without her. He would kill Ruiz with his bare hands before he would let the bastard hurt her.

Mat surged to his feet, swaying with sickening dizziness. He thought only of one thing—to keep Susanna safe. He dove at Ruiz, bringing him down. They rolled in the dirt, tangled together, their blood dripping into the dust.

Both were nearly spent, their blows clumsy and slow. Desperation gave Mat the strength to blot out the pain. With a final surge from muscles that felt as though they were bursting, he rolled Ruiz to his back. Before the other man could react, Mat landed a bone-jarring blow to the man's jaw.

Buck's neck snapped back, plowing his head into the dirt. With a groan, he went limp, his eyes rolling back in his head. Mat tried to get up, but his legs failed him, and he sank to his knees, his head hanging.

Susanna flew to him, her tears nearly blinding her. "Oh, Mat, my darling, Mat," she cried as she knelt to take him in her arms. "I was so afraid. Where does it hurt? Tell me."

Mat buried his face against her shoulder, too tired to raise his arms to hold her. Her tears bathed his bruised cheek. Her hands were gentle on his battered muscles.

For a long moment he allowed himself to give in to a fierce longing to stay in her arms. He wanted to wake up next to her and go to sleep curled around her small body. He wanted to love her.

Slowly he raised his head, blinking to clear his vision. "Rifle . . . in the truck. Get . . . it."

"Yes, I'll get it." Her hands touched his face, wiping away the blood. "Are you hurt? Can you breathe?"

Her face wavered in and out, and a roaring began in his ears, drowning out her voice. He fought to keep the gray fog from enveloping him, but his strength was gone. He tried to say her name, to tell her . . .

"Bobby . . . not your fault," he managed to say. "Mine, only mine."

He pitched forward into the black void.

Flat on his back, Mat floated, moving toward consciousness, from black to gray in slow stages. His body ached. His head was fuzzy, and his throat burned.

"He's coming around." It was a man's voice. Unfamiliar, speaking English.

Mat opened his eyes, feeling slightly disoriented. Steeling himself against the various aches and pains that were beginning to make themselves known, he quickly reconnoitered. He was in his own bed, his nakedness covered by a warm blanket. A stocky, dark-haired man in jeans and a rumpled green smock stood at the end of the bed, returning bandages and gauze to a large black bag. Mat frowned, then recognized the clinic doctor. Greenleaf.

Susanna was closer, perched on the side of the bed less than an arm's length away, her face white, her bangs pushed aside to reveal a wide strip of plastic adhesive. A thin red line slanted across her throat where Ruiz had cut her. Her shirt was dotted with blood, and one sleeve was ripped at the shoulder.

At the sight of her small still face, Mat forgot his vow to clean up his language and swore long and creatively, his fury evenly divided between Buck Ruiz and himself. When he ran out of breath, he sank back on the pillow and tried to ignore the pain in his side.

"Sounds like he's on the mend," Greenleaf muttered with an appreciative grin as he shut his bag with a snap.

Mat inched his shoulders higher on the pillow. He was tired of waking up flat on his back, half-dead and covered with bruises.

"Ruiz?" he ground out impatiently. If the man had gotten away, there wouldn't be enough ground for Ruiz to cover, enough places for him to hide. No matter how long it took, Mat would find him and make him pay.

Greenleaf glanced at Susanna, who answered softly, "After Brad patched him up, Two Skies locked him up in the cell in your office. She said you had to decide what to do with him."

Mat scowled. "If it were up to me, I'd put him up against the wall and shoot him, but it's not. It's up to the Tribal Court to decide what to do with the bastard."

He raised his hand and looked at the heavy thickness of tape binding his knuckles. It was his right, the one he thought of now as his good hand.

"That hand is broken," the doctor told him in the same slightly unctuous tone Mat had come to detest. "Come by tomorrow as soon as you can manage and I'll cast it for you."

"The tape'll do fine."

The frustration in his voice tore at Susanna's already shredded nerves. Mat didn't deserve to be hurt any more.

"Not if you want to regain full use of that hand, it won't."

As he passed by on his way to the door, Greenleaf gripped Susanna's shoulder in friendly support. "Don't let him do anything strenuous for the next forty-eight hours. Otherwise, he might end up with a punctured lung from those broken ribs."

"I'll make sure he stays in bed," Susanna promised.

"The hell you will," Mat muttered, furious at ending up flat on his back in front of Susanna again.

Silence settled between them. Susanna stared at her own hands folded loosely in her lap. One of her nails had been torn to the quick in her desperate scramble for the knife, and two of her knuckles were bruised. She didn't know how that had happened.

"You look tired," Mat said after the silence grew thick.

As her head came up, she managed a smile. "It's been a stressful day."

Mat thought about the way the day had started, and a leaden fear settled in the pit of his stomach. Paradoxically, in spite of his flawed memory, he remembered every word she'd said to him.

He stirred restlessly, trying not to wince at the pain every movement cost him. "Where are the kids?" he asked, looking past her to the open door.

"Next door with Grandmother."

"Missy okay?"

Susanna nodded. "She's so proud of herself."

Mat raised his one undamaged eyebrow. "She is? Why?"

"As soon as Ruiz dragged me out of the house, she went to the phone and started calling all the emergency numbers you'd put by the phone. Finally she reached John at home, and he . . . he called out the troops."

"Meaning Two Skies and Spruce?"

"Yes, and several of the elders who were at Headquarters for a meeting."

Mat sent a dark look toward the ceiling. "That's just great," he grated with thick sarcasm. "I imagine they were impressed as hell at the sight of their police chief spread-eagled in the dirt."

"More like awestruck, I should say," she told him with a private smile of pride. When he'd pitched forward into her arms, she'd known she would never love anyone as she loved Mat. She only hoped it wasn't too late for them. But the way he looked at her, so expressionless and cold, gave her little hope.

"According to Garcia Crowe, Buck Ruiz once took on three bikers in a bar and knocked them all on their . . . fannies. If you want a raise, now is the time to ask."

"At the moment, that's the last thing on my mind." Gritting his teeth, he eased himself into a sitting position against the piled-up pillows. A dozen different pains shot through him, making him gasp.

"Where was Ruiz taking you?" he asked when he could draw breath again. Her thigh was only inches from his. Her hand was closer, and yet she had made no move to touch him.

Susanna cleared her throat. "Actually, I was taking him."

Mat forgot his aching ribs as he barked out, "You *what*?" Agony exploded in his side, making him suck in his breath. "You what?" he managed more softly.

Susanna cast an anxious look at his ashen face. She was afraid he was going to pass out again. "I told him I knew where you were. That I'd take him there."

A thunderous frown settled between his sooty eyebrows. "To where? You didn't know where I was."

"But Buck thought I did." She twisted her fingers together. "I planned to drive as close to headquarters as I could, then ram into the nearest solid object. I figured he was too macho to use a seat belt, and if I hit the brakes just right, he'd smash his head against the windshield, and then—''

Mat's unbandaged hand tunneled under her hair to curl around her neck. With one swift tug she was in his arms, his mouth hot on hers, his arms crushing her. His kiss wasn't gentle. If anything, it was almost brutal, fired by his realization that he'd almost lost her before he had a chance to make things right.

"You little idiot," he managed against her mouth. "You're enough to drive a man to drink, even after he's sworn off." His mouth settled over hers again, gentler this time, but no less volatile.

Susanna clung to him, her breasts pressed against his pounding heart, her hip angled over his hard thighs. Her senses gloried in the intimacy, reeling from the potency of his not-quite-perfect mouth.

This was the man she loved. The only man she had ever wanted. His strength was much greater than her own, his superior size and rawhide toughness so wonderfully overpowering, and yet she sensed a rough male tenderness in him that was there only when he was with her.

She responded to his kiss with a savage demand that rivaled his own. Whatever happened, she would never be sorry that she had loved him. Nor that she had borne a child from that love. How could she, when Bobby was the one link neither regretted?

She twined her arms around his wide torso, feeling his breathing become hers, his heartbeat dictate the rhythm of her own.

Mat felt her small fingers press his spine, warm and strong and, he fervently hoped, possessive. She was so close, he wanted to believe she was a part of him.

Desperately aware that this might be all he would ever have of her, he took it hungrily, greedily, like a man facing life in solitary confinement.

But when she moaned deep in her throat, he came to his senses. She had just been through a day filled with enough trauma to lay out most men. He had no right to take advantage of her shaky defenses. Not again.

With a control that cost him dearly, he slid his hands to her shoulders and gently pushed her away. Her mouth was full and moist, her eyes glazed with a depth of passion that made him groan silently. But the faint blue crescents under her eyes and the small lines between her arching brows told him that she was near the end of her emotional rope.

"Damn, I didn't mean to do that," he muttered, his voice raw. "But I saw you dead, because of me, and I... It hurt."

"You saved my life," she said in a shaky voice. "No, don't look at me like that. I saw the look in your eyes when Buck's knife drew blood. You wanted to kill him."

Mat clenched his jaw. "I promised you he wouldn't hurt anyone again. But he hurt you." He raised his unbandaged hand and brushed his bruised knuckles over the fragile curve of her cheek. "I kept thinking about you while we searched Diego's place. I kept seeing your face when you were talking about Bobby. I had to come back."

Mat took a deep breath, struggling to find the words to express the fiercely knotted tangle of feelings inside him. "You did the right thing, Susanna. The only thing you could do. Because you loved Bobby, you had to let him go. Sometimes... sometimes that's the only thing you *can* do, even though it's the one thing that hurts the most."

Susanna dropped her gaze, seemingly fascinated with the weave of the blanket beneath her. "I was afraid you'd hate me."

Mat swallowed hard. "That isn't possible."

Holding his breath against the pain in his ribs, he leaned forward to slide open the small drawer in the stand by the bed. Trying not to wince, he withdrew a tattered notebook and closed the drawer. Without a word he handed it to her.

"What is it?" she asked, her tone reflecting the same confusion she knew must be in her eyes.

"A journal of sorts. I kept one for each year, until I got out of the habit in Brazil. Read the last dozen or so pages."

Susanna flipped to a spot close to the end, her stomach fluttering at the familiar sight of his handwriting.

The words were cryptic and blunt, like the man who had penned them. They told of his mother's death, his request for emergency leave. And then the pages were filled with a description of their love affair. "Susanna asked me about love. Told her I didn't believe in it. Afraid I hurt her, but she has to know I can't make promises I can't keep. Hell of it is, with her I want to believe."

Her cheeks burned as she read of his desperate hunger for her, his longing to share himself with her in ways that were new to him, his fascination with her laugh and her smile and her spirit. His words painted a picture of a man fighting his own needs in order to behave honorably. Fighting and, ultimately, because of his own desperate loneliness and need, losing.

The man who had written those words was arrogant, yes, and full of himself as young men often are, but he was also as caring and sensitive as she had believed him to be.

Tears came to her eyes as she read of his sadness at their parting. "Feel guilty as hell because I didn't tell Susanna about Trina. But as soon as I get back to the post, I intend to tell Trina I can't marry her. Not when I know it's Susanna I really want."

Susanna bit her lip, turning the pages now with fingers that shook. "Saw Trina tonight. She's pregnant. Baby due in seven months, she says. Claimed she used the Pill. Not that it matters. Threatened to have an abortion if I don't marry her."

The next entry was dated a week later. "Married yesterday morning. Trina's family came up from Hillsborough, looking anything but happy to have an enlisted man in the family. And an Indian, to boot. Damn, I feel sick inside. Kept seeing Susanna standing next to me instead of Trina. But the thing is done, and I intend to be a good husband to her."

There were gaps in the dates, a few terse entries dealing with his work. And then close to the end she read, "Susanna wrote—she's expecting a child. Read the letter three times, tried to tell myself it wasn't true, but Susanna wouldn't lie. The baby is mine, and there isn't one damn thing I can do about it. If things were different, if I were free, I'd be on the next plane, but Susanna would hate me if I abandoned Trina. A marriage under those circumstances would be hell for both of us. Damn thing is, if the situation were reversed, Trina wouldn't give a damn about Susanna. God, I hate myself."

There was one more entry, on the last page of the book. "Talked to the chaplain. Had to talk to someone. Thinking about Susanna so far away, waiting to hear from me, was driving me crazy. Chaplain told me I had to tell her the truth. Said I had to let her go so that she could get on with her life. So that she could find someone else. Someone who would love her and take care of her and the child. My child. Is this God's revenge for my sins? If it is, He couldn't have found anything that would hurt more."

Susanna was crying openly now, her tears splashing on the black ink. Mat kept his gaze on her face, a feeling of dread crystallizing inside him. If she turned away from him, if he lost her... He clenched his jaw, refusing to think about the possibility.

As she turned the page, Susanna felt Mat's gaze probing her face. But she couldn't allow herself to look at him, not until she knew it all.

"Serving two tours in 'Nam was hell, but writing to Susanna was worse. She'll hate me now, and that's the way it has to be. I can never see her again. It would kill me to walk away again. But I'll never forget her. A part of her will be with me until I die."

The journal ended there. The last page was wrinkled, the cardboard beneath it indented, as though a fist had smashed against it.

"Why didn't you show me this weeks ago?" she asked in a low voice.

"It was packed away with the rest of our household goods." A self-conscious smile softened one side of his mouth. "I had a hell of a time making myself read it. I thought... I was afraid to find out I was a worse bastard than you thought I was. If that was true, I sure as hell didn't want to let you find out."

"Then why did you read it?"

He took a slow breath, hearing the thunder of his agitated heartbeat in his ears. "I had to know what it felt like to be loved by you."

"Oh, Mat," she whispered helplessly, clutching the book to her chest.

"I'd give anything to remember," he said in a low voice that throbbed with sincerity and deeply felt pain. "But I'll never have those years back, Susanna. Just as I'll never really know all the things I felt then. All I know is what you read, that I wanted you, that I would have married you." He raised her hand to his mouth and kissed her ring finger. "I wish I could tell you I loved you then, but I can't."

"It wouldn't make any difference," she said softly. "There's nothing you can say that will change the way I feel about you."

Mat went cold inside. Was this it, then? Had he offered her everything and still lost?

Susanna saw his mouth flatten, saw his jaw clench, saw him prepare himself for the worst. "I love you, Mat. The man you are now."

Mat's breath came shuddering from deep inside, from that private part of him where he locked away his hurts and regrets and insecurities.

"I don't know much about love, Susanna. After a while, with Trina, it seemed like a dirty word, a symbol of all the things that were wrong between us, all the things that she wanted me to be that I wasn't."

"I'm not Trina," she said gravely. "And I'll never try to change you. To me you're perfect just the way you are."

"I'm not perfect, Susanna," he said in a rough voice. "I can only be the best man I know how to be."

"The man I love dearly."

Her hand shook as she touched the imperfect half of his face, her fingers tracing the rough places on his jaw. When her fingers brushed his mouth, it trembled beneath her touch.

His smile was so beautiful, she thought. As though he'd just been given something very precious, something he'd thought he would never have.

He drew a ragged breath. "Think you can teach a beat-up ex-soldier about love?" He asked the question lightly, as though he were teasing. But Susanna heard the note of raw emotion in his deep voice.

"Absolutely," she said, her mouth curving into a smile. "Of course, it might take me years and years to get it right."

Looking into her golden eyes, seeing her smile warm until it blazed with welcome, Mat realized that she already knew all there was to know about love. Love's name was Susanna. And he would never let her go.

Epilogue

"Why do we have to go to Albuquerque now?" Susanna asked for the third time since leaving Santa Ysabel in the early-morning hours. It was Saturday, and traffic was light on Interstate 40.

Mat looked away from the long ribbon of freeway in front of him to smile tenderly at his wife. "Because we do," he said gently, returning his gaze to the road. It wouldn't be long now. Less than an hour. He only hoped she wouldn't hate him for what he was about to do. If she did . . .

He shuddered inside, where she couldn't see it. After living with her for nine months now, he couldn't bear the thought of losing her.

Beneath the floppy brim of her hat, Susanna's brow puckered into a stormy frown. "I don't know why you're being so stubborn about this. Aurora is already half-frazzled because Morningstar is cutting her first tooth. She doesn't need two more kids to take care of."

Mat heard the soft whisper of maternal concern in her voice and smiled to himself. Susanna hadn't been away from their children for more than a few hours at a time since their honeymoon, and she was as fluttery as a mother owl hovering over her two little nestlings.

"John will be there, sweetheart. And it's only for one night."

With a sigh, Susanna told herself to relax. She'd lived with him long enough now to know that whenever Mat braced his shoulders and set his jaw in that hard obstinate line, nothing changed his mind. Not even her.

"We could have taken them with us. Cody would love a trip to the zoo, and Missy needs clothes."

"You need a break, sweetheart."

"But—"

"And so do I."

Silently admitting defeat, Susanna settled back against the seat and studied his craggy profile through the lace of her lashes. For weeks now he had been preoccupied, wrestling with some private demon, something that had knotted his jaw with tension and returned the shadows to his eyes.

"I'm sorry," she said with the soft smile Mat never tired of seeing. "I know you've been under a lot of stress. It's just that I...I worry about Missy and Cody when we're not there."

"They're in good hands, sweetheart. Missy will beat the pants off John in Chinese checkers, and Cody will trail after Aurora, trying to figure out why Morningstar can't get down and play trucks with him."

Susanna laughed, her amber-gold eyes shimmering with so much love that Mat wanted to stop the truck and pull her into his arms. Instead, he lifted her hand from her lap and settled it on his thigh. After today he might never have the right to touch her again.

Resting her head against the seat, she watched the scenery speed by. It was early September, a fine clear day. The trees were still green, but here and there she saw a wash of fall color covering the aspen leaves.

What did Bobby see when he looked at the autumn leaves? she wondered with a private sad sigh. Did he remember how she used to hold one under his small nose so that he could smell its pungent scent? When he heard a lullaby, did he remember the way she'd crooned to him when his gums were swollen and aching? Or did he feel only hatred for her because she had given him away?

She inhaled a shaky breath. Every time she tucked Cody into bed, she bled a little inside. Every time Missy snuggled against her to whisper one of her desperately important little-girl secrets, she wondered if Bobby had someone to listen to his secrets, to give him advice, to heal his small wounds, to love him even when he was naughty or stubborn or angry.

Deep in her soul she wanted so many things for him. Health, happiness, joy. Most of all she wanted him to know how much she loved him. But she could never tell him. And that was tearing her apart inside.

Closing her eyes, she sank into the soothing motion of the Bronco. Mat was right. She needed a break.

Mat slanted her a worried look, his gut tight with a tension that had been there for days now, since he'd made arrangements for this trip.

With every dawn that broke with her nestled in his arms, he loved her more. With every sunset they watched together, he thanked the benevolent spirit that had brought her back to him. Happiness had only been a word to him before Susanna brought it into his life. His world was perfect.

But not hers.

It wasn't anything she said, or anything she did, really. But sometimes, in the night, he would jerk awake to discover her crying in her sleep.

She claimed it was just the pressure of her job, but with the sensitivity that loving her gave him, he knew it was more than that. In spite of the love she gave unstintingly to Missy and Cody, and the love she gave to him that made his life complete, a part of her was closed off, reserved for the son she missed so desperately.

Mat sighed, then checked his watch. In twenty minutes he would know if he had done the right thing.

* * *

"Sweetheart, wake up. We're here."

Susanna sat up and yawned, blinking at the unfamiliar surroundings. "Where exactly is *here*?"

"De Anza Playground."

"De Anza *what*?"

Mat laughed at the befuddled look on her face, but even as he helped her from the Bronco, his gut began to twist with nervousness. Please understand, my dearest, he begged silently as he led her past a clutch of squat adobe buildings to the soccer pitch in the rear.

Susanna stared in rising dismay at the scene in front of her. The game was already in progress. Twenty-two boys, half of them wearing red jerseys, the other half in white, ran up and down the field, forming and reforming into complex patterns that only they understood. On the sidelines, a fair number of spectators—proud parents, she assumed—shouted encouragement.

Was Mat out of his mind? she thought, her temper beginning to simmer. Or was this some kind of a bizarre joke?

"A soccer game? You brought me all the way from Santa Ysabel, made me leave Missy and Cody, to watch a soccer game between a bunch of kids?"

Mat slipped an arm around her waist and pulled her closer. It took all of his considerable strength to voice the words that he had been repeating in his head since they'd left the pueblo.

"I love you more than my life, Susanna. And I can't stand to see you blaming yourself for something that wasn't your fault."

Her heart began to race. Her hands grew clammy.

"Bobby?" she whispered achingly.

He nodded, holding himself very still. This was as painful for him as it was for her, maybe even more so, because this was the only memory he would ever have of his son.

"It wasn't easy, but I called in a few favors with some people I know in the Pentagon and I found him for you. I thought…I hoped that if you knew he was happy, you could let him go."

Susanna's face lit up. "Oh, Mat, which one is he?" she begged in a breathless voice, her nails digging into his arm. The joy in her eyes made him hurt inside.

"Number seven on the red team," he said quietly.

With an eagerness that tore at his heart, Susanna frantically searched the field. "There he is," she whispered hoarsely. "Oh, Mat. He's so big. He's...he's almost grown."

The boy was lean, like his father, with the same imposing shoulders and strong legs. The baby softness was gone from his face, replaced by an angularity that promised to mature into striking good looks.

Tears collected in her throat, making it difficult to breathe.

The coach shouted something, and Bobby looked up, his hair flopping over his brow. "He still has a cowlick," she said through her tears. "He would get so impatient with me when I brushed his hair. I...I remember how he'd jerk his little chin at me and scowl like the very Dickens."

Mat felt the pain settle hard inside him as he struggled to see the baby Susanna described in the half-grown boy streaking up and down the field. But he couldn't, and that would always be his deepest regret.

"He's so beautiful, so perfect." Her voice caught. "He's going to be so handsome someday."

Mat inhaled slowly, feeling as though he were being ripped in two. "I'm told he's the best player on the team. The coach...the coach says he's a natural athlete."

"Like his father," she whispered.

"Yes."

Susanna kept her eyes riveted on the tall boy in red, exulting over each powerful kick, each skillful play. His face was alive with the joy of competition, his black eyes sparkling, his grin flashing again and again.

Suddenly the black-and-white ball spurted away from the shouting, kicking tangle of boys, streaking with surprising speed straight for her head. Before she could duck, Mat moved in front of her, catching it on the fly with one large hand. His left.

A whistle shrilled.

"Red, side out," shouted the referee.

Number seven separated from the others and jogged toward her. Mat hesitated, then took her hand and placed it on the ball. She clutched it tightly against her, warming the leather with the heat of her body.

The boy with the bright, happy eyes stopped a few feet in front of her and held out his hand. Susanna's gaze devoured his features, searching for the face of her son. For Bobby.

She found traces, in the high arch of his black eyebrows, in the jut of the chin, in the sweetness of his smile. But the adorable little baby she remembered was gone.

"Ma'am? Is something wrong?" The boy's smile faltered, and his gaze darted toward the tall, fierce-looking man standing so still and rigid in front of him.

Susanna made herself smile. "You're very good." She couldn't let him go. Not yet.

His grin flashed, going straight to her heart. Their eyes met. Susanna held her breath, searching those dark depths for a glimmer of recognition. Please remember, she wanted to beg. Please know your mama.

The overweight referee came puffing up to them, an impatient scowl on his beefy face. "What're you waiting for, Begay? An engraved invitation?"

"Yeah, let's *go*, Jimmy," shouted one of his teammates.

With shaking hands Susanna passed him the ball. His fingers brushed hers, and she fought down a sob. "Good luck," she whispered.

"Thanks." He turned away, his mind back on the game, already forgetting the small woman with the white face and shaky smile.

Play resumed, and he was gone, charging toward the goal with the same powerful stride that Mat had once possessed. He passed off, shook off two defenders, took the ball again. With one powerful kick, he sent the ball spinning into the net.

That's my son, Mat thought with a thrill of pride, his throat tight. He hugged Susanna closer, offering her silent support. He could feel her shaking, but there was nothing he could do but love her and wait. This was her battle to fight, and she had to do it alone.

The crowd exploded in sound. The boy's teammates crowded around, hugging him, thumping him on the back, hugging each other.

Arms raised in triumph, he ran directly toward a man and woman who stood slightly apart from the others a few yards distant from the spot where Susanna and Mat were standing. She was small and blond, he was shorter than Mat, but with the same Native American heritage stamped on his dark features.

Susanna felt as though she were drowning in sadness as she watched them embrace the boy. Their son. Seeing the pride in their eyes, her own eyes flooded with tears. Hearing the love in their voices as they congratulated him made her heart lurch.

"They love him, Susanna, and he loves them," Mat said in a voice that was thick with the tears he couldn't let himself shed in public. "Be happy for him. Let him go."

She turned into his strong arms and buried her face against his shoulder. "I can't, Mat. He's a part of me. And he's a part of you. Our son. Bobby."

His arms tightened. "No, Susanna. His name is James Frederick Begay, and he's not ours anymore. Or yours. He's a part of the two people who have taken care of him and worried about him and loved him when we couldn't. Just as Missy and Cody are a part of you now."

Susanna took a shaky breath, then another. In her mind she saw Missy's shining eyes when she had introduced Susanna to her classmates as her mother. And she heard Cody's sleepy voice calling to her in the morning, confident that the woman he knew now as Mama would always be there for him.

Gradually, as she listened to the strong steady beat of her husband's heart, a healing peace settled inside her. Finally, after all the years of self-doubt and pain and guilt, she was able to let Bobby go.

Be happy, Jimmy Begay, she murmured in her heart. I'll always love you.

Raising her head, she looked into Mat's eyes. A wave of tenderness overtook her when she saw the unmistakable sheen of tears glistening in their obsidian depths. "Oh, Mat," she whispered. "I love you so desperately. You will always be part of me, even though I have to let our son go."

A lone tear escaped his control and slid down Mat's hard, scarred cheek. Susanna wiped it away gently, her hand lingering against his beautiful, perfect face.

"Take me home, my darling," she whispered. "Our family is waiting."

*   *   *   *   *

Star-crossed lovers?
Or a match made in heaven?

Why are some heroes strong and silent . . . and others charming and cheerful? The answer is WRITTEN IN THE STARS! Coming each month in 1991, Silhouette Romance presents you with a special love story written by one of your favorite authors—highlighting the hero's astrological sign! From January's sensible Capricorn to December's disarming Sagittarius, you'll meet a dozen dazzling heroes.

Sexy, serious Justin Starbuck wasn't about to be tempted by his aunt's lovely hired companion, but Philadelphia Jones thought his love life needed her helping hand! What happens when this cool, conservative Capricorn meets his match in a sweet, spirited blonde like Philadelphia?

The answer leads to THE UNDOING OF JUSTIN STARBUCK by Marie Ferrarella, available in January at your favorite retail outlet, or order your copy by sending your name, address, zip or postal code, along with a check or money order for $2.25 (please do not send cash), plus 75¢ postage and handling, payable to Silhouette Reader Service to:

In the U.S.
3010 Walden Ave.
P.O. Box 1396
Buffalo, NY 14269-1396

In Canada
P.O. Box 609
Fort Erie, Ontario
L2A 5X3

Please specify book title with your order. Canadian residents add applicable federal and provincial taxes.

 *Silhouette Books*®

JANSTAR

DIAMOND JUBILEE CELEBRATION!

It's the Silhouette Books tenth anniversary, and what better way to celebrate than to toast *you*, our readers, for making it all possible. Each month in 1990 we presented you with a DIAMOND JUBILEE Silhouette Romance written by an all-time favorite author! Saying thanks has never been so romantic....

If you missed any of the DIAMOND JUBILEE Silhouette Romances, order them by sending your name, address, zip or postal code, along with a check or money order for $2.25 for each book ordered, plus 75¢ for postage and handling, payable to Silhouette Reader Service to:

In the U.S.
3010 Walden Ave.,
P.O. Box 1396
Buffalo, NY 14269-1396

In Canada
P.O. Box 609
Fort Erie, Ontario
L2A 5X3

Please specify book title(s) with your order.

January:	ETHAN by Diana Palmer (#694)
February:	THE AMBASSADOR'S DAUGHTER by Brittany Young (#700)
March:	NEVER ON SUNDAE by Rita Rainville (#706)
April:	HARVEY'S MISSING by Peggy Webb (#712)
May:	SECOND TIME LUCKY by Victoria Glenn (#718)
June:	CIMARRON KNIGHT by Pepper Adams (#724)
July:	BORROWED BABY by Marie Ferrarella (#730)
August:	VIRGIN TERRITORY by Suzanne Carey (#736)
September:	MARRIED?! by Annette Broadrick (#742)
	THE HOMING INSTINCT by Dixie Browning (#747)
October:	GENTLE AS A LAMB by Stella Bagwell (#748)
November:	SONG OF THE LORELEI by Lucy Gordon (#754)
December:	ONLY THE NANNY KNOWS FOR SURE by Phyllis Halldorson (#760)

Hurry! Quantities are limited.

SRJUB-1AAA

Take 4 bestselling love stories FREE

Plus get a FREE surprise gift!

Silhouette Special Edition

proudly presents
the long-awaited ''prequel'' volume of

★ LOVE AND GLORY ★

by
LINDSAY McKENNA

Dawn of Valor

In the summer of '89, Silhouette Special Edition premiered three
novels celebrating America's men and women in uniform: LOVE
AND GLORY, by bestselling author Lindsay McKenna. Featured
were the proud Trayherns, a military family as bold and patriotic
as the American flag—three siblings valiantly battling the threat
of dishonor, determined to triumph . . . in love and glory.

Now, discover the roots of the Trayhern brand of courage, as
parents Chase and Rachel relive their earliest heartstopping
experiences of survival and indomitable love, in

Dawn of Valor, Silhouette Special Edition #649.

This February, experience the thrill of LOVE AND GLORY—from
the very beginning!

DV-1

Silhouette Books

"Maybe your memory will come back," Susanna said.

"Maybe it will."

But did she want it to? Did she really want him to remember the foolish, adoring girl who'd all but begged him to marry her?

No, she thought. This way she was safe. This way, *she* had the advantage.

"Maybe you could help me fill in the blanks," Mat said, his voice dipping into the seductive huskiness she'd once loved. "Were we friends?"

Pain tore through Susanna, almost as fresh as it had been ten years before. It isn't fair, she wanted to shout. She wanted to tell him the truth, to rail at him, to recite his own words back to him, the cold, cutting words that had shattered her dreams.

But she didn't dare. It was better to keep the past buried.

"No," she told him. "No, we weren't friends."

Dear Reader,

The holidays are almost here, and with snow whipping through the air and cold winds blowing—at least in my part of the country!—I can't think of anything I'd like more than to escape to a warm climate. Let Barbara Faith help you to do just that in *Lord of the Desert*. Meet an American woman and share her adventures as she is swept into a world of robed sheikhs and sheltering desert dunes. You may not want to come home!

This month's other destinations are equally enticing. The Soviet Union is the setting of Marilyn Tracy's *Blue Ice*, and intrigue and danger are waiting there, despite the current spirit of *glasnost*. Paula Detmer Riggs returns to New Mexico's Santa Ysabel pueblo in *Forgotten Dream*, the story of a man who has forgotten much of his past and no longer has any memory of the woman he once loved—and is destined to love again. Finally, reach *Safe Haven* with Marilyn Pappano. When Tess Marlowe witnesses a murder, her only refuge is a secluded house in the Blue Ridge Mountains —and the embrace of Deputy U.S. Marshal Deke Ramsey.

In coming months, look for new books by such favorite authors as Nora Roberts, Heather Graham Pozzessere and Lee Magner, as well as a special treat in February: four brand-new authors whose debut books will leave you breathless.

Until then, happy holidays and may all your books be good ones.

Leslie J. Wainger
Senior Editor and Editorial Coordinator